PRIVATE PROSECUTION

PRIVATE PROSECUTION
LISA ELLERY

FREMANTLE PRESS

Lisa Ellery was raised on a sheep, cattle and barley farm at Gibson near Esperance on Western Australia's south coast. She studied law and arts at the University of Western Australia before returning to regional WA in 1998 to commence her career as a lawyer in the gold mining city of Kalgoorlie–Boulder. She soon fell in love with Kal and its people and in 2008 established her own law firm there. She works predominantly in commercial and mining law and employs a dozen staff in her busy Hannan Street practice. Lisa is married to Simon Ellery, a geologist. She divides her time between managing her law firm, running in the Goldfields bush and writing.

For Dad

PROLOGUE

I liked what I saw.

Maybe five-foot-six with long brown hair, she filled out a figure-hugging dress that made her seem sensuous and carefree. She smiled as she flirted with another suit at the bar. He was much older than both of us; she was cruising for a moneyed lover.

Her smile was easy and warm, creating a dimple in the cheek I could see from across the room. The man in the suit looked enthralled.

I decided to cut his grass. I threw my jacket over the back of the bar stool next to them and ordered a beer.

~

'I'm not pretty,' slurred Lil, taking another sip of her chardonnay and spilling a drop onto her front. Up close, she had muddy irises and freckles. I liked freckles.

'You are,' I insisted, as she wiped at the drop of wine with her tissue. 'I think you're beautiful.'

'I'm fat.'

'Beautiful.'

She laughed, those dimples arresting me again. 'So, what ... what's your name again?'

'Andrew.'

'What do you do for a living, Andrew? You're all dressed up in a big, flash suit like a little kid at his mother's wedding.'

'I'm a lawyer.' I didn't usually like to break this to potential lady-friends too early in the evening, since some didn't find it as attractive as others. But Lil didn't look too fazed.

'No, really? My brother-in-law's a lawyer, and he's a total arsehole.'

I nodded. 'Yeah, there are a few of them around.' A change of subject was probably called for. 'How about you? What do you do?'

'I'm a florist.'

'Cool.' It wouldn't have mattered if she said she was a slaughterhouse throat-cutter, I still would've been enthusiastic. We were playing the niceties game in anticipation of sex. 'A creative mind.'

'Well, in training, anyway. I'm not ... you know, it takes a lot of practice.'

'That's funny your name is Lil – is it short for Lily?'

'It is, but lilies are funeral flowers.' She stuck out her tongue to express her disgust. 'I prefer to imagine I was named Lilium, for Lilium Asiatica. Queen of the Night.'

'I don't suppose there's any flowers named Andrew?'

She laughed. 'What's your middle name?'

'Barney.'

'Well, then we're a good pair. A florist named Lily and a lawyer named Barney.'

She grinned, having amused herself. I felt slightly offended. 'There's a lot more to being a lawyer than just arguing with people.'

'Well, it's a good name for flora too. There's a day lily called Barney. And a nineteenth-century American botanist known as E.E. Barney.'

The light behind her eyes as she imparted her knowledge almost had me convinced that floristry wouldn't be a bad career choice if ever I had to give up the law. It wasn't typical for me to get too enthralled by anything a potential sexual partner had to say. But Lil was intriguing. She was working hard to better her skills and knowledge in a field for which she had obvious passion. She seemed like someone who had their shit together.

She pulled out her phone and started scrolling through pictures. 'See,' she said, passing the phone to me. 'That's one of my arrangements.'

I glanced at the picture. A bunch of flowers.

'That's great, Lil,' I enthused. 'Beautiful.'

She beamed, then leaned across to scroll through some more. 'This is my favourite.'

'Pretty.'

'Yeah.' Sensing my lack of appreciation for the finer details of her craft, she took the phone back. She was about to cancel out of the photos when it rang.

I glanced away politely as she took the call but found myself looking back when she spoke to the caller. Her voice had become heavy and cold.

'I'm out, Sam. I don't have time to talk with you.' She gave me a fleeting apologetic smile. 'Yes, tomorrow. That's fine. I don't know what we have to talk about, but yes. Fine.' She ended the call, her expression clouded. 'Fuckhead.'

'Someone hassling you?' I felt it was polite to ask, but I crossed my fingers under the bar in the hope that the conversation wouldn't need to go anywhere too intense.

'Nah. Just ...' She shrugged. 'Yeah, just someone who can't take no for an answer.' She seemed to pull herself together. 'Come on, Barney, I am the Queen of the Night. And the night is young, right?'

'Right,' I agreed. 'Let's get out of here.'

~

In the morning I woke early, as was my habit. Lil was still asleep, her dark hair lying across the pink pillows of her sweat-stained bed.

The sex had been hot. Intense. Just how I liked it.

It was Thursday, and I had to work. I left her a nice note with my phone number, which would hopefully ensure she wouldn't be too pissed off to find me gone, then collected my stuff and vamoosed.

I hoped she would call. I wanted to make her smile again. Not just to see her dimples.

CHAPTER 1

'Andrew, you're wanted.'

A wave of irritation washed over me. 'I'm so close to getting this statement finished.'

Sally didn't much care. She was fifty-five; she'd been a legal secretary for nearly forty years. The only thing that annoyed her more than poor time-management skills was twenty-nine-year-old junior prosecutors who thought they were important because they had a law degree.

'It's Rufus,' she clarified.

I sighed and saved my document. It'd been a long day. Mainly because I'd had quite a few drinks before Lil took me back to her apartment in Northbridge last night, then of course I hadn't done much sleeping over the course of the night and was up before the crack of dawn. Then my mother had been on the phone early about my brother Rodney's upcoming wedding. Something about a most ungrateful young lady who should consider herself lucky she's going to be part of our family. And Rufus had been at me all day to do something about the Schneider matter. The District Court was getting stroppy and Schneider's counsel, a ferocious barrister named Audrey Simons, was threatening to apply to strike out the charges for want of prosecution. The problem was that it was starting to look like the cops might have screwed up the investigation from beginning to end, starting with seizing a whole heap of evidence from Schneider's house without a warrant. Or, at least, not one that they could now produce. They reckoned they'd lost it. I was having trouble trying to work out if there was a case that would stick among the mess. Rufus was threatening to nail my balls to the wall if I didn't get swiftly to the bottom of whether we would have to discontinue the charge at hideous expense to the state and justify the decision to the victims and the media. As I frequently found myself saying since I'd joined the Office of the Director of Public Prosecutions, it wasn't my fault, but it was my problem.

Two detectives loitered in Rufus' office. I knew them both. Detective Sergeant Richard Simms had been a police officer for longer than Sally had been a legal secretary. He was old-school. He had no patience for lawyers and never held back when it came to making the fact known. He regularly announced that in forty-three years of policing, he'd never come across a good lawyer. He was always happy to declare that in front of me or any of my colleagues. We consoled ourselves with the thought that perhaps he was talking about defence lawyers. Broadly speaking, the DPP was supposed to be on the same side as the cops, although as a general rule they treated us like the enemy. This was because we were always asking them unreasonable questions like 'Where's the warrant?' and 'Did you give him his rights?'

Detective Senior Constable Jessy Parkin was young, a little younger than me. She had a reputation for being a dedicated cop who was excellent at her job, and was quite severe though undeniably cute. She kept her white-blond hair practically shaved so no one could grab her ponytail and, despite being no more than five foot five, she frightened lawyers and crooks alike with fierce green eyes. We'd worked together last year on *State v Aaron Thomas Urquhart*, a long and boring drug-trafficking case, the appeal process in respect of which had only just wrapped at the beginning of the week. I'd been intending to give her a call and deliver my congratulations on the eventual verdict and ask her out to dinner. I probably would've done it last night if I hadn't got lucky with Lil. And I wouldn't call her now if things went well with Lil. I was hoping they would. She hadn't called me yet today, but I was putting that down to her being not-overly-desperate rather than totally uninterested.

Neither Richard nor Jessy were particularly involved in the

Schneider matter, so I wasn't sure what they wanted. Rufus didn't seem to be about to enlighten me.

'Can I help you officers?'

'We'd like you to come down to the station and help us with some enquiries,' Richard intoned.

I laughed. 'Why didn't you bring the files?'

'No, it's not about a prosecution, Andrew,' Jessy interjected. 'It's an investigation. There's been a crime ... and you're implicated.'

My heart began to pound. *Holy fuck.* I'd no idea what they were talking about, but my gut told me clearly: *no good can come of this.*

'What crime? What's happened?' I tried not to sound too panicky. It was important to stay cool when dealing with the cops. They were already convinced we were just a bunch of namby-pamby pen-pushers. Frightened squeaks emanating from my lips would only reinforce this impression.

'A murder,' said Richard, and watched for my reaction.

Out of the corner of my eye, I saw Rufus wince.

'I'm implicated in a *murder*?' I yelped, feeling the blood draining from my head. 'How? How can that be?'

'Come with us now, and we'll have a chat about it on video.'

Rufus laid one hand on my shoulder. 'Now, you know you don't have to talk to them.'

My hands were starting to shake. 'If I was guilty of murder, I certainly wouldn't talk to them.'

'Do you want someone with you? I can get you a good defence lawyer.'

I felt like I was in greater need of a doctor than a lawyer. 'No. I'm fine. Really, I'm fine. Thanks. Thanks Rufus.'

'Stay calm now, Andrew,' Rufus went on. 'It's probably just some big misunderstanding.'

Probably? What did he mean, *probably*?

'Let's go,' I snapped. 'The sooner we get this interview finished, the better.'

~

The photograph smacked down on the desk. I'd seen dozens of them before. A classic crime-scene pic. A gruesomely twisted figure, gut-churning wounds, a face that belonged to no one, bereft of life.

I picked it up.

No one had bothered to tell me who the dead guy was. During the long and uncomfortably quiet car trip down to the cop shop, I'd pondered the possibilities. There was Martin Pfizer, a rapist I'd fought hard to bin six months ago who'd just had his conviction overturned on appeal. I could see how they might have considered me a suspect if he'd been offed. Or Harry Anderson, a drug lord who'd threatened to have my existence terminated if I went ahead with his trial, which I was presently doing. Maybe the cops suspected I'd got in first. None of these guys seemed like a brilliant fit, to my mind. Maybe someone had actually framed me, as payback for a conviction. Maybe some dickhead had written a note saying 'I, Andrew Deacon, hereby confess that it was me who killed this guy' and stuck it on the dead guy's chest. Even if they didn't suspect me of the killing, it would certainly be grounds to haul me down to the police station and question me as to who might have the motive to have written such a thing.

I'd convinced myself in the car that that was exactly what I was going to see when I looked at the photo: a dead guy, completely unknown to me, with my name written on his chest, *Da Vinci Code*-style.

The dead guy was a woman.

I stared hard at the photo.

When I recognised her, I found myself dropping the picture like it was infected, and a kind of repulsed grunt came out of my mouth.

'That's Lil,' I whispered.

Richard's voice was cold. '*That's* Lily Constantine. Twenty-three years old. Two brothers, two sisters, two devastated parents. Stabbed. Fifteen times.'

I had experienced what you'd have to describe as a blessed life, to date. I grew up on a sheep farm near the coast in the south-west of Western Australia. I had two loving parents who helped me with my homework and took me to sport and funded my city-based secondary studies and university education. From that springboard I was able to catapult myself into a coveted career, working days and nights for the Director of Public Prosecutions. I'd been at that for four years, and I was doing well. I was having success. People were talking about me as some kind of up-and-coming next big thing. I had a bright future ahead of me.

Well, it was bright, right up until the moment I recognised last night's hook-up in a crime-scene photograph.

'She's a florist,' I rasped. I looked up at the two police officers. Both were staring at me. 'That's all I can tell you about her.'

'We don't need to know about her, Andrew,' Jessy murmured, her eyes focused and still. 'We know who she is. What we need to know is why you killed her.'

Oh, God. 'I did not kill her.'

I looked back at the photo. I couldn't believe now that I hadn't recognised her straight away. The position in which she lay was not so different from the position in which I'd left her first thing this morning, lying curled up on her side with her glossy hair across the pillow. Only now her hair was knotted and sticky with blood, and there were grisly wounds to her chest and stomach, bruises to her neck.

'How do you know this woman?' Jessy continued. 'What is she to you?'

'She's ...' I paused, swallowing painfully over razorblades. 'She's nothing to me. I met her last night. I had sex with her. Once. Last night.'

Jessy's eyes narrowed. I suspected she was grossed out by my admission. Geez, a hook-up was not the most heinous crime in the world. Everyone did it. I was young and single. I hadn't done anything wrong. And I'd left a nice note. Oh yes, the note.

'You found my note.'

'Your phone number made it pretty clear who was there.'

I nodded. 'Yes, and when you do all the forensics, which no doubt you have your people diligently and competently sorting right now, you'll find my DNA too.'

Jessy shuddered. 'You're agreeing to provide a sample?'

'Of course.'

Richard disappeared and returned moments later with a kit. He used a swab to take skin cells from the inside of my cheek. It was an intimate experience.

'Why didn't you use a condom?' Jessy asked.

'We did. But I'm expecting you won't have too much trouble locating it in the bathroom rubbish bin. In any case, it was very intense sex,' I informed her. 'Very physical.' I would have felt embarrassed about telling Jessy this much about my sex life if I had anything to lose. It wasn't like there was much point in trying to impress her now, given that she was about to charge me with murder.

'We get it, thanks Andrew,' said Richard, clicking his police-issue pen impatiently. 'So you spent the night at Lily's apartment in Northbridge. What did you do when you woke?'

'I got dressed. I threw water on my face, wrote the note, grabbed my stuff, and left.'

'Did you speak to her before you left?'

'No.'

'Did you touch her?'

'No, I didn't. Not after I woke up.'

'How did she look to you when you last saw her?'

'Asleep.' I shuddered. 'Alive, and asleep. I wrote the note because I hoped to see her again.'

'What time did you leave the apartment?'

'Before dawn. There were only those filmy white curtains on the windows. I woke when it started to get light. Whatever time that was. Maybe a bit after five. I texted my friend to say I was skipping our run as I left the apartment. I can check my phone and tell you the exact time.'

'Did you lock the door on your way out?'

'Yes, I pulled it shut. The door locked itself. I checked it.'

'Did you see anyone else at the apartment while you were there?'

'I had the feeling she had a flatmate, but I never saw anyone while I was there.'

'Did you return to the apartment at any time today?'

'No.'

'Where did you go when you left the apartment?'

'I got a coffee at Zoomer's then I went straight to work. I showered downstairs, and then I started working and I stayed at work all day. I think it was around six thirty in the morning when I got to work. You can get Rufus to check my pass card on that one.'

Richard nodded. 'Don't worry, we will.'

'Just make sure you get a warrant.'

Richard frowned, as if he suspected – correctly – that I was having a go. 'Don't worry,' he snapped. 'We will.'

~

I'd thought I'd had a hard day at five in the afternoon. By ten o'clock that night I was starting to reconsider my definition of a hard day. Jessy and Richard were obviously used to this kind of workload as they didn't seem to be tiring in the slightest. I was willing to think about conceding that cops possibly did work at least equally as hard as prosecutors.

Jessy was like a dog with a bone, gnawing at the same points over and over. How did you meet? Where did you meet? What did you talk about? When did you leave the pub? Which nightclubs did you go to? What time did you get to the apartment in Northbridge? What time did you get up, what time did you leave the apartment, what time did you go to Zoomer's for coffee, what time did Sally tell you that you were a lazy brat, what time did your mother ring, how was Lily lying when you left the apartment, how much did you have to drink, how much did she have to drink, did you kill her, did you stab her, did you thrust a kitchen knife into her chest and her breasts and her guts and drain the blood from her body?

'I didn't do this,' I told Jessy through gritted teeth. 'I'm sorry ... I know you're just doing your job and, honestly, I'm not going to blame you once this thing is over. But I think you really ought to know that I'm not a psycho killer. I love women. I don't hurt them, I don't hit them, I don't abuse them. I have a great relationship with my mother and my sisters, and I have a great relationship with my lovers. I've got exes who can vouch for me.' Well, I was pretty sure they would tell Jessy I was a nice guy. Just a bit ... immature. 'I really hope you two aren't the only ones on this job, and there are other cops out there now following up other leads.'

Jessy leaned across the desk and our eyes locked. I searched hers for any sign that she believed me. There was nothing there.

'What other leads, Andrew?' she said quietly. 'You got any ideas for us? Because all the signs are pointing to you. There's no one else in the frame for this.'

I felt like my eyes were flitting all over the place in response to the steadiness of hers. I couldn't seem to stop them. 'She said something about a guy who was hassling her.'

Jessy almost laughed. 'Really? How helpful.'

I found myself pinching my forehead as I tried to focus. 'Well, she didn't use the word *hassle*. I think I used that word.'

She looked like she found my stupidity tiring. 'So, tell me what happened.'

'We were still at the bar, and she was showing me some photos on her phone. She got a call, some bloke wanting to talk to her. She said she was out, didn't have time, but she'd talk to him tomorrow. She didn't know what they had to talk about, but she'd talk to him tomorrow.'

'Can you remember her exact words?'

'Sam: that's the name she called him. *I'm out Sam, I don't have time to talk with you.* Or something like that. Then she said they could talk tomorrow and hung up on him. She said it was just someone who couldn't take no for an answer.'

'Tomorrow ... as in today.'

I felt sick. 'Yeah. Today.'

'Could you hear what Sam said to her?'

'No. Far too much noise in the bar. I could only hear her side of the conversation.'

Jessy raised her eyebrows but said nothing. Maybe she was more excited by this lead than she was letting on. It probably wouldn't do to let the suspect think you're not still all over them.

'Why didn't you mention this call earlier?'

'I honestly don't know. I'd forgotten all about it. I was thinking about my own problems. I just ... I forgot about it, I'm sorry, Jessy.'

She stared at me as if she'd like to smack me around the head. Our intimate moment was interrupted by Richard's arrival back in the room. He pulled Jessy aside and they spoke in low murmurs. Then she turned back to face me.

'Andrew, we've got the time of death. It's much later than we thought. Close to ten this morning.'

'Oh, that's...' I wasn't sure what it was. Good news for me, I supposed. If a woman's time of death could ever amount to good news.

Richard smiled, as best he could. 'Your alibi is good for hours either side,' he said. 'We appreciate your time. We may have some more questions later, but for now you're free to go.'

CHAPTER 2

I stared at my computer screen. The last Schneider statement hovered before me like the words on a heads-up display. I couldn't make any sense of them. I was having trouble believing they were written in English. I contemplated ringing IT and seeing if my computer had a virus that had mutated everything into Klingon.

The more I thought about it, the more I really did believe that I'd given Jessy the name of Lil's killer.

Sam.

Sam was the despicable piece of shit who'd robbed a beautiful young woman of her life at the age of twenty-three. She had freckles and dimples and all she wanted to do was arrange flowers. How could anyone do what I'd seen in that photograph to a woman like that?

Jessy had been unequivocal when she dropped me off in the underground car park near my work after our interview wrapped last night.

'Listen, Andrew, you're in the clear. This is all an unfortunate mess. You're bloody unlucky. But you need to forget all this ever happened and move on, yeah?'

I nodded. 'Of course.'

'I mean, you fucked this woman once. She wasn't your girlfriend. Like you said, she wasn't anything to you.'

'I understand. What do you think I'm going to do?'

'Oh, I don't know. Try and do my job for me?'

'I can't wait to put it all behind me, starting right now. You can follow up the Sam lead. I'll just forget this ever happened.'

'Good.'

I clicked the unlock button on my BMW's remote. 'It was good seeing you again, Jess.'

She laughed. 'Yes, let's do a five-hour interrogation again some time, shall we?'

'Well, it's sexy the way you do it.'

'Good to see you've bounced back. You really are incorrigible.'

So now I was back to my normal life, back to work in the office, back to Schneider, back to Sally giving me a hard time about my attitude. I told Rufus what he needed to know about what'd happened. He said I had a very promising future with the DPP and as far as he was concerned the matter would go no further. He was the one who'd provided the details of my alibi, and no one else even knew I'd been interviewed, so there really was no need for it to go any further. Life would just continue as normal. No problems. All good.

Just as soon as Jessy charged Sam.

~

'What do you mean?'

Jessy and I faced each other across a table at Zoomer's, the café midway between my work and hers, a week after Lil's death. It was seven o'clock on a Thursday morning and I'd once again forgone my usual run after Jessy agreed to meet for an early coffee. Zoomer's was popular in the mornings so if you wanted privacy you had to go out to the beer garden, which resulted in wet-bum syndrome on days like today when dew coated every surface. A flock of corellas had taken over the giant fig trees from where they screamed cockatoo obscenities and threw branches at patrons. I was pretty sure they were going to get shot soon, as it was all getting a bit out of hand. But for now, the corellas ruled the beer garden at Zoomer's.

'Pretty much what I said,' said Jessy.

'A dead end? Are you telling me there's no Sam? She said he was a man who couldn't take no for an answer, an ex-boyfriend, maybe, or a friend who wanted more.'

Jessy sighed like she was dealing with a pouty child. 'According to your statement a week ago, she never said Sam was a man.'

I was confused. 'What?'

'You told me her only words to you about the caller was that it was *just someone who can't take no for answer*. So that could be a man, or a woman. Samuel or Samantha, and maybe a few other possibilities as well, I guess.'

I stared at her. 'She said ... I don't ... I'm not sure now what she said.'

'It doesn't matter. What you said at the time means we can't rule out either possibility, even if you change your story now.'

'So, is there a Sam? Male or female?'

'There is a Sam, but it looks like he's not the killer.'

'*What* are you talking about? Who is he?'

'Samuel Godfrey, SC.'

'Sam Godfrey.' I frowned. 'I know that name.' I clicked my fingers and pointed at her, both actions clearly irritating her. 'He's a defence barrister. I haven't been up against him myself, but he represented – he was on Rose. And Hadley. And that rape case ... you know, the stockings guy.'

'Reilly.'

'Yeah, Reilly. And I'm pretty sure I saw Godfrey's name in the paper recently – he's been representing that James Millan, the guy who set his girlfriend on fire but reckons his sentence was too harsh 'cause actually she's not as fucked-up as she claims.'

'Godfrey is Lil's brother-in-law. He's been married to her sister Amanda for ten years. He's the only Sam in her life, so far as we can work out. We're still making enquiries but at this stage it really looks like there just isn't anyone else she knows by that name.' Jessy shook her head. 'And the Constantines won't hear a word against Godfrey. They're not well-off themselves; they're a hard-working immigrant family. The shine of their eldest daughter marrying a wealthy Australian barrister is far from wearing off. Lil's mum and dad run an Italian restaurant in Northbridge. It nearly went bust last year but Sam bailed them out. He's a great husband and a great dad. As far the

LISA ELLERY

Constantines are concerned, he's their golden boy.'

'Have you pulled his phone records?'

'And Lil's. The call she answered when she was with you was from a payphone in the city.'

'Seriously? A payphone?'

'People don't realise they still exist and actually there's quite a lot of them, more than you'd expect. Travellers use them as wi-fi hotspots, but you can absolutely still stick some coins in one and make an anonymous phone call. Couldn't pull any useful prints unfortunately. That was always a long shot. We're still checking surveillance footage. Anyway, there are no calls from Godfrey's phone to Lil's that night. There are very occasional calls from him to her on previous occasions. Maybe once a fortnight? At appropriate times. Like a brother-in-law might call his sister-in-law. Nothing like you'd expect if they were having an affair. We checked her phone for texts – nothing.'

'Maybe he deleted all her texts before he left her apartment after killing her.'

'Maybe. There are no emails in Outlook on her computer or his. Maybe they used webmail, but Sam's given us access to his Hotmail address. It's got tons and tons of history. It's clearly the address he uses every day. But there's nothing on that except perfectly innocuous emails between them. Perhaps he has another one. The techies are working on that and trying to get into hers but that's not an easy thing.'

'What are the innocuous emails about?'

'She asks him for legal advice about setting up her own florist's shop. She was planning to call it Full Bloom. Anyway, he gives her the advice. There are a few other emails where she asks him a few further questions about Full Bloom, and he responds. There's nothing particularly overfamiliar in the emails.'

'Could he have arranged for her to write those? Or written them himself from a webmail address he'd created? Maybe he thought they might be needed in case his wife found them out, to provide him with a cover story?'

Jessy looked up and nodded thanks as our coffees were delivered. 'Maybe, but we've spoken to all her friends, all her work colleagues, her family – no one knows anything about her being in a relationship with Sam or anyone. If she was having sex with her sister's husband, she didn't tell a living soul about it. Not even her best friends. Not even her friends living overseas. And everyone who knew the family said that they seemed to have an innocent and normal friendly family relationship. The conversation you've recounted sounds like it was with a different person. Another Sam. A Sam we haven't found yet.'

'She said her brother-in-law was a lawyer and an arsehole.'

'Well, if that's the case, you're the only one she's told she feels that way about him. Ever.'

I understood why Jessy found it hard to believe that a woman would confess an intimate secret to some strange bloke she'd picked up that night in a bar. But maybe she had, just casually without thinking, *because* I was no one. It was a secret; she couldn't tell her family and she couldn't tell her friends.

Maybe I really was the one and only person in the world to whom this funny, ambitious young woman had given just enough information to enable her killer to be caught.

Justice for Lil Constantine was in my hands.

'No.' Jessy was firm.

'What do you mean?'

'No, I can see what you're thinking. This is *not your problem*. Leave it to me. Richard and I are the police officers. We will do the investigation. You are the last root she had and that's it.'

'Yeah, but what if –'

'For God's sake, Andrew,' snapped Jessy. 'You're starting to piss me off. I shouldn't have told you anything.'

'Jessy, I'm only trying to help you catch this guy.'

'I'm not giving you any more information.'

Shit. 'You have to,' I whined. 'Come on, Jessy, you have to keep me updated.'

She stood and thrust five dollars into my hand to cover her coffee, then tried in vain to unstick her pants from her bottom. 'Forget it. You're not a cop; you've no right to this information. And as a witness and a one-time suspect in the case, I very much doubt you will be the one handling the prosecution when we ultimately find who did this.'

For a cop, that was an impressive level of insight into legal niceties. 'Is there any more DNA? Apart from mine?'

'No,' snapped Jessy, glaring down at me. 'There isn't. Don't bug me about this anymore, Andrew. I mean it.'

CHAPTER 3

The next morning, I jogged away from my apartment at a quarter past five for my last run of the working week. I was due to meet Russell in Kings Park at five thirty. It was early April and starting to get a bit nippy in the mornings. We'd just begun to push our runs out a bit later to have enough light to see by in the park. When I arrived, there was a bunch of runners waiting for their friends or preparing to run, all stretching against a curb or jogging on the spot. Russ was sitting on a park bench with one ankle crossed over the other thigh, as if he didn't feel the cold, reading the *West Australian* by the dim light coming out of his Garmin watch. He looked up as I jogged towards him and then grinned, getting to his feet and leaving the paper next to the bin for someone else to grab. Russ didn't really believe in warming up.

'Did you run yesterday?' I asked as we took off together down Fraser Avenue.

'Yeah. Went faster without you.'

'My meeting was a total waste of time as it turned out.'

I first met Russ four years ago running the City to Surf marathon. It's a fairly tough course with some gnarly hills. I was in good condition. I'd run a race over east in just under three and a half hours about a month prior and, though that'd been hard, I'd been fantasising since then in a dark corner of my mind that I might be in with a chance for a sub-three if I wanted it badly enough. I was only twenty-five at the time and I knew it took many men until well into their thirties, forties or even fifties to drop under three hours, but the advantage of youth of course is a certain degree of cluelessness about one's limitations. So yeah ... I dared to hope. When the pack thinned out a little as we approached the first hill at the top of St Georges Terrace, I noticed a skinny, goateed man running ahead of me. He looked to be around my age. He looked like he was running strong, just a bit quicker than what felt comfortable for me, so I thought I'd see if I could hold him for a bit.

Thirty-eight kilometres later, I was still holding him. It'd become apparent a couple of hours earlier that he was probably treating this as a training run for a bigger race and was cruising along pretty comfortably. I, on the other hand, was – to put it mildly – struggling. *You never feel so alive as when you're nearly dead*, Russ likes to say, and if that was the case, well then, boy, was I alive. I was pretty sure I'd been in the red zone for long enough to give any cardiologist who might stumble across my Strava stats a heart attack. I'd been reduced to repeating *I can do this* over and over in my head, one word per footfall, just to try to gain the most miniscule psychological advantage. Despite this, I felt a strong urge to quit every thirty seconds or so. With four kays to go, I was mentally vacillating between four kays being in fact not much, or the longest and most impossible distance ever attempted by man. My mind flip-flopped hopelessly on the issue until I realised that this was just stupid. I couldn't do this. I was not the kind of runner I was pretending to be. You can't fake a marathon, for fuck's sake. I didn't need to stop, just back it off a smidge. Just a smidge. It'd make practically no difference to my overall time. A minute or two probably, over four kilometres. Probably only a minute.

Russell, running beside me, sensed my plan before I'd even executed it. He had a runner's intuition. He spoke the first words he'd said to me over the course of the entire race.

Come on man. You've got this.

After that, the desire to not let down some random stranger who believed in me pushed me forward. As we crossed the line at City Beach a quarter of an hour later, I stopped my watch. I hadn't so much as glanced at it the whole run because I knew I had nothing left in the tank, whatever it said. By the time I'd wiped enough sweat from my eyes to see the bloody thing, it told me I'd run the race in two hours and fifty-eight minutes, and ten seconds.

I looked up and saw the skinny guy grinning at me. *Nice run, bro,* he said. I felt like hugging him. Instead, I reached out to shake his hand and thanked him for getting me over the line. Then I ducked behind a tree and threw up.

Russ and I had started training together after finding out we both liked to run in Kings Park in the mornings before work. For the past four years we'd run most weekday mornings, as early as the sunrise allowed.

'What happened?' said Russ as we picked up our pace at the roundabout. 'Why was it a waste of time?'

I'd told him a short version of the story by text when I bailed on yesterday's run. 'So now they've found out who Sam is,' I said, picking up where I'd left off. 'Or they think they have, unless there's some other Sam literally no one knows about, who could be male or female apparently, according to whatever I said after five hours of interrogation. But anyway, the only Sam they can find in Lil's life is her brother-in-law and they don't think he did it. There's no evidence at all implicating him.'

'Could have been just a phone call.'

'Yeah, there's just a few things about it that are not sitting right for me. She was shitty with the Sam she spoke to. According to her family she gets along just fine with her brother-in-law, but she told me her brother-in-law was an arsehole. So what's that about? That's one thing. The other is that the Sam who rang Lil, rang her from a payphone. The brother-in-law probably makes a million bucks a year. I expect he'd have a mobile phone and it wouldn't be often he'd run out of credit.'

'That's only suss if it was the brother-in-law that called.'

'I think it's suss generally. I think the person who made that call knows exactly who did this.'

Russ increased our pace again as his lungs and legs began to embrace the workout. 'I do agree it seems like a grim coincidence this lady would get a call from a payphone the night before she winds up murdered,' he said. 'And from someone who clearly wasn't a friend.'

'As far as evidence goes, it feels to me like they have everything they need to know who did this, and so far, absolutely nothing they need to convict him. He's not the only Sam in the world, a fact he'll have no trouble proving. And if by some miracle prosecutors did manage to establish he called Lil that night and she was pissed off at him, he'd have an explanation for both. With a good enough story, he should be able to convince a jury that using a payphone does not amount to proof beyond reasonable doubt that you're a murderer.'

'Do you think the cops will bother?'

'What?'

'You know, looking for evidence against him? Will they give up, or keep trying to run him down?'

'I dunno. Jessy got mad at me for pressing her on it. Now she reckons she's not telling me anything.'

'Do they have another suspect?'

'No.'

'Have you met this guy Sam?'

'Not really. I know who he is.'

'Maybe you should go and have a chat to him.'

'Maybe.'

Russ' ideas were often ill-advised at best, but generally just downright reckless. As a young male myself, I was not well-equipped to resist them.

'You can tell a lot about a man if you look him in the eye,' he said.

Part of me thought he was right. Probably mostly the young male part, but I supposed if it went pear-shaped, I could talk my way out of it. Or run my way out of it. Whichever was required. It wouldn't be the first time I'd sprinted down St Georges Terrace in my suit and tie.

Of course, a more mature part of me didn't think so much of the idea. What I should do, if I had any brains, was forget about Lil Constantine. I should show some respect for Jessy, who I knew was a good cop and a diligent one. Jessy had this under control. She didn't need me second-guessing her.

'Wanna do some intervals?' I said. 'Five hundred on, five hundred off?'

'Sounds good. We can go off my watch.'

The first day Russ and I ran together, the day after the City to Surf, I told him I worked for the DPP. He told me he worked in a sports store in the city and had a wife, Cindy, and two little boys. I told him that I had the hots for someone from work, and he informed me matter-of-factly that he suffered from a mental illness. Specifically, schizophrenia. Well, schizoaffective disorder, whatever that was. Quietly, I'd shat myself because I knew nothing about it then. It seemed extreme. It wasn't like confessing you had the occasional asthma attack and might need someone to give you a puffer. He'd looked at the expression on my face and laughed. *I think it's important you accept you're gonna have to fight me*, he'd said. *'Cause you sure couldn't outrun me.*

He was joking, though I didn't know it then. He had a pretty fucked-up sense of humour. On his Facebook page he described himself as: *Paranoid schizophrenic with delusions of grandeur.* Lots of people wrote that kind of thing as a joke, but of course with Russ, the joke was, it wasn't a joke. Well, he might've been exaggerating about the delusions of grandeur. He was certainly an overachiever, so you could argue he was just stating facts.

I looked it all up anyway as soon as I could get to my phone. I found out that most schizophrenics aren't violent at all. Nevertheless, I quietly hoped he wouldn't contact me again, but it was a forlorn hope. He was keen to run again the next day. He had a lot of friends, but not many who could come anywhere close to keeping up with him. I couldn't say no without admitting I was an ignorant dick. I had to run, and I did run, that day and pretty much every day since. I asked Russ about what happened when he had an episode and he was more than happy to talk about it. The worst time, he said, was when he was burning alive. Cooked skin was sloughing off. He could smell his hair on fire. He explained that when this kind of thing happened, he would look at the people around him. If no one seemed worried, he knew it wasn't real, and he just had to endure it. I was impressed by his faith in people. What if no one seemed worried because actually no one gave a fuck? I didn't mention that to Russ though. Really, his innate faith in other people, even strangers, was incredibly fortunate. It was that faith that enabled him to manage this beast.

He was keen to turn me into a better runner, and he always encouraged me to try bigger things. He loved to run, and he truly loved to help others. Within six months of running with Russ, a sub-three-hour marathon was pretty much assured each time I raced.

It was about seven o'clock when I swiped back into my apartment complex. I got myself a drink of water. The intervals had been hard, thanks to the influence of my running buddy. I felt good. I was still sweating far too much to have a shower, so I picked up my mobile phone.

'Hey Jessy, it's Andrew.' I knew she'd be at least at Zoomer's by now.

'Hi Andrew.' Jessy sounded busy. Maybe she was already at work. Of course, cops did work quite hard.

'Listen, I wanted to tell you that you're right. I'm sorry I've been difficult about this Constantine thing, demanding that you fill me in on the investigation and that sort of thing. You're totally right. It's none of my business and nothing to do with me. And I'm sure you're doing a great job.'

'Thank you, Andrew.' She sounded like she wasn't sure whether I was being sarcastic or not. 'The investigation is thorough, I can assure you.'

I glanced at the bunch of blue-mauve hydrangeas I'd pinched from the central garden at my apartment complex. I'd poked them into an old marmalade jar (itself a recycled pasta sauce bottle) and positioned it at the centre of my dining room table. It gave a sort of softness to the apartment which was usually fairly stark, with its stacks of *Financial Review* and *Australian Muscle Car* magazines on the coffee table, posters stuck on the walls with blu-tack and complete lack of interior design. I was sure my mother would be pleased to see I'd taken to displaying flowers in my apartment. Though it was probably best if no one found out about it, since there was a group email from the chair of the body corporate threatening to report the theft to the police just as soon as he ascertained who was responsible.

'Jessy, I was wondering whether you might be prepared to come to a family wedding with me in Esperance next weekend. It's my brother's wedding. I kind of need a date.'

'You're asking me out?'

She sounded incredulous. I couldn't believe she hadn't already felt the vibes. 'Yeah. If that's okay.'

'But ... your family will be there. You're going to introduce me to your *family* on our first date?'

I was starting to rethink the whole idea. But I was pretty sure she'd get along okay with my family. They were country people. My father was an intelligent, practical man who drove a Landcruiser ute with fishing-rod holders welded to the bullbar, which he fixed himself if it broke down. He'd taught all us kids to do the same. He bought the newspaper every day and read it front to back and did the cryptic crossword. He was hardworking, organised and disciplined. And he was brave, too. When I was only about ten or eleven years old, I'd been with Dad in the passenger seat of his ute on the way back from a clearing sale to which he'd allowed me to accompany him as a reward for doing the dishes all week. It was mid-winter; a biting southerly had blown all day, occasionally punctuated with blustery rain. Dad and I were in the middle of a competition which involved seeing how long we could endure hurtling into the icy wind with both the windows down. There was, of course, little point to it, but it seemed like fun to me at the time. As we approached the railway crossing not far from our place, Dad swore under his breath. I followed his gaze and saw up ahead an iron-ore train had collided with a car on the railway crossing. The train had derailed and the car was upside down, its tail-lights still on. Dad accelerated towards the crossing before coming to a screaming halt, yelled at me to stay where I was, then leapt from the ute. I watched as he tried to open a door, then smashed a rear window with a rock. The train driver must've been a pretty good runner because he arrived not long after in a steelcap-booted sprint, and the two of them together dragged a woman out of the wreck.

The car exploded into flames not thirty seconds after they were clear of it.

It turned out the woman was the sister of one of my teachers. To thank my dad for saving her sister's life, Mrs Broom organised a trip to Perth for my whole class later in the year. We went to Scitech and ice-skating. After that it wasn't just me who thought my dad was a hero. The entire school did.

My mother was what I'd always termed a *free spirit*. She was hard-working, like Dad, but she wasn't what you'd call organised. Like nature itself, she was unpredictable and she never showed up to anything on time. She never actually started getting ready until the thing had started. It drove Dad mad that he always missed the first half of the footy and the first four races of any horseracing meet. But you couldn't speed Mum up, any more than you could slow Dad down.

Mum always gave the impression she was a bit ditzy, but I knew from experience that she was the one person you wanted in your corner when shit got real. Dad knew that too.

Both my parents were straight shooters, just like Jessy. And Jessy was a country person too. She'd grown up in the gold-mining town of Kalgoorlie–Boulder. Her dad was an underground bogger operator, she once told me, the sort of bloke who could end a twelve-hour shift buried up to his thighs in a rockfall and not think to mention it at dinner.

'But it's not really a big deal,' I said. 'I mean, I'll tell them you're just a friend who's agreed to be my arm-candy for the weekend. I just don't want to turn up in my hometown on my own, you know? My sisters will try to set me up with their friends.'

'Well, since you put it so romantically, how can I resist?'

'Sweet.'

'Are you hoping I'm going to indulge in pillow talk about Constantine?' She certainly didn't mince her words.

'No, like I said, I've forgotten about that. Cross my heart. I couldn't care less what happens with that one.'

CHAPTER 4

'So, Richard,' I said airily as Richard Simms and I wrapped up a lengthy proofing session on Monday morning in relation to an aggravated burglary charge against some meth-addled young lady, the outcome of which wouldn't make much difference to her life or anyone else's either way. 'Don't s'pose they found any dirt on Sam Godfrey?'

'Jessy said I was to tell her if you raised this subject.'

Shit. Shit. 'Oh, please don't do that,' I begged, electing to abandon all pretence at indifference. 'We're going on a date this weekend. We're both taking Friday off. If you tell her, it will ruin everything.'

'No kidding.' Richard looked at me like he did feel a little bit sorry for me. 'I'm going to give you one chance, son, but you've got to take Jessy's advice. Back off about this.'

I nodded vigorously. 'I understand.'

Richard rolled his eyes. I knew he thought I was an idiot, but he also sensed I was sincere. Or at least I hoped he did. 'Look, I'll tell you this much. At the apartment we've got no unexplained DNA, no second person's blood, fibres, anything. It's the cleanest crime scene I've ever seen. There's no weapon, of course, and nothing to give us a clue about what might have motivated this killer. There were no other injuries, no sign of a head strike or much of a struggle, just fifteen merciless stab wounds. On top of that, there are no obvious suspects: no family feuds, no stalkers, no disgruntled ex-lovers. We've got no texts, emails, unusual communication of any sort, with Sam Godfrey or anyone. Pretty much our one and only clue so far is the call. Someone rang Lil the evening before her death from a payphone and there's a chance that caller was the killer, or someone associated with the killer. But we've got no fingerprints or DNA from the phone or useful footage of it, so the only evidence suggesting that Sam Godfrey was that caller is that one pissed witness – you – thinks they heard Lil say the name Sam. The thing is, she could've said Stan, or Pam. She could've said San, short for Sandra or Sandeep. It was a noisy bar. And we don't know if the caller said: "Hey, it's Sam here," or if she identified him or her by voice. If the latter, there's no guarantee Lil's identification of that caller was reliable. Let's face it, she was pissed as well. If we assume the caller was definitely someone called Sam, that narrows it down to one of the five hundred and fifty million Sams in the world. But if you got the name wrong, or if she misidentified the caller, the caller could be any one of the eight billion people on the planet.'

That sounded like bullshit to me. She knew the caller. It was someone called Sam, and it was someone she knew. But I nodded. 'Okay.'

I couldn't believe they really did have nothing to go on. How could someone just waltz into a locked apartment and brutally slash the occupant without leaving a trace of DNA or a single solitary clue behind? Wouldn't she have fought for her life? Surely, she must've drawn a drop of his blood somewhere? Scratched a fragment of his DNA?

Did the killer sneak in, and attack her as she slept?

'I locked the door, Richard. I locked the door when I left. There was no forced entry, right?'

Richard began signing each page of the statement I'd printed out for him on the agg. burg. charge. He made a point of correcting a typographical error made by me and initialling his changes. 'Right.'

'What did her family say about whether she would open the door to a stranger?'

Richard shook his head. 'She wouldn't have done that. Apparently.'

'So, we know she knew her killer.'

'Unless someone had a key, that's how it's looking.'

To my mind, there could be only one person in the frame for this. The caller was the killer, and the caller was the only Sam in Lil's life.

A man she didn't want to talk to, but who wanted to talk to her. A man who wouldn't take no for an answer. A man she described as *a total arsehole*.

'I suppose he has an alibi anyway,' I said, knowing Richard would give me this information only if he felt like it.

'He does. A watertight one, as it happens. But it wouldn't matter if he didn't, because there's no evidence against him.' Richard put the pen down and pushed the wad of pages in my direction. 'Every single member of her family is convinced of his innocence, Andrew. As tempting as it is to hang a defence lawyer out to dry for this, we just don't have a thing on him.'

~

'I'm just heading down to the District Court to have a word with the Registrar about Schneider,' I told Sally as soon as Richard left.

'Fine,' she said. 'I'll cover for you.'

'You make it sound like I'm planning to do something wrong,' I protested. I was, but it was spooky how she knew that.

She shrugged. 'They've invented these things called telephones,' she said. 'Busy people find them useful for communicating.'

'It's a lengthy matter.'

'I've already said I'll cover for you.' She glared at me. 'Get moving before I change my mind.'

I decided not to push my luck and headed downstairs and across the street to the car park. My new Beamer had been my twenty-ninth birthday present to myself last year. She was a beautiful creature, befitting my social and professional standing these days. And the ladies liked her a lot. Well, what was not to like? I found myself smiling whenever I sat in her plush leather driver's seat and watched my phone hook up via Bluetooth and cranked up my stereo. The car screamed over-the-top, ostentatious moneyed wanker, which was exactly what I loved about it. Ah, it was no wonder Sally hated me.

My brother rang while I was cruising down the terrace, which was great, as it enabled me to use the Bluetooth.

'Hey, Drew, how's it going?'

'Marvellous. If you don't count the five-hour police interrogation the other day.'

There was a short silence. 'What?'

'I was, briefly, a suspect for a murder. I'll tell you all about it this weekend.'

'So, did you murder someone? No, hang on, don't answer – this phone could be tapped.'

I laughed, marking the first time I'd found anything about this shit even slightly funny. 'No, it wasn't me. I was just unlucky enough to be the last person to see the victim alive.'

'That's hardcore, man. That's even more intense than what I'm going through right now.'

'What are you going through?'

'Two words. Bride. Zilla.'

'I'm pretty sure that's one word.'

'What about Motherzilla?'

'Oh, she's harmless.'

Rodney gave a humourless laugh. 'Easy for you to say, Drew. You're not in the thick of it here.'

'I've organised a nice young lady to bring along to the wedding. That'll cheer up Mum.'

'Well, I sincerely hope you're not anticipating this lady will accept your calls after this weekend. I'm not confident our family is going to make a great impression.'

I vaguely recalled telling Jessy that I loved the women in my life and had a great relationship with my mother. Hopefully Jessy would feel the love even if my family was having a battle royal over the potato rosti and red wine jus. The last thing I needed was to be reinterviewed over lying to the cops. I wondered whether the wedding might proceed more smoothly if I explained that we all had to get along nicely this weekend, otherwise I could be in trouble with the police.

In accordance with Sally's prediction, I didn't go to the District

Court. I went to the Supreme Court, where an appeal in the matter of James Anthony Millan was being argued today, according to this morning's paper, in Court 7. This was the guy who was sure his ex-girlfriend had at least seventeen and a half degrees of movement in her right arm following her third-degree burns, not the fifteen degrees she was claiming.

I scored a street park on Terrace Road, right behind a car I wouldn't be surprised to learn belonged to Mr Godfrey SC. A quad cam V8 gunmetal grey Lexus. 'Mercury', I was pretty sure they called that colour. The marketing guys were obviously supremely confident that naming the hue after a deadly toxin would be attractive to their target clientele.

Court 7 was an open court and there were a few interested parties sitting up the back. I took a seat behind them.

Sam Godfrey was what's known as a 'silk', a ranking signified by the SC, or Senior Counsel, that he was entitled to follow up his name with. It was a clear indication to all that he was supremely knowledgeable, experienced, hideously expensive and totally the bloke you wanted on your side if you were a guilty-as-sin drug trafficker with a lifestyle to which you'd become accustomed. SCs had at one stage been called QCs before the Queen was unceremoniously evicted from the title a couple of decades ago. I was pretty sure those SCs would have been pissed off about that. Although the prospect of any of them ever actually being asked to counsel the Queen was fairly slim, it did have a pompous ring to it.

There wasn't much to see of Sam Godfrey from the rear. He was tall, as tall as me maybe at around six foot. He wasn't overweight but was well built with an athletic physique, and he held himself with an air of aristocracy. His voice was steady and composed, and not the voice of a particularly old man. He was blessed with a full head of nearly-black hair, greying just slightly at the sides.

I caught a glimpse of his face when he turned to refer to some papers on the bench behind him. He had movie-star classic good looks and I would've guessed he'd be about fifty years of age. Quite a few years older than Lil. Either his wife was a fair bit younger than him – not out of the question at all – or Lil was much younger than her sister. I found that idea quite plausible too. She had the kind of naïve sweetness of a much younger sibling, an afterthought in the family, viewed as a blessing.

He was not a small man. He would have effortlessly overpowered Lil, disabling her with the first thrust of his knife and not losing a drop of his own blood.

I narrowed my eyes. It just didn't seem that far-fetched to me that this man could have been the killer.

'Mr Godfrey,' I said, jumping to my feet after he'd wrapped up his argument, the judges had reserved their decision and the judges' associate had closed the court for morning tea. 'Sorry, sir, I just wanted a quick word.'

He'd been in the process of packing a stack of papers into his briefcase. He looked up without putting down the documents. His eyes settled on my face. It was clear he didn't know who I was.

'Yes?' His expression revealed not more than a vague level of interest in whatever it was I was about to say. He wasn't going to bother with niceties. I wondered whether he did that even for his own clients.

'I just wanted to say ... I knew your sister-in-law Lil, and I wanted to pass on my condolences.'

Godfrey glared at me, hardly moving a facial muscle. 'Right. Thank you. Who are you?'

'My name is Andrew Deacon.'

A muscle twitched just below his steely eye. 'Andrew Deacon,' he said. 'The boy from the DPP.'

'Yes. That's where I work.'

He smiled suddenly, in a crocodilian kind of way. 'You're the nice young man whose inebriated pre-orgasmic recollections saw me detained for ten hours of interrogation two Fridays ago.'

'Ah, yes.'

'I'll send you the bill for my time.' He grinned as if sharing a joke, cocking his head slightly to the side. The grin disappeared abruptly, and he turned his attention back to the mountain of documents. He recommenced thrusting them into the case.

'Yes, well, I just told them what I heard.'

He didn't look up from his task. 'Of course. It's important to assist the wheels of justice. We should all be so public-spirited.'

'So, I guess you weren't having an affair with your wife's sister? I mean, she was pretty cute. And great fun in the sack, I thought.'

He stopped and stared at me for a moment before taking a step closer to me, his shiny Guccis almost touching my own shoes. I could feel his breath on my face.

'Stay the *fuck* out of my life, Andrew Deacon, or you'll regret it,' he hissed under his breath. 'Am I making myself clear?'

I nodded. 'Clear as day, sir.'

Without another word, he snatched up his case, turned, and strode for the door.

I followed him down to Terrace Road. He opened his car – the Lexus I'd parked behind – and tossed his briefcase across to the passenger seat before climbing in and slamming the door. I watched him pull the Lexus out into the traffic.

CHAPTER 5

'We're driving? I thought we'd be flying.'

I grinned as I dropped Jessy's bags into the boot of my car. 'We're driving, firstly, because this is a road trip and it's going to be fun, and secondly, because I always drive. I love my car.'

'Road trip,' she muttered. 'Excellent.'

Jessy looked sensational in casual get-up. Needless to say, I'd never seen her in anything other than a suit. In a sarong and singlet and with sunglasses perched on the top of her head she looked as fresh as a daisy.

The thing was, I wasn't positive I had the guts to actually make a move on Jessy. Granted, she'd agreed to a date – a pretty serious one, really – but something about her manner gave me the feeling that she'd break my balls if I tried anything. Our relationship was complicated. Professionally, it'd been fine, plenty of sexual tension and so on building up over the course of the drug trial, but the murder investigation had changed things a bit. She'd interviewed me doggedly for five hours. She'd seen me at my most vulnerable and maybe, somewhere in her mind, she'd doubted me and wondered if I really was a psycho killer.

The interview had only made me want her more. But maybe she was still assessing whether this was really such a good idea from her point of view. I decided to take it steady and create some new history for us to launch a relationship from. If nothing else, this weekend would give us new history. I hoped my family behaved themselves.

Jessy warmed to the idea of the road trip after a while, even though it was a seven and a half hour drive each way and we were only going for a long weekend. She put her feet on the dash and I didn't tell her off. It was a dangerous precedent to set, but they were cute feet and luscious legs and now was not the time to fill her in on the full extent of my neuroses.

The sun was starting to sink towards the horizon as we approached Esperance. The temperature, as it always did there in the late afternoons, dropped drastically and the air started to smell like cold damp foliage. I drove the Beamer gingerly up the gravel driveway, taking great care not to bottom it out on the crests where Dad had graded it in honour of the wedding, or shock it too badly on the corrugations that stubbornly remained, and we pulled up at the farmhouse. There we were greeted by two bounding kelpies, one of whom I hadn't actually met yet but who still loved both of us unconditionally, and two Cavalier King Charles spaniels I'd never seen before, both with little jumpers on. They were followed by Mum (who, to my great relief, squealed when she saw me and proceeded to express lots of love for me in front of Jessy), then Rod and his fiancée Ellen. Ellen picked up one of the spaniels and gave it a slightly confronting kiss on the mouth.

'This is my friend Jessy,' I said as I hauled our bags from the boot. 'My mother, Deirdre, my brother, Rod, and this is my nearly-sister-in-law, Ellen.'

As if she was a ninety-year-old lady in a nursing home, Mum grabbed both of Jessy's hands and squeezed them. 'Jim's just finishing off one more yard of drenching, but he's very excited to meet you Jessy,' Mum assured her, causing me to groan inwardly. I should have explained beforehand that Jessy and I weren't engaged yet. Actually, I was pretty sure I had done that.

Ellen put down the dog and delivered hugs for me and Jessy. She did look stressed, poor thing. I was sure Rod was being unnecessarily hard on her, describing her as Bridezilla. Any young woman would be driven insane if they had to share organising duties with my mother, who would have a hard time organising a game of pin the tail on the donkey on her own.

'Are these your dogs?' Jessy asked Ellen. 'I love their jumpers.'

Ellen gave her a grateful smile. 'Their names are Mimi and Jimi. I know the jumpers look funny, but they do get cold.' She lowered her voice. 'You're the only one who's been nice about it.'

'Course they do,' said Rod. 'Don't worry about people who take the piss, love, they're just jealous 'cause their dogs don't have jumpers.'

Rod was a doctor, training to be an anaesthetist in fact, but as a general rule holding the lives of trusting patients in his hands on a daily basis didn't seem to inspire him to be any less irresponsible. In classic inconsiderate groom style, he'd launched the boat and checked the slalom course with a view to enjoying a twilight water-skiing session, the day before his wedding.

'Surely there are things you need to do around here?' I proffered weakly, when Ellen seemed to have been rendered speechless by the announcement.

'Nah, everything's sorted, right, Mum?' said Rod. 'There won't be any time after the wedding, and I want to catch up with my big bro. I've been doing a fair bit of work on the 351 this week. She's running like a dream and you have to check out the mods.'

Jessy looked amused.

'I checked the water's deep enough, we're all set to go,' Rod went on blithely. 'Come on, ladies can come too, as long as you wear bikinis.'

Ellen stared hard at Rod. 'Do you know what, I think that's a marvellous idea,' she said. I was pretty sure she didn't mean the bikinis. 'You and Drew go for a ski. Deirdre and I will stay here and finish organising the food, wine, table decorations, photographer, flowers, name tags, DJ, champers with strawberries and gifts for the guests.'

'It will probably be easier without them hanging around,' Mum agreed. 'Jessy, you can join us if you like.'

~

Rod had done a pretty amazing job with the non-marinised 351 Cleveland engine in his ski-boat, converting it from points to electronic ignition and installing a heat exchanger.

'Next, I'm going to install an over-the-transom race boat exhaust system,' he enthused. 'It'll be like it's got eight individual exhaust pipes coming straight out of the engine and the thing will sound like a 747 taking off.'

'Cool,' I agreed. 'What sort of carby are you running?'

'I'm sticking with the Holley 650,' he said. 'You can over-carb an engine. People don't realise.'

Out on the lake in the south-east corner of the farm, as the afternoon sun threw long shadows across the paddock, I slipped easily back into my trusty old Connelly water-ski and had a red-hot crack at the slalom course. I was secretly pleased that Jessy wasn't there as I didn't seem to be reliving past glories.

'So, what's this business about a murder investigation?' said Rod, idling the boat back to the dock. 'Sounds like serious stuff.'

'It's all over and done with, really. There was this woman, Lily Constantine. Lil. I picked her up at the bar the other night and we went out for a bit and then ended up back at her place. I pissed off early in the morning, and by the afternoon the cops were around at my work wanting to talk about the fact she'd been found dead later that morning. Stabbed multiple times by some psycho.'

'Shit,' breathed Rod. 'So, you're in the clear?'

'Yeah, they put time of death at around ten in the morning, which was a bit over five hours after I left her place. As far as I'm concerned, it's all over. They interviewed me, but that's it.'

'Did they find who did it?'

'Not so far as I know.'

'I suppose they wouldn't tell you if they did. After all, why would you care? She's just some root you picked up.'

'Yeah.'

Rod switched off the engine and moored the boat. 'Lucky you weren't there when the psycho showed up. He might've killed you too.'

'I reckon he wouldn't have done anything if I'd been there.'

He squinted at me against the setting sun. 'Is this thing bugging you?'

I shook my head. 'No. No. I mean ... I guess. A bit.'

'What's the problem?'

'I think I know who killed her, and the cops aren't going to do anything about it.'

'Why not?'

'They reckon they've done everything they can. There's no evidence against him. It's just a gut feeling I have, and the cops can't do much about that.'

'What makes you so sure he's the killer?'

'I introduced myself to him. His name is Sam Godfrey. He's a big-shot defence lawyer. I stood toe to toe with him – literally – and I just ...' I shook my head. 'I dunno, Rod. I just felt he did it.'

'A lawyer with connections could make life very difficult for you.'

'I know.'

'Why does it matter?'

'Her family believe he's innocent. I know she was nothing and no one, just a root or whatever. But, to be honest, I'm starting to feel like I'm the only one on her side.'

Rod pulled himself out of the driver's seat of the boat and jumped onto the jetty. 'If it was me, I would just move on.'

'That's what the cops keep saying I should do.'

'It's not worth your career, Drew. And that might not be all you lose if you don't leave that lawyer well alone.'

~

Rod agreed he wouldn't say anything to Jessy about our conversation. But first I had to convince him I wasn't having him on when I said that she was one of the cops who'd interrogated me.

'That's kinky, man.'

'Yeah, I reckon so too. She's just taking her time getting into the naughtiness of it.'

'There'll be happy days ahead for you ... handcuffs and batons and those cute uniforms.'

'She's a detective so she only wears suits.'

'How disappointing.'

'Don't worry, we'll adapt.' I wasn't as confident as I was making out that Jessy would let me get as far as dress-ups, but still, I was enjoying making Rod jealous of my lifestyle the day before his wedding.

By the time we got back to the house, Dad had arrived home and showered, and my sisters Jodie and Anne-Marie had turned up with their respective husbands and a lot of children. I hadn't committed to memory the exact number of them, but it was a full house. Jessy and Ellen had bonded over the course of the afternoon, and everyone seemed happy and relaxed.

'You've done a great job, there, diffusing the tension between Mum and Ellen,' I whispered to Jessy as we all sat down to a drink on the patio late in the afternoon. 'They seem to be getting along.'

'It took every skerrick of my people-management skills,' Jessy confirmed. 'Thank you for the acknowledgement.'

I grinned. Nice work, Drew.

Together once again, my family laughed and chatted through a huge barbecue and a fair bit of the grog purchased for the purposes of the wedding. Even Ellen seemed to have rediscovered her feelings for Rod and snuggled up to him as we finished dinner. Ah, the bliss of the first night of family togetherness. We were all so excited and full of stories.

By the time Jessy and I staggered into my childhood bedroom, her eyes were glinting. The room, these days, sported a very grown-up queen-sized bed, although the walls were still covered with Transformers posters.

'I had a great evening,' she told me as she rummaged in her bag for her toiletries. 'Thanks for inviting me.'

'Hey, my pleasure.'

'We're going to be sleeping in the same bed.'

I nodded. 'I'll behave myself though. If you want me to.'

She laughed. 'Are you suggesting you might do what you're told?'

'I am capable of it,' I assured her. 'I just don't choose to go that way very often.'

We climbed under the bedding together, her in her cute little nightdress and me in my boxers. In the moonlit room Jessy pulled the covers up to her chin and stared at the ceiling.

'I know it's easy to say now, but Andrew, I promise, I honestly never believed you killed that woman.'

I swallowed uncomfortably. 'I suppose you'd have been entitled to wonder.'

She shook her head. 'I never even ... I never even wondered. I've been a cop for a few years now, you know. You can smell a killer.'

'Yeah, I'd imagine you'd know what they smell like by now.'

'You just know.'

I wanted to ask her if she had been the one who'd interrogated Sam Godfrey for ten hours. I would love to have known if she smelt the killer in him. But I knew if I asked her that, it would be curtains on the rest of my plans for the evening. And right about now, those plans were my priority.

Jessy rolled over, smiled, and reached out to touch my face.

CHAPTER 6

'I hear you're on with Jessy Parkin,' my colleague Matthew Bridges announced to the entire office first thing on Monday. Like me, Matthew was a junior prosecutor. He was born, raised and educated in this city. He once proudly told me that he had never in his lifetime travelled further than the Perth Hills. It wasn't like I'd exactly climbed the Matterhorn or backpacked around South America for a year, but I had at least been further than Mundaring Weir. 'Nice one. She's a real hottie.'

'How'd you find out about it?' I demanded, dropping my car keys on my desk and shrugging off my jacket.

'She works with detectives, Andrew,' Matthew scoffed. 'When she goes off on a dirty weekend, they're going to find out with whom.'

'And blab it to everyone.'

'Not everyone, just a select few offices. Obviously, ours was the first likely to be interested in this particular bit of gossip. I'm a bit devastated, actually. I was going to ask her out myself.'

I ignored him and sat down to read the paper. I knew no good could come of it, but I turned to the notices and checked to see if there was any word on Lil's funeral yet. It'd been two and a half weeks since her murder. Usually I could rely on the police to give me any information I wanted on anything: when the forensic pathologist was expected to complete the autopsy; when the Coroner would release the body for burial; when the funeral was to be scheduled. But, of course, the police were being less than helpful in relation to this particular matter.

Whether I would actually be able to go to Lil's funeral was another matter. Sam Godfrey would no doubt have a complete conniption, and so would all the other members of Lil's family if they knew who I was, which they would, thanks to Sam. Furthermore, Richard and Jessy would probably both be there given the chance the killer would attend. When they saw me there, they'd blow a gasket. Especially Jessy. Richard might just shake his head and draw the conclusion that I was too stupid to deserve any more chances, but Jessy would probably dump my arse. Things in Esperance had gone extremely well. We were now definitely on in every sense of the word, and the last thing I wanted to do was blow it with her.

But having said that, I wanted to meet Lil's parents. I wanted to speak to them myself and tell them what Lil said on that phone call, tell them that they had to keep the police focused on searching for any evidence that might incriminate Sam Godfrey. I'd found no listing for them in White Pages online or an account on Facebook, they didn't own their own home, Jessy and Richard weren't about to give me their address and there just wasn't any way I could think of to find them other than by going to the funeral.

There was a funeral notice. This coming Thursday, the eighteenth of April, at two o'clock in the afternoon at Our Lady's Assumption Catholic Church in Dianella.

~

'Listen, Jessy, I don't want you to go nuts, okay. But I want to go to Lil's funeral.'

Jessy stared at me across the table at Zoomer's, her spoonful of pumpkin soup hovering halfway between her bowl and her mouth. It was lunchtime on a sunny Tuesday, so now everyone was in the garden and the only spot offering any privacy was inside.

To her credit, she didn't lose it completely.

'Why?'

'Not because of what you think,' I lied. 'It's nothing to do with Sam

Godfrey. I just ... I know we weren't really friends, but you know, I liked her. I thought she was sweet. I just wanted to pass on my condolences to her parents.'

Jessy brought the spoon up to her mouth and took a sip. 'Tell me you're shitting me.'

'No, I –'

'You are not going to her funeral.'

This wasn't going well. 'Jessy, I am going to her funeral,' I said quietly. 'I'm sorry if it's not what you want. But I'm just letting you know.'

She glared at me for another moment then lowered her forehead into her hand.

'Of course. Anyone can go if they want to go. Pass on their condolences.'

'I'm glad you understand.'

Her eyes were huge and round as she looked up at me again. 'I just ... I feel like things are going well between us.'

'They are.'

'I like you.'

I grabbed her hands. 'I like you too. A lot.'

She swallowed uncomfortably. 'I just don't know if it's a bad sign, you know, that you keep thinking about Lil Constantine.'

I laughed. 'I could hardly be in love with her, Jessy. We only spent one night together.'

'Yeah, I know.'

'I don't think it has anything to do with Lil. To be honest, I think it has more to do with me. She's a stranger, but I'm the only one who can help her.'

As I said the words, the image of my dad and the train driver pulling that woman from the wreckage of her car pushed its way into my mind. It was something I thought about less and less as I got older, but each time it came into my mind, the memory seemed just as crisp and clear, as if I was watching it on the television.

I hadn't told Jessy the story and I didn't particularly want to, yet.

In fact, I didn't think I'd ever told anyone the story in my life. Every-one back home already knew it, so there was nothing to tell. In Perth, well, I hadn't really met anyone I thought would be interested. After all, it wasn't a story about me. It was about my dad. No one in Perth gave two shits about my dad.

I said to Jessy: 'If there was a stranger in an overturned car, and you were the only one who could get them out, wouldn't you want to do that? Wouldn't you be … compelled to do that?'

'So, it is about Sam Godfrey.'

I stared at her. 'Yes, it is. Are you okay with that?'

She gave a watery smile. 'I suppose,' she said. 'For now.'

~

A stranger in an overturned car.

The woman Dad saved had survived. Did that make a difference? I wasn't sure.

'If you make a scene,' Richard warned me on the phone on Wednesday, the day before the funeral, 'I'm going to have your guts for garters.'

'I can't really see you in garters, Richard. Oh no, hang on – now I can. And that image is going to stick with me for the rest of the day.'

'I'm serious, Andrew. You're not to speak to me or to Jessy at the funeral or give any hint to anyone that either of us might have sanctioned you showing up to this thing.'

'Got it.'

'Because we haven't.'

'I understand.'

'If it looks like it's going to blow up, do the right thing and make yourself scarce, okay?'

'I will.'

'Bloody hell,' he said, 'I can't believe Jessy's agreed to this. She's gone soft in the head since she's started spending time with you.'

CHAPTER 7

I turned up a few minutes early to Lil's funeral service. The church was already close to full. I and many others stood at the back of the room, with the seating, apart from a row of close family members at the front, reserved for the elderly.

Sam Godfrey sat in the front row, looking snappy in an Armani suit and tie. A dark-haired woman sat beside him – Amanda, I guessed – and two young children, a boy and a girl in their Sunday best, fidgeted beside her.

Lil's father, bushy-browed and berry-brown and at least forty kilograms overweight, gave the eulogy. He spoke about his daughter in clipped tones, his gaze shifting between his page and Lil's coffin, which was smothered in white flowers just below where he stood. He seemed to be trying desperately to restrain his emotion but in so doing he only showed the depth of his grief.

'Lily loved life,' he told the assembled crowd. 'She was passionate about her career and about her family, above all else. Those who knew her know that she was hot-headed at times with a bit of a temper – I'm not sure where she got that from.' He paused to allow polite, subdued laughter. 'But she was always deeply protective of her family, her sisters and her brothers, from a very young age. No one could hurt us and get away with it. She had enough love to fill a city.' He paused again, this time to bleak silence. 'She was my girl,' he finished, his voice cracking. For a long time, he stood without speaking. Then he raised his handkerchief to his face. When he looked up again his eyes were red.

'All we wanted was our family, together. Now we cannot have that. Now, we want nothing more than for our daughter's killer to be found, so she may rest in peace.' His eyes scanned the crowd, as if he was searching for the person responsible. 'Thank you all for coming,' he said eventually. 'This means a lot to us.'

Godfrey I was sure would've been watching for my presence, though I never caught him glancing in my direction. Jessy and Richard were studiously ignoring me. I followed the mourners to the graveside without having spoken to a soul.

Lil's father stood by a woman who I assumed was his wife as the pallbearers lowered Lil's coffin into the ground. Lil's mother was tall, pale, with frizzy blond hair cut in a bob at the base of her thin, white neck. Lil's father was a good three inches shorter than his wife. They threw rose petals into the open grave, and then Amanda and another, younger woman and two men who had been pallbearers – Lil's brothers, I guessed – did the same. Once the six turned away from the grave, the other mourners began to toss the flowers also, and then they approached the family to offer their condolences. I took a few petals from the proffered basket and stood to join them.

'Mr and Mrs Constantine, my name's Andrew Deacon. I'm so sorry for your loss.'

Lil's mother seemed as though she might blow over in the breeze that wafted across the cemetery. Her two sons were driving the same style as their old man, but without the extra weight. Lil also took after her father, but somehow features that were unremarkable in his sons had translated into smouldering beauty in his daughter. In all three of his daughters, in fact. Up close I could see that Amanda was both much younger than Sam and quite a bit older than Lil. The other sister, also a stunning brunette, seemed even younger than Lil, maybe only nineteen or twenty. Both women watched me as I addressed their parents. Sam Godfrey had joined his wife, and his gaze was fixed firmly on me.

'Thank you, Andrew,' said Lil's father, giving the impression he didn't instantly recognise my name, though I assumed the police had filled him in on the details of their investigations. 'Were you a friend of Lil's?'

Amanda snorted derisively. 'You could say that, Dad. This is the guy who left her the note.'

Mrs Constantine visibly recoiled. 'Oh. I wouldn't have expected ...'

'If we're lucky, a few more of her one-night stands might turn up to pay their respects,' Amanda went on. 'It's of some consolation to learn that my slutty little sister occasionally picked up sensitive guys like Andrew here. You fuck her, fuck off and then turn up at the fucking funeral. That's so woke.'

Lil's mother turned to Amanda in horror but seemed to have been rendered speechless by her daughter's tirade.

'I'm sorry, Mrs Constantine,' I said quickly, sensing the situation deteriorating in a way that would not please Richard Simms one bit. 'I really didn't want to upset anyone.'

'Maybe you should just leave?' suggested Sam helpfully. None of the venom he'd sprayed in my direction in the courtroom last week was present now. He was on his best behaviour.

'This is the guy who accused Sam of murder,' said Amanda. 'I think leaving right now would be a good idea.'

'I only told the police what I heard.'

'What you think you heard,' she spat. 'You were thinking about nothing except getting laid. And you were drunk.'

'I want you to know,' I said, turning back to Lil's parents, 'that I know what I heard. Amanda's right about me and I know I shouldn't be here. But I want you to know that *I know what I heard*. Please tell the police they must keep hunting for evidence.'

Both parents stared at me. 'There are two police officers here,' said Mr Constantine eventually. 'If you don't leave right now, I'm going to call them over to escort you from this service.'

I nodded. 'I understand. I'm going. I'm sorry. I'm sorry for being here, and I'm sorry for your loss.'

The nameless younger sister's eyes followed me as I turned away from the family group.

I reasoned that at least Jessy and Richard would have to be happy with the fact that no one had cried, screamed, or thrown anything. Nevertheless, I still felt like a bit of a prick. I crossed to the edge of the cemetery and then out onto the street where I'd parked the Beamer.

'Hey,' a voice spoke behind me as I unlocked the doors. I turned.

It was Lil's younger sister.

'Hi,' I said. 'Listen, I'm sorry. I feel like a real arsehole.'

'I understand. You are an arsehole.'

'What's your name?'

'Angie.'

'Angie, I hope your parents won't be too upset.'

She shrugged. 'I guess you turning up to Lil's funeral is not the worst thing my parents have had to endure over the past three weeks.'

'I guess not.'

'Why'd you show up here?'

'I wanted to tell them in person what I know. Lil got a call and she recognised the voice as someone she knew, and she called that person Sam. She said the caller was someone who couldn't take no for an answer. It was obvious they weren't friends. Whoever that caller was, it was someone she hated. And she told me her brother-in-law was a lawyer and a total arsehole. How many brothers-in-law does she have?'

Angie's eyes narrowed. *She looks so much like Lil.*

'Do you really believe Sam did this to her?'

'I believe it was him, Angie. I've got no evidence. All I know is what I just told you. But I believe it was him.'

'It's just, I –' She stopped abruptly and shook her head.

'What?' I took a step towards her. 'What? Do you know something? Was Lil in a relationship with Sam?'

She held up her hand as I approached. 'Please don't – please just stay there,' she commanded. 'Please.'

'Sorry.' I knew my voice was rising. I didn't want to frighten her. 'You have to tell the cops if you know something.'

'I'm going to think about it,' she said. 'I'm going to think about what I know.'

I nodded, not wanting to discourage her. 'That's good. Great.'

'Stay out of our family business, Andrew.'

'I will. I will, from now on. I promise.'

~

In the morning I got into work early and, with my coffee steaming on the desk in front of me, undertook a few basic enquiries to determine what kinds of assets Sam and Amanda Godfrey held. I found there was more than enough residential and commercial real estate held in their names and the names of companies they controlled to make any bloke nervous about the possibility of divorce.

Had Lil threatened to reveal the affair to Amanda? Was that what had got her killed? The thing was, it seemed that any affair between Sam and Lil was well and truly over by the time of the phone call. He was ringing her, but it was clear she wanted nothing more to do with him. She didn't seem like a spurned lover to me. Based on what I'd heard, I couldn't imagine her making wild threats to talk to the wife. Could Sam Godfrey really be nutso enough to kill a woman just because she didn't want him anymore? Like some psychopath with a mortally wounded ego. *If I can't have her, no one can.*

I didn't get a lot of work done during the day, so was forced to work late. By the time I returned to the car park it was only an hour shy of midnight, and I was exhausted.

The first blow was to my upper back, and it dropped me like a sack of shit.

CHAPTER 8

My briefcase flew out of my hands and smashed open on the concrete, the contents scattering. I looked around me. There were three of them. Strong, male figures, balaclavas shrouding their faces.

Holy shit.

One carried a cricket bat, the weapon they'd used to bring me down in the first place. Now he threw that away and they laid the boots in.

Oh, this is not good. Not good.

I knew there was no point in fighting. One-on-one would be the only way I'd stand a chance. Instead, I curled up into a ball and tried to deflect the worst of the kicks away from my face, head and groin. I realised I was going to survive this only if it was intended I would survive it.

The beating went on and on. I heard my ribs crack and blood started pissing out of my mouth and nose in a thoroughly scary way. In trying to protect my head I managed to get my right forearm – the one on top – badly mangled. I wondered whether I really was completely fucked. I was now trying to protect my head with a shattered flappy flipper. This was grim, grim, grim.

Please, God, let them be instructed not to kill me. Let me be meant to survive this.

A boot thudded into the side of my jaw and, mercifully, it was lights out.

I didn't know how long I was unconscious for, but when I woke again, the thugs were still standing there, my view of them sideways as I lay on the ground. The beating had stopped.

One of them spoke.

'Next time, you'll get what you deserve.'

Through foggy, blood-smeared eyeballs I watched the speaker walk over to the Beamer, smash the passenger side window with the cricket bat and toss a can of liquid across the plush leather seats. Then he lit a match and threw it through the window, and she went up like a bonfire.

Then all three of them walked calmly towards the lifts.

My head was stuck to the concrete with my own blood. I tilted it to look around. My phone had been in my briefcase. Maybe it was around somewhere. I spotted it maybe three metres away. I lifted myself onto my good elbow and then began to haul myself across the gritty surface towards the phone. Until then the pain had been bearable as my body pumped adrenalin into my system, but now, dragging my skinful of broken bones into motion almost blew the circuits of every nerve to my brain.

'It's only pain,' I mumbled sternly, reflecting on the fact that the last time I'd said this to myself was when I was playing year twelve rugby, which was hardly the same thing.

Come on, Drew.

It wasn't only pain, really. It was there for a good reason. Why couldn't they have finished with me just a bit closer to my stuff? By the time I got to the phone, my humour was at an all-time low.

You never feel so alive as when you're nearly dead.

Right?

I rang 000 and garbled my sorry situation through the blood still pissing out of my mouth.

'Ambulance and police and fireys are on their way now,' the operator confirmed. 'The police are expected in three minutes. Ambulance in ...' She paused and checked her information. 'Five.'

'Well, that's good,' I said. 'That's great, actually.'

'What are your injuries?'

'I've got broken bones and a broken face and also broken balls,' I said. 'It doesn't feel like there's anything that isn't broken at the moment. There's blood everywhere. And my car's burning really close. If it blows up there'll be more injuries to report.'

'Can you move?'

'I suppose I could. Death seems like an easier option.'

'Do you know your blood type?'

The police showed up first, by which time I was starting to feel faint again. The officers were two uniforms. I didn't know if I knew them or not. I couldn't tell who they were because my eyes weren't working. They carried me away from the car while I bawled from the pain, then started racing through their first-aid procedures.

'You're going to be okay,' they told me.

'You say that to everyone.'

'Just try to stay awake until the ambulance gets here, and we'll get you some more blood, and you'll be right as rain.'

~

My first visitor at hospital in the morning was Jessy.

'Oh, Andrew, I can't believe this,' she shrieked, obviously not having been briefed to take the official line, which was that it was no big deal and I was going to be fine. 'I can't believe someone would do this to you.'

'Apparently, it's not a big deal,' I assured her. It hurt my mouth to move it.

'Your parents are going to catch a flight this afternoon and Rod is cutting short his honeymoon to get back here.'

'Really?' That seemed a bit extreme. 'I *am* alive. Aren't I?'

'They're worried about you.'

'There's no need to cut short the honeymoon. What's he going to do, sit around and chat about his boat engine for hours? Would you mind calling him and telling him not to do that?' My right forearm was encased in a weighty plaster cast, which made me look like an oversized ten-year-old boy. Even if I knew where my phone was, it wouldn't have been easy to manage it.

She frowned as she sifted through the contents of a reusable plastic shopping bag she'd brought with her. 'Uniforms collected your personal belongings at the scene,' she explained. She found my phone and scrolled down to Rod's mobile.

'He's pretty messed up but he's awake and talking,' she said when he answered. 'He asked me to tell you he doesn't want you to come back here. He says it'll just be sitting around, and it'll be boring.'

Jessy held the phone away from her hair while Rod spoke. She was, I assumed, grossed out by the dried blood smeared all over it from my busted head when I made the emergency call.

'He wants to speak to you,' she said eventually, and put the phone up to my ear.

'Listen, Drew, was this that lawyer?' Rod demanded before I could even say hello.

'I assume so.'

He sounded cross. 'I don't know what the bloody hell is going on here, but I want my brother alive, you understand?'

'Yes.'

'You back off about this business. It's over. I'm not going to explain to Mum and Dad why their firstborn son is at the bottom of the Swan River in concrete boots or whatever the bloody mafia does to people these days. I'm telling you now. *You back off.*'

'Just because they own an Italian restaurant doesn't mean they're the mafia. That's quite racist, Rod.'

'Drew, I'm serious.'

'All I did was go to her funeral.'

'I don't care. He obviously took it personally. Now you promise me that this is the end of it, that I don't have to say anything to Mum and Dad about who did this to you, that I'm *never* going to have to say anything to Mum and Dad about that lawyer or that woman you fucked, or, I swear, I'm getting on the next plane and coming to make you promise me in person.'

'I promise,' I said. 'This is the end of it.'

Rod seemed relieved. 'Good. I'll cancel my flight. You better mean it.'

'I will. I don't want to die.'

Jessy hung up the phone for me. 'What'd he say?'

'He told me to stop bothering Sam Godfrey.'

Jessy winced. 'Do you really believe he did this to you?'

'Well, perhaps not him personally.'

'Andrew, I've got to tell you ... Richard doesn't think it's likely.'

These cops were really starting to piss me off. 'Why not?'

'It seems a bit extreme. He's no longer a suspect as far as the police are concerned. Why would he want to draw attention back to himself now?'

'Why would he stab a woman fifteen times?' I snapped. 'That seems a bit extreme also.'

'We're cross-referencing prison records now to see which of the guys you prosecuted have been recently released –'

'There's no point, Jess.' My face was starting to throb.

'Andrew, come on.'

'There's no point, because I'm not going to make a complaint anyway.' I looked away from her. 'It'll just be a waste of resources which I would prefer you to utilise trying to get Sam Godfrey for murdering Lily Constantine.'

'Andrew, you know what those men did to you is a serious criminal offence.'

'This isn't about me.'

'You're crazy. Look at the state you're in.'

'Sam Godfrey is the one who did this to me,' I said, trying to keep a check on my emotions. I tried to swallow, but it seemed more painful than it should be. 'And he'll be punished if he goes down for Lil's murder. That's not an impossible task, not like trying to link someone to those blokes in the car park.' I needed to change the subject. 'Do you know what's wrong with me? They told me when I woke but I can't remember what they said.'

'It's actually a lot better than we expected,' said Jessy. 'One badly broken arm, some broken ribs and teeth and of course the busted nose ... and a ruptured spleen. That's about it.'

'My kidneys hurt.'

'You'll be pissing blood for a week, but you'll recover. They tell me you've got a good surgeon.'

It was good to know my legs were okay. I'd be able to walk out of here. Though the ruptured spleen sounded serious, I found myself not really caring how grim things were from the waist up. I was just grateful I'd retained the ability to get myself the hell out of hospital. I tried to sit up. Bolts of pain across my chest slugged me back to the pillow. 'Holy shit.'

Jessy looked worried. 'Richard has called Rufus to explain the situation. You're not expected at work. You have to rest for a while, Andrew. Seriously.'

CHAPTER 9

'Nah, nothing important,' Matthew informed me when I called him on Wednesday. I should have called him first thing on Monday morning for a handover, but I'd pretty much done nothing but sleep since Jessy left the hospital on Saturday morning. Even when my parents were visiting, I slept. It had taken me about half an hour to make this one simple call, despite nearly five days having passed since the beating. Just lifting my good arm to grab my mobile phone sent white-hot spears through my rib cage. I resolved to ask for help with phone calls from now on. 'A couple of anxious cops, a couple of pushy lawyers.'

'Yeah, I'll worry about them later.'

'So, I hear you're in hospital.'

'Yup.'

'I hear you got beaten up.'

'Yeah.' There was no point in fantasising for one second that this information wouldn't have spread like wildfire across the police, detectives and DPP offices. Even the cleaning staff and the IT department would've been appraised of the situation.

'You got any idea who did it?'

'Nah.' It wasn't easy lying to a lawyer. Usually only the naïve attempted it. I felt I had a chance of getting away with it since we were on the phone and he couldn't see my face. 'They reckon probably someone I binned.'

'Well, I would've thought definitely, wouldn't you? Unless you do a bit of drug dealing or loan sharking or illicit gambling on the side.'

'Yeah, not really. Well, I'm trying to give up.'

'Whatever, Andrew. You're way too squeaky-clean private school choirboy to indulge in anything too dodgy.'

'Piss off. I can be dodgy.'

'I hear they torched your car.'

'Yeah.' I really loved that car. 'I suppose insurance will cover it.'

'Maybe.' Matthew seemed to have lost interest in the conversation. 'Oh, someone interesting did call on Monday. A woman, sounded young, apparently. Wouldn't tell Sally what it was about. Just asked her to get you to call her.'

'Did she leave a name?'

I could hear Matthew flicking through the pile of messages I knew would, by now, be caking my workspace. Most people received their messages by email these days, but Sally didn't believe in it. She thought emails were too easy to ignore and preferred little notes torn from a pre-printed message pad she had to order online from China. While I waited, I took the phone away from my ear to read the text I'd received from Russ on Monday morning. I'd only noticed it when I went to ring Matthew.

Where were you this morning? Left me hanging. I nearly got picked up by some guy who looked like Boy George. The current version. Couldn't wait any longer.

Matt said something.

'Hey?' I said, manoeuvring the phone back to my ear.

'I said: Her name was Angela Constantine.'

Angie Constantine was another thing I'd forgotten about.

When we'd met at the funeral, I had no idea of the lengths to which Sam Godfrey was prepared to go to stop those he perceived as a threat. But now it was clear to me that if she spoke up, if she said anything at all to Amanda or to her family about what she might or might not know or suspect, then there was a risk that he would do to her what he did to me. Or what he did to Lil.

If I tried to call her, that would be a phone call which could very easily get me killed, if not by Sam Godfrey then definitely by my brother Rod. Or probably both. There was no arguing that it wouldn't qualify as a breach of my promise to Rod. But I could hardly just lie here knowing her life was in danger and there was something I should be doing about it.

'Would you mind texting me the number? I don't have a pen or paper or the ability to manage either at the moment.'

'Sure.'

'Did Sally tell Angie where I was?'

'I don't know. I don't think so. It's not her practice to tell people where we are. We're just out.'

'Yeah, thanks Matt. Could you put me through to Rufus? I think I'm going to be out of action for a little while longer.'

~

After lunch, I saw a doctor doing her rounds, who seemed surprised to see me not sleeping. She told me I wouldn't be going back to work for another month. The plaster cast would remain on for four to six weeks. Once I got out of hospital, I should keep the arm elevated if possible and avoid driving, sports and any heavy lifting. I should rest as much as possible. I asked her to help me with a phone call, but she said she was too busy and would send someone around.

Twenty minutes later a chaplain named Phil turned up. With his help, I phoned Russ. I could've had Phil call Angie, but I expected Matthew would have included her name alongside the number in his text and I didn't want the chaplain or any nurses and definitely not Jessy to see I was calling her.

'What the hell? We don't call each other, man. We don't have that kind of relationship.'

'Yes, look, I'm sorry, I can't text right now. It requires me to push too many buttons.'

'What?'

'I'm in hospital.' I squinted as I read the signage on the opposite wall. 'RPH. If you get a minute, drop in and see me.'

'Is everything okay? I'm not a big fan of hospitals, I gotta tell you.'

'Look, don't come if you don't feel comfortable, but yeah, if you can ...'

'What's happened?'

'Well, I'm ... injured.'

'Did you stack it?'

'I got beaten to a bloody pulp.'

'*Beaten?*'

I realised everyone was going to make a similar fuss about this. Suddenly, I felt tired. 'I'm sorry, Russ. I'm not going to be much good for a while. Let's just say I don't think I'm going to make the Melbourne Marathon this year. Maybe next.'

He did show up, later that afternoon after he finished work, with an expression on his face like a cat that thinks you're going to put it in a cage and take it to the vet to get its temperature taken. I looked at his tall, lean body and felt jealous of how well it was functioning. While I was lying in hospital for five days, after being broken in pieces and put back together on an operating table, he'd have been loping effortlessly through the park, putting distance between himself and Boy George as easily as if he were riding a bike. For someone whose mind was definitely a bit touch-and-go, it was almost funny what a fine specimen he was physically.

'Mate, you look really grim,' he said.

'Listen, Russ, would you mind grabbing my phone? Can you have a look for a text from a guy from work for a number I'll get you to dial?'

He found the phone, found the message, called the number and put the phone up to my ear.

I waited for Angie Constantine to answer and prayed that she would.

CHAPTER 10

Angela Constantine wore her dark hair in a ponytail which swept across her shoulder blades as she moved. Just like Lil, Angie's eyes were huge and brown, her cheeks dimpled and, even in jeans and a ratty old jumper, her figure delectable. Luckily, although I'd been in hospital for a week now, I was still a bit too sick to get terribly distracted, which only showed how sick I was.

She stared at my strapped chest and plastered limb.

'What happened to you?'

We hadn't said anything much to each other over the phone, as Russ held it up to my ear. I just told her where I was, and she said she was coming to see me. I was worried the phone was tapped. Was it irrational to think the phone was tapped? The phone was not tapped. Sam Godfrey had neither the inclination nor the opportunity to tap my mobile phone. But I was starting to learn that getting walloped to within an inch of your life does strange things to your powers of reasoning.

That phone call was three days ago. I'd been convinced she'd decided not to come, but then she showed up.

'Some blokes beat me up in a car park.'

She shook her head, confused. 'Why? Who?'

I decided to play it cool for the time being. 'I don't know.' I gestured with my fingers for her to take a seat on the brown vinyl guest's facilities. 'Would you like a small carton of orange juice? There's one in that bar fridge. Or help yourself to some warm scheme-water out of that beige jug over there.'

'No thanks.' She seemed reluctant to sit down, as if she didn't really want to be here at all.

'How are you all holding up? Your mum and dad ... are they okay?'

'They're okay. They're still ... they're in shock.'

'You seem like a very close family.'

'We are. This has hit all of us hard.'

She began playing with the beads at the end of the strings that ran through the hood of the jumper she was wearing. Her fingers were long and delicate. And shaking.

'You wanted to talk about something?'

She smiled hesitantly. 'Yes. I guess I did. I'm sorry, Andrew. This seems really stupid. But I haven't got anyone else to talk to. Like Amanda says, you're just some bloke who Lil brought home for one night ... but I feel like you do care about her. About finding out who did this to her.'

'I do.'

She slid to the very edge of her chair. 'Andrew, Lil was not having an affair with Sam.'

I stared at her, cautiously. 'Right.'

'It was me. I was ... having sex. With him.'

My revulsion for Sam Godfrey SC ratcheted up a couple of notches. She couldn't have been older than twenty. 'Oh, Angie,' was all I managed to say. 'Why?'

The moment the question was out of my mouth, I realised the answer was none of my business. 'Listen, you don't have to talk to me about –'

'About a year ago I was working at my parents' restaurant,' she said, as if I hadn't spoken. 'The tables were always full, but the business was struggling, more and more each week. And the reason why was because I was stealing from it. More and more each week.'

I shut my mouth.

'I knew it was wrong.'

She seemed to be on the verge of tears. This frightened me because usually when a woman cried, I just gave them a big hug and said: 'everything is going to be okay' and that tended to do the trick.

However, at present I was still having major difficulties moving my upper body. I'd have to speak to her instead; say the right thing. Like I said. Frightening.

'I never wanted them to go broke. I just couldn't think ...' She pulled a tissue out of her handbag and dabbed furiously at her eyes. 'Sam agreed to loan them some money. But he insisted on looking at the books. He worked out what I was doing. He told me he would keep my secret. But there would be a price. I never wanted to have sex with him at all. Ever. But I had no choice.'

'Angie, that's –'

'Do you understand? I had no choice, Andrew. If he told my parents what I'd done I could never face them again.'

I stared at her. I wasn't sure if she really understood what was happening to her. 'Angie, that is so illegal. That's rape.'

'I kept hoping he'd tire of me ... but he always wanted more. It wasn't nice sex either. Amanda would never let him do that to her. I begged him to leave me alone, but he always said if I backed out of our deal, everyone would learn I'd stolen from my family. I knew I could tell them what he'd done to me, but it wouldn't help me if I did. I'd still be a thief. One who was willing to betray her sister to cover it up. I knew he would deny threatening me. He'd say it was an affair. They think he's wonderful. He'd tell them I seduced him, and they'd believe it.'

It crossed my mind that Sam Godfrey was possibly a psychopath. I'd come across a few in my time. A lot of them were violent criminals, repeat offenders. Just as many were corporate high-flyers. It wasn't the case that the latter group had any aversion to violence. They'd be more than happy to use it if it suited them and they were unlikely to be caught. They were just slightly more long-term in their thinking than your garden-variety raging brawler. With a shiver, I realised I really was lucky to be alive after that bashing. It made me wonder if perhaps one or more of the assailants didn't have the stomach for what Sam had ordered them to do. Not all career thugs perhaps?

Angie looked utterly miserable. 'Then after he'd explain all this to me, he'd send me flowers and expensive gifts like it was some kind of *relationship.* It was so foul, Andrew. I hated myself so much. Eventually I told Lil what was happening. I had to tell someone. I spoke to her on Tuesday night, and she was killed the following Thursday morning.' She dissolved into proper sobs then, her shoulders shaking.

'Do *you* think he was the one who killed her?' I asked as gently as I could. My mind was racing. Lil was protective of her younger sister. I knew that from what her father had said at her funeral. Irrespective of what her sister had done, that Godfrey was abusing Angie would have enraged her and she may have confronted him. She may have threatened to report him to the police. Or at the very least to tell Amanda what he was doing. Godfrey had obviously convinced Angie she had more to lose than he did. But I wasn't sure I agreed. Angie's parents probably wouldn't press charges over the theft, and they'd forgive her eventually. Godfrey, on the other hand, would lose his marriage, access to his kids and, if convicted of any of various possible charges around the sexual assault, his career and probably freedom. Had Lil thought the same? Had she called his bluff?

I remembered Lil's words. *Just someone who can't take no for an answer.* I'd assumed she was talking about her own *no.* But she was speaking on behalf of her sister.

Angie shook her head, blowing her nose. 'I think he was probably in court that morning. He'd said he was going to spend that morning with me, because Amanda was going to be at a conference, but he cancelled when some appeal was listed at the last minute. He could have been lying about that, but I don't think so, since the cops have bought his alibi. But Andrew, if he didn't do it, I think he knows who did kill her. I think they did it because he ... asked them to.'

'Have you told the cops any of this?'

'No.' She fished for another tissue in her handbag. 'I don't know what to tell them.'

'Tell them the truth.'

'I've already told them a bucketload of lies. They're saying: "Do you know anyone named Sam who might want to hurt your sister?" and I'm like: "No, officer".'

'Yeah, but they'll understand. They'll appreciate that you're coming clean now.'

'Andrew, don't you get it? If you and I are right, *I'm* the one who got her killed. My actions got my sister killed.'

'No way, Angie, you can't think like that.'

She found her tissue and dropped her bag back onto the floor. 'Maybe she was on borrowed time when she spent the night with you. Maybe the killer came around then but heard voices inside and decided to come back the following morning.' She blew her nose again. 'Maybe you gave her one extra night, Andrew, but the reality is I'm the one whose selfishness got her killed.' She stared at me through swollen, red eyes. Then she shook her head slowly. 'If I tell the police, everyone will know it.'

'You didn't stab her, Angie. Whoever did that was a monster, and there's nothing you or anyone else could've done to help Lil. You can't blame yourself for this.'

She wound the jumper strings tight around her fingers. She looked up at me. 'Andrew, who did this to you? Was it Sam?'

'I think so. Men he sent. Maybe Lil's killer was one of them.'

'So, Lil pissed him off, and he stabbed her to death, and you pissed him off, and he smashed you to pieces. What's he going to do to me if I go to the police and tell them *the truth*?'

'I don't know.' It was exactly what I'd worried about. But I was feeling anger rising. 'If you don't tell the police the truth, he'll just keep on messing up anyone who gets in his way, I guess. We must fight back, Angie. The police will protect you. I will protect you.'

She looked doubtful. 'Only one of your arms works, Andrew, and you can't get out of bed.'

I stared at the hospital's white ceiling. 'He cannot get away with this,' I said, only partly to Angie. 'He just *cannot* get away with what he's done to all of us.'

She frowned. 'I've got to go,' she said, picking up her handbag. 'I'll call you.'

CHAPTER 11

I checked out of hospital that day.

'You can't check out,' a nurse informed me crisply, ten minutes after Angie had left. 'You're nowhere near well enough.'

I pushed my two t-shirts, two pairs of jocks and one pair of tracksuit pants into the gym bag my parents had lovingly packed for me when they'd arrived in town the afternoon after the bashing. 'On the contrary, I am an adult and I can check out any time I like.' I'd been in hospital for a week. That was enough.

'You'll have to wait until the doctor's seen you this afternoon.'

She clearly wasn't listening to me. 'No, I won't. I'm leaving right now.'

'You will if you want to take any painkillers with you.'

It was Saturday, so I spent the rest of the afternoon watching a game of football on the television above my hospital bed, even though the footy bored me to tears. It was a derby, the Eagles versus the Dockers. The Eagles were Dad's favourite team, the Dockers officially his second favourite team. A lot of people put the Dockers last if they were Eagles fans, but not my dad, he was loyal to the state of Western Australia, the place he was born and where he'd worked the land his whole life. Watching a derby had always been his least favourite thing to do because it annoyed him that they'd just injure each other, leaving both teams worse off for advancing the cause of the homeland. There seemed to be a bit of that going on. Someone did a hammy and someone else a suspected ACL. They were both Dockers. I supposed that was something.

Finally, at about three o'clock in the afternoon a doctor came around.

'I'm checking out,' I informed him.

He reluctantly gave me a box of a drug called Vicodin and a repeat script. 'Don't take any more than two every six hours, maximum,' he instructed. 'Try to just confine it to two in the morning and two at night if you can.'

I nodded. 'Thanks for that.'

He frowned. 'Try to take it easy, Andrew.'

~

I popped a couple of the Vicodin when I got home and lodged an insurance claim for the Beamer before enjoying a fairly peaceful night's sleep. The following morning, I got on Gumtree to find myself a new car. I settled on a 1979 XD Falcon with a crossflow 6, automatic transmission, after-market mags and a glued-on spoiler. I rang the guy and convinced him I was legit and coming around shortly, then took a couple more Vicodin and got an Uber to the address he'd given me in Canning Vale. The car was a bit of a reduction in status from my previous wheels, but I decided it could be argued that it had some vintage cred. The main point was that it was only two hundred bucks and I was a bit worried that the continuation of Operation Get Sam could see the same thing happening to my next car. Explaining that to my insurance company would not be straightforward.

The Falcon had after-market suspension too which, in 1982, would've been as flash as Michael Jackson. Sadly, the XD's Konis, like Mr Jackson's personal legacy, weren't really cutting it anymore. I was in a lot of pain by the time I swiped into the underground car park at my apartment complex and parked between a 200 Series Landcruiser and a late model Audi. I accidentally slammed the Falcon's door into the Audi before heading upstairs.

There, I took more drugs, then rested on the couch for the remainder of the day.

~

At nine o'clock on Monday morning I rang the Supreme Court and asked to speak to my friend Trish in listings. Trish wasn't really what you'd call a friend. She was a sixty-year-old lady I'd been charming for the past year with a view to making my life easier when it came to convincing the court to cooperate with me. If they didn't like you down there, it could be nearly impossible to get anything listed on an urgent basis or find out what was going on with a given matter (particularly if it wasn't, in a technical sense, your matter). I'd devoted on average fifteen minutes per week to chatting with Trish about her grandchildren, her renovations, her husband's weekly successes or failures at lawn bowls, and what she thought about the rules forbidding people to smoke within fifteen metres of the front door (an outrage, I thoroughly agreed). I was hopeful this was all about to pay off.

'What did you have listed in the Court of Appeal on the morning of Thursday the twenty-eighth of March?' I asked her.

'Why do you ask?'

'Trish, come on. We're friends, right?'

There was silence on the other end of the phone. 'I'm waiting,' she prompted me eventually.

I didn't know what she wanted from me. I really had done everything I could possibly be expected to do before attempting to ask a favour. Just one, singular favour. 'Please?' I offered.

She tutted in frustration. 'I'm waiting for you to give me a good reason why you are asking me for this information.'

I thought for a moment. 'I'm off work today,' I said. 'I have the old lists at work, obviously, but I thought it might be quicker to ring you.' That sounded pathetic even to me. I forged on. 'I was trying to remember the name of this matter on that date. Rufus had asked me to speak to the victim and gave me a phone number, and I thought I'd get it done today, but the name of the accused just escapes me for the moment, and I don't want to ring the victim without knowing it. I know there were probably a lot of matters listed on that day, but Sam Godfrey was on the other side, if that helps.'

Trish said nothing for a long moment. Eventually, she said: 'That'll do.' She began typing.

'Thanks, Trish. How'd Bill go at scroungers last weekend? Have you completed the full set of coffee mugs yet?'

'No, all he got was a frozen chook.'

'Shame.'

I waited while she searched.

'Mr Godfrey appeared in the General Division that morning, in the matter of O'Callaghan,' she said. 'It was an appeal from the Magistrates Court. Wendy Everingham is on the record for the DPP.'

'Yes, that's it,' I enthused. 'The General Division, yes, that's the one. Thanks so much for that.'

'My pleasure, Andrew.'

~

'Oh, do you have that transcript for O'Callaghan?' I asked the ladies at the front desk as I wandered past in my suit pants, collared shirt and tie with my jacket draped over my plastered arm. I'd donned the outfit purely for the purposes of going down to the Supreme Court and pulling this stunt. In fifteen minutes, I'd be back out of it again and flat on my back on my couch. I wasn't anticipating that this was going to be particularly challenging, since the ladies on the front desk, unlike Trish, were generally fairly easy to manoeuvre into giving you what you wanted. It wasn't like we *intimidated* them as such. I preferred to think of it as impressing them. Wendy Everingham, on the other hand, would not be so easily impressed. I couldn't see myself getting a transcript out of her about a matter I had no legitimate interest in, at least not without answering fifty million questions first which I had no intention of answering.

'I emailed it to Ms Everingham yesterday,' one of them told me, confirming that it existed, which was great news. I didn't think the cops were interested enough in Sam Godfrey as a suspect to actually order a copy of the transcript at considerable expense to the taxpayer, and Wendy wouldn't have ordered a transcript unless she was considering a further appeal. Appeals by the DPP against decisions of the Supreme Court were not common, since usually Supreme Court judges knew what they were on about, whether we liked it or not. So, it was a long shot, but worth a crack.

'Oh, that's odd,' I observed, feigning confusion. 'I spoke to her this morning and she said she hadn't received it. I offered to check with you guys while I was down here.' I flashed them a grimace which I hoped would pass for a smile. 'Perhaps you could just give me a copy, just in case. We have been having some troubles with our computers, actually. I've had quite a few emails go missing.'

'No worries. I'll just grab it for you.'

Five minutes later, I unlocked the XD, then felt the door handle snap in my hand when I tried to open the door. It proceeded to just dangle there. I'd need to get another one from the wreckers. In the meantime, I got into the passenger side and clambered across the centre console. That was a painful exercise. I felt like I may throw up, but I took a couple of Vicodin and my stomach settled as the pain ebbed. It was an unspeakable relief to be off my feet.

I took the document from its envelope.

On the morning of Lil's murder, Sam Godfrey SC was arguing an appeal by a certain Mr Justin O'Callaghan against a magistrate's decision to convict him of a drink-driving offence. The submissions were long and complex, revolving around the question of whether the police prosecutors in the Magistrates Court had managed to prove the time of driving beyond reasonable doubt, thus enabling the court to be satisfied that the accused was breathalysed within four hours of the time of driving as required by the *Road Traffic Act*.

The transcript clearly stated that the hearing of the appeal took place on the date of Lil's murder and involved SAMUEL GODFREY SC for the accused and WENDY EVERINGHAM for the DPP. There wasn't a victim, as such, but I was hopeful that Trish wouldn't even look at it and if she did, she wouldn't take my improper request any further.

The transcript began at nine in the morning and concluded at one o'clock in the afternoon, and littered throughout were words spoken by Sam Godfrey, with his name followed by a colon printed at the commencement of each line enunciated by him.

It was, I had to agree, about as watertight as alibis got. I flicked through the document. Even where he wasn't speaking for a while, there was no chance he wasn't there. Although there have been many occasions on which I would have loved to, it wasn't possible to just duck off for a bit while the other side is rabbiting on, without it showing up in the transcript.

I was about to toss the document onto the back seat when I noticed that the transcript had recorded a half hour break at ten o'clock, due to the court needing to hear another urgent matter.

Lil wasn't living far from the city centre.

If he drove like the clappers, he could have got to Lil's in time to kill her and then get back to court. Maybe there was no hit man. Maybe he really did do this himself.

I started the XD. I needed to talk to Richard and Jessy about this.

Angie called me on my way to the police station. It would have been great to be able to speak to her on the Bluetooth, but of course, that was no longer an option. Even illegally using my mobile phone while driving was tricky, as I usually used my good hand to steer, but I couldn't hold a mobile phone with my right fingertips due to my thumb being stuck too far away. My only option for illegal phone calls was to use all available digits poking out of my plaster cast on my right hand to delicately manoeuvre the steering wheel and handle the mobile with my left. The cops would throw a fit if they saw it.

'I've decided I will go back and talk to the police again,' she said.

Yes. 'That's good. That's the right thing to do.'

'Will you come with me?'

'Sure. Of course. Listen, I can't talk now because I'm driving. But I'll come pick you up and take you down there if you like.'

'Thanks, that'd be great.'

I diverted to her place which was, I was surprised to find out once I followed her directions to the address she gave me, Lil's place.

'You weren't here when I ... when Lil and I ...'

'I was out,' Angie explained, her eyes skipping away from mine as we stood in the doorway of the apartment. 'These days I work as a barmaid at The Den. I knocked off work at about midnight the night you were here, but some of my friends were going out and I decided to join them. I crashed at my friend Kelly's house. I didn't get home until midday the next day. That's when I found Lil. Her work said she'd called in sick that morning, otherwise she wouldn't even have been home at ten o'clock in the morning.'

I winced. 'It was you who found her?'

Angie's jaw tightened. 'Let's go, hey? I want to get this over with.'

CHAPTER 12

I peered through the one-way glass between the observation area and the interview room, perched on the edge of my chair trying to minimise my discomfort. I had taken six Vicodin already today and it was only midday. At times the pain was verging on ridiculous.

Beside me, Richard kicked back in comfortable recline.

'Angie, do you want to make a formal complaint about this?' Jessy asked quietly. 'Sam's abuse of you amounts to serious criminal offences. I can take a statement –'

'There's no proof.' Angie's eyes were anxious, her face tightly drawn. 'He never put any threats in writing. It would be my word against his.'

'Most rape cases are.'

She shook her head. 'I just want to tell you what he did to me in case it helps you find out what happened to Lil.'

'Okay. But have a think about it. We can talk about a complaint any time. Just remember it doesn't matter about the theft. What he did to you is illegal even though you'd also committed a crime. People think they can threaten others and get a free pass because their victims have also broken the law. Not true. Blackmail is illegal.'

'I understand.'

Jessy gave Angie a moment to compose herself. 'So how long ago did this abuse start?' she asked eventually.

'Perhaps a year ago. The bank threatened to take our family home in April ... Sam paid the money before the end of April and I first went to his and Amanda's home about a week after that.'

'You were eighteen?'

'I was at the time. I'm nineteen now.'

'What a slimeball,' Richard observed.

'No kidding.' I was fishing around in my backpack for my drugs. 'He could have shagged any number of perfectly willing young ladies if he wanted some nasty sex he couldn't convince his wife to get into. But he chooses to blackmail his wife's sister.'

'Does add a certain degree of vulgarity,' Richard agreed. 'Maybe she was more willing than she's letting on.'

I knew he was trying to wind me up. 'Or maybe he prefers it non-consensual.' I found the packet and took a couple more pills. Now I only had to wait another few minutes and the throbbing would ease off. I stood up and started pacing the tiny observation room, figuring that getting my blood flowing might speed up the process.

'Did he have a key to your apartment?' Jessy asked.

'Yes,' said Angie. 'He demanded one and I gave it to him. He still has it.'

'You never changed the locks?'

'No.'

'Drew, you're stressing me out,' said Richard, not looking in the slightest bit stressed. 'Sit down.'

'I'm right, thanks.'

'You said you wanted to talk to us. What do you want to talk about?'

I pulled the transcript out of my backpack and tossed it down on the bench in front of him. 'This.'

He glanced at it only momentarily before turning his attention back towards the interview. 'Seen it,' he said. 'Told you he had a watertight alibi.'

'It's not watertight,' I insisted. 'See look, there's a thirty-minute recess at ten in the morning. Enough time for him to go to Lil's unit, kill her and get back to court by half past.'

Richard sighed, as if contemplating whether now would be an appropriate time to announce that in forty-three years of policing, he had never come across a good lawyer. 'Andrew, even if he did manage to get his car out of the car park in record time, race out to Lil's place, stab her fifteen times, change into a new identical non-blood-spattered suit and then belt back to court in time for the transcript to show the court reconvening thirty minutes later, there's this.'

He opened a cheap manila folder sitting on the bench and pulled out a document which he thrust in my direction. It was a colour photocopy of a speeding ticket. 'Uniforms pulled him up speeding in South Perth. He gave his licence details; the uniforms identified him. The whole process took somewhere between five and ten minutes.'

I stared at the ticket. Nearly a hundred in a fifty zone on Mill Point Road at eleven minutes past ten in the morning on the day of Lil's murder. This was nowhere near the route he would've had to have taken to get to Lil's place in Northbridge in the time he had.

How mighty, mighty convenient. I felt anger rising.

'He did this deliberately,' I said. 'He hired someone to kill Lil. He'd planned to have a watertight alibi for himself for the whole morning so he couldn't possibly be implicated. When the court called a thirty-minute recess right about the time he'd planned for this hit man to be doing the job he shat himself. He realised that if his defence was not going to rest solely on the spurious recollection of some kid at the reception counter who may or may not recall not seeing him leave the building, he was going to have to organise another alibi. He got in his car and drove in the opposite direction from Lil's place until he found a cop car on patrol, then set about breaking the land speed record in front of them. *Voila!* Watertight.'

Richard actually turned in his chair then and looked at me. 'Andrew, let me explain this to you *again*,' he began, labouring every word as if I was a child. 'We have *nothing* on this guy. On the strength of your inebriated recollection, itself based on Lil's inebriated incomplete identification, which let's face it is really all we ever had, we have turned his life upside down trying to find something, just the tiniest hint of a suggestion he might have been involved in Lil's death. We've been through his private and business bank accounts, we've been through his private and business emails, we've chased rabbits down holes a hundred and fifty times because you asked us to, and now Jess is doing the same thing *again* in there now, *because you asked her to.*'

He glared at me, his expression making it clear I was not to attempt to speak.

'He did *not* kill Lil himself,' he went on, after taking a breath. 'And I think I'm going to have to tell you even though you're not an investigating officer and you're not the bloody prosecutor on this either and never fucking will be, he did *not* hire anyone to kill Lil. We've double-checked all his financial records and *no funds changed hands.* People don't do this kind of shit for love, Andrew. They almost invariably require money. Quite a lot of money if they're going to provide any kind of a reliable, quality service, and I don't think Godfrey is the type of bloke to give some drug-fucked dropkick a hundred and fifty bucks and cross his fingers the guy doesn't roll on him at the first hint of heat.'

'He could've been squirrelling cash.'

'Are you hearing this interview? Angela is saying Lil only found out about this shit with her and Sam two days before the murder.'

'Maybe he's been setting up secret accounts in anticipation of divorce, and he just dipped into one of them to pay the killer.'

'Maybe. But it's one thing to have an account that's kept secret from your wife and another to keep one secret from the police. He'd have to have set up a completely false identity. Hiding money isn't as easy as you think, Drew. Why do you reckon drug dealers find it so hard to reliably stash cash in bank accounts? Everything suspicious flags with the anti-money-laundering guys these days. An account with no withdrawals but repeated cash deposits is going to raise AML alarm bells. And he's just not really in a cash business. As a barrister he deals with law firms, not crooks direct. I don't know how he could get his hands on large amounts of cash. Do you?'

I didn't have an answer to that.

In the interview room, Angie sat with her arms wrapped around her knee. Tears spilt down her face and her soft voice broke as she continued to answer Jessy's gentle but persistent probing.

'How did Lil respond when you told her what had been going on?' Jessy enquired.

'She was shocked,' Angie admitted, her lips brushing against her knee as she spoke. 'She'd had no idea anything was happening. She told me I had to bring it to an end it once and for all, however he reacted. I told her I knew that.'

'Did she say she was going to speak to Sam about it?'

Angie shook her head. 'No, I begged her not to. I didn't want him to know she knew anything about it. I was worried what he might do to her. She agreed to say nothing to him but told me I had to straighten him out. I had to ring him and tell him this was ending for good and he wasn't to send me any more flowers or try to call me, and he could tell people whatever he wanted to about me.'

'And did you?'

'Yes.'

'When?'

'Right there and then. Lil and I sat together; she held my hand while I rang him, and I told him exactly that.'

'What phone did you use to call him?'

Angie unravelled herself to pull a mobile phone from her handbag. 'This one. It's a prepaid Sam gave me. He rang it when he wanted to see me.'

'Do you mind if we keep it for now?'

'That's fine. Of course.'

Angie's hands shook as she handed over the phone. *You didn't kill your sister,* I told her silently. *Sam Godfrey did.*

'So, there you have it,' Richard observed. 'There's nothing to suggest Lil ever confronted Godfrey about what he was doing to Angie. There's nothing to suggest he would have had any reason to even suspect she knew about it.'

I turned towards Richard. 'You're giving up, then, are you?'

Richard pursed his lips. He didn't look away from the interview.

'Of course we're not giving up,' he said. 'We'll find whoever killed Lily Constantine. But it wasn't Sam Godfrey.'

CHAPTER 13

'Jess, is there any chance Angie could go into witness protection?'

Jessy looked up from the omelette she was making for us both. She wore nothing but white lingerie, which is pretty much what every red-blooded bloke wants to see on a hottie standing in his kitchen in the morning. I cursed the fact that I was still in so much pain most of the time I'd hardly been able to see to Jessy's needs at all. What had happened between us since the beating was pathetic and demoralising. It felt like the performance of some old codger on his sixtieth wedding anniversary.

'We have limited resources.' She used an eggflip to expertly fold the omelette.

I nodded. 'I understand.' I'd been to Angie's place last night and had checked out her security situation. I got a tradie in to install new locks on all her doors and windows, but there was no way that was going to be enough to ensure he couldn't get at her. 'It's just a worry.'

Jess' mouth was a hard line. 'I'm not talking about this case with you anymore,' she said. 'Neither is Richard.'

I nodded. 'I understand. Sorry, Jess.'

She turned away from me then and grabbed a couple of plates from the cupboard above her head. Momentarily, her negligee rode up to reveal the curve of her bottom. When she turned around again and looked up at me, her eyes were shining. 'Drew, are you really sure that this is a good idea? Us, I mean?'

Oh, man.

'Jess, I know I haven't been much of a lover –'

'That's irrelevant,' she snapped. 'You should know I wouldn't dump you just because you're unwell.'

Ouch. 'You're dumping me?'

She didn't reply. It didn't matter. She didn't need to spell it out.

'What do you think is the problem?' I pressed.

She put my half of the omelette down in front of me.

'Thanks Jess, that looks awesome.'

'It's like we're on opposite teams at the moment,' she said. 'I'm doing the best I can to find out who killed Lil Constantine and bring him or her to justice, but, honestly Andrew, I feel like you think you're the only one who wants to solve this case. You're obsessed about it.'

'I know you're doing a great job.' I stared at her. Man, I really wanted to keep this woman. She could easily be the best thing that'd ever happened to me. But she was slipping out of my grasp and I couldn't hold onto her.

'Maybe once this investigation is over ... maybe then, Andrew, we could get together again and go out for dinner, you know? See if there really is anything worth pursuing.'

I nodded, but I felt like I was sliding into a hole. I hadn't had my breakfast Vicodin, that was the problem. I looked around for the packet.

'How many of those do you take each day?' Jessy asked as she passed it over to me.

'Four,' I lied. 'Two in the morning and two at night.'

'Good. You don't want to overdo it. They're pretty serious drugs.'

'Jessy, I don't want to lose you,' I said. I could hear a beseeching edge start to creep into my voice. I couldn't believe it. I'd never begged a woman not to leave me in my life. 'I reckon we do have something worth pursuing right now.'

The problem was, I knew where she was coming from. Hadn't I squirmed when I'd thought that Lil might have baggage? Hadn't I contemplated slamming into reverse and burning out of there the moment I'd anticipated the possibility that she might try to offload on me, that she might try to render our date anything other than laughter and light? If I dated a woman and she went all weird and obsessive about some dude she'd slept with once, I'd dump her so hard and fast I'd give myself whiplash.

'I really don't believe now is the right time, Drew. I'm sorry.'

~

I dressed and showed up at work. Rufus was visibly surprised to see me.

'What are you doing here?'

'It's Tuesday.'

'Your medical certificate said you'd be off until the twenty-fourth of May. That's nearly a month away.'

'Right. But I'm bored.'

He stared at me like I was some kind of gargoyle. 'Drew, you're … you're clearly not well.'

'I'm alright.' I'd had to acknowledge my face looked a little drawn in the mirror this morning, but I thought I looked okay. Suitable enough for work, anyway. The plaster cast was a bit clunky, but I was sure I could work around it. I only typed with four fingers at the best of times.

Rufus shrugged. 'It's up to you, I suppose. You're back in time to deal with Schneider, which is one good thing.'

'What's happened?'

'It got set down for a directions hearing. Nine o'clock this Thursday. The police found the original warrant, but Schneider's lawyers have sacked Audrey Simons and hired a new barrister, and he's trying to get all our evidence knocked out before the trial.'

'Great, sounds fun.'

'Do you need some help with … typing, and stuff?'

'I'll be fine. Thanks, Rufus.'

He looked doubtful. 'Schneider is important.'

'I'm on it,' I assured him.

'Alright. Good. Great. Thanks, Andrew.'

I returned to my office and found a pile of Sally's handwritten messages about a foot high smothering my desk. I used the cast on my right arm to sweep them all into my empty wastepaper basket. I would retrieve them from there over the course of the day and return all those calls. Unless, of course, the cleaners unexpectedly arrived in the meantime and accidentally took them all away.

Matt had wasted no time, upon learning of my presence in the building, returning the Schneider file to my desk. I opened it.

Rocco Schneider was a twenty-three-year-old factory worker and not a bad-looking bloke, if you were into that kind of thing. Since he fancied he was a bit of a stud, he didn't bother with grooming teenage girls on the internet, which could take weeks to pull off. He preferred to seduce them at the shopping centre or the flicks and take them and/or their friends back to his place for sex within an hour of meeting them. What ensued he inevitably filmed and photographed, and he sold the videos and pics to like-minded buddies. The girls were rarely older than fourteen or fifteen. All in all, he was a pretty despicable character and I understood why Rufus was so determined that he was going to go down.

The file featured a CD of Schneider's latest productions seized, according to my police witness statements, from his home computer where he had them stored on his desktop in an unsecured folder named 'Naughty Pics'. He lived alone. I'd never been sure why he was defending these charges, but assumed it had something to do with the fact that he was certain to go to jail for quite a while if and when he was convicted and, when he got there, life would not be pleasant. He had little to lose by giving it a tilt.

Pinned to the front of the file was a copy of Schneider's new barrister's notice of acting, informing the court and the DPP of who they were now dealing with.

I stared at it in disbelief. Schneider's new barrister was Sam Godfrey SC.

CHAPTER 14

Of course, it wasn't so unusual that a crook would hire Sam Godfrey SC to represent them in court. I just couldn't believe that of all the dozens of potential barristers this guy could have gone with, it just so happened that my nemesis was the bloke he selected. I wondered irrationally whether *Godfrey* had selected *him*. Whether he'd found out that this was my file, then approached Schneider's lawyers offering to act for a greatly reduced fee. As a barrister Godfrey was far superior to Audrey Simons. She was strictly small-time and would never in a million years earn the right to add 'SC' to the end of her name.

I sighed. Of course Godfrey hadn't deliberately set out to face-off against me in court. That was the whacks to the head talking again. It was just bad luck, and it was up to me how I decided to deal with it.

Neither Matt nor Rufus, nor any of the people I worked with knew anything about the slight personal differences I was currently experiencing with Sam Godfrey. Asking to bump the file to someone else was out of the question.

So, if turning and running was not an option, maybe the time had come to stand up to him. Figuratively, at least. Actually being on my feet all day Thursday was going to hurt, there was no two ways about that. Perhaps I might seek special dispensation from the judge to sit down to examine witnesses. Godfrey would have to have a bit of nerve to object to that.

I called Godfrey's office straight up and asked his secretary if he was going to be filing anything before the directions hearing, given it was listed in two days time. Within half an hour Godfrey himself had emailed me an inaptly named 'Outline of Submissions' – a forty-seven-page document.

The directions hearing was on the admissibility of the evidence seized pursuant to the police warrant from Schneider's computer. That evidence was critical to our case. Godfrey's document made it pretty clear that he wasn't just complaining about whether the warrant had been properly issued, signed by a justice of the peace, issued in time or served appropriately on Mr Schneider. No, he was accusing the police of having fabricated the warrant entirely, after the event, and lying when they said they'd possessed it and served it prior to seizing the evidence. The JP who'd signed the warrant was Reg Thompson, a retired local government town clerk. I knew Reg well. He loved fishing and horseracing and was a lifetime member of the local footy club. He had been a gunner in Vietnam, where he'd lost his brother and a fair few of his mates. He was a straight-down-the-line type of bloke and not a person I would want to accuse, to his face, of conspiring with corrupt police officers to backdate a warrant. Like every JP I'd ever met, he took the role incredibly seriously and the reality was you'd be battling to convince him to backdate a birthday card.

Schneider had been aware of the issues with the warrant, as was the court. Until the police had finally found it, Schneider had been under the impression that the DPP was going to drop the charges, just as soon as they'd done a proper review of the file. He'd have been bitterly disappointed when the warrant was relocated. I didn't have a lot of sympathy.

~

'Mr Thompson, do you recall signing this warrant?' Godfrey demanded ten minutes into the directions hearing on Thursday morning, as Reg Thompson faced him from the witness stand. In a crisply ironed robe, Godfrey towered over Schneider's lawyer and the diminutive Rocco Schneider, who sat beside him nodding in response to pretty much everything he said.

Reg was looking mightily unimpressed to have been dragged into court to justify himself. He wasn't used to being second-guessed. Godfrey wasn't in the least bit put off by Reg's glare of disapproval. It wouldn't have made any difference to Godfrey whether Reg had killed a thousand men in the jungles of wartime Vietnam or whether he'd been an ice-cream salesman his whole life. As far as Godfrey was concerned, he was just a witness. There to be driven into a state of confusion and aggravation by the manipulation of his words.

'Yes, I do.'

'On what day did you sign it?'

'On the ninth of February.'

'What day was that?'

'I don't know.'

'Well, do you remember signing it or not?'

'Yes, I do.'

'So what day was it? Monday? Tuesday?'

Reg's eyes narrowed. He didn't really need the sarcastic clarification of what a "day" was, but of course that was all part of the tactic.

'I remember signing the warrant. I don't remember what day it was when I signed it.'

'Yet you remember the date?'

'Yes.'

'That's convenient, isn't it?'

Reg shrugged. 'I suppose.'

'What did you have for breakfast that day?'

'I don't know.'

'Lunch?'

'I don't remember.'

'Did you go anywhere that day? Catch up with anyone?'

'I don't remember.'

'Can you remember a single solitary thing about the ninth of February except for the fact that you signed this particular warrant on that day?'

'No.'

Godfrey glanced down at his papers, as if to give the witness the impression he was starting on a new tack. In fact, he was working up to the finale on this one.

'The police told you the ninth of February was the date written on the warrant, didn't they?'

Reg hesitated. 'I don't know what –'

Godfrey sighed, as if he was tired of dealing with an idiot. 'They spoke to you before court today, or some time in the past week, didn't they? To organise for you to come to this hearing. They said, "This is the warrant you signed, Reg. See it's dated the ninth of February. Mr Schneider's lawyers will ask you questions about it, but you just have to say you signed it on the ninth of February."'

Reg paused. 'Yes. But –'

'Thank you. No further questions.'

I got to my feet and gave a bit of a dramatic sigh of my own, partly to indicate derision for Godfrey's *tactics*, and also because my body hurt. It had been weird, to say the least, to see Godfrey's steely eyes dart in my direction as we entered the court, to see him look me up and down and register my gaunt appearance, my obvious injuries. To note his own handiwork.

'Mr Thompson,' I began. 'How do you know you signed this warrant on the ninth of February?'

'Because that's the date on the warrant. I have never in my life signed a warrant without dating it, and I have never in my life signed a warrant that didn't have the correct date on it, as inserted by me at that time. That's how I know I signed this warrant on the ninth of February.'

'Thank you. I have no further questions, Your Honour.'

~

'I'm going to allow this evidence to go before the jury,' Judge Grainger informed the court after a short recess. 'I don't accept that it is sufficiently unreliable as to justify being ruled as inadmissible at this stage. The jury can be cautioned in relation to some of the concerns you've raised, Mr Godfrey. And you will, of course, get the opportunity once again to cross-examine the prosecution's witnesses.'

'Yes, of course, thank you, Your Honour.'

It didn't surprise me that Godfrey had lost this argument. He didn't actually *have* anything to go on. He didn't have any evidence or even anything to suggest that the warrant might have been backdated other than that it had been missing for a while.

In insisting on a directions hearing he didn't realistically have a good chance of winning, Godfrey had arguably damaged his client's chances of success at trial. Yes, he could cross-examine the witnesses again before the jury on these issues, hoping to create doubt about the integrity of the warrant. But now those witnesses had had a dress rehearsal. They knew his tactics. They'd be better prepared and he wouldn't find it so easy to bamboozle them. Meanwhile, Schneider, on his modest income of fifty-five thousand dollars a year, had been denied Legal Aid and would have to pay Sam Godfrey's bill for the half-day directions hearing himself. He'd be lucky if he got any change from thirty grand for that alone.

'Congratulations, Mr Deacon,' said Godfrey after the judge had left the room, furnishing me with another of his spine-tingling smiles. 'A competent win.'

It was on the tip of my tongue to spit *I know all about what you did to Angie, you lowlife*, but I restrained myself. It annoyed me more than I could possibly have imagined that he would speak to me like that, as if nothing had happened. As if the near-bloody-mortal wounds I carried weren't inflicted *on me by him*. Next thing he'd be bailing me up in the robing room: *Oh, g'day Andrew, just wondered how you were old chap, those bones healing up alright? Glad to hear it. Yes, a busted spleen can be a right pain in the backside, I had one myself once, playing footy back in the eighties.*

'Not really,' I said tightly. 'I don't know why you insisted on the directions hearing in the first place.'

Godfrey winked conspiratorially. 'Ah, I have my reasons.'

'Of course you do,' I snapped, then regretted it. 'How's Schneider going to pay for it? Cut it out in kiddie porn?'

Godfrey's face clouded over, and I was interested to see that I'd got to him. That was totally unexpected. But as soon as the blackness had descended, it lifted again, and he smiled his usual dazzling smile. 'It's lovely that you concern yourself with poor Mr Schneider's finances, Andrew,' he said, using my first name in order to belittle me. I knew that if I called him 'Sam' now it would just sound puerile. Instead I turned away from him and grabbed my stuff. It seemed pointless to tell him to leave me alone. 'Leave me alone' was something you said to an annoying co-worker who kept taking sips out of your coffee, not to someone who had already flogged you with a cricket bat-wielding team of helpers.

'Since you care so much,' Godfrey went on, speaking to my back, 'perhaps you would attend on me some time before we list the trial to discuss minimising Mr Schneider's costs by having some witness statements go in by consent.'

'Fine,' I snapped. 'But if you want defence witness statements to go in by consent, *you* can attend on *me*.' What an arrogant prick.

'Fine. When?'

'Tomorrow at two.'

'Good. See you then.' Godfrey disappeared without another word.

My ribs and arm were starting to burn again. I'd already had eight Vicodins today. If I was still alive by tonight, I'd take another two for bed. After all, if eight didn't kill me, then ten wasn't likely to either. At this rate I would run out of drugs tomorrow afternoon. Fortunately, I had an appointment with my GP tomorrow evening for another script.

CHAPTER 15

'I just need a script, thanks doc,' I explained to the GP, after waiting half an hour for him. The appointment was scheduled for six o'clock and I'd taken my last two Vicodin at half past three that afternoon, so my patience for delays was low. 'I ran out.'

The doctor frowned as he looked at my file on his computer screen. I couldn't remember his name. He'd seen me after I crashed and burned on a trail run last year and bent my knee sideways. Prior to that, I'd never had any need for a doctor, so this bloke had become my doctor. He was short and fat and a bit sweaty, and a stack of medical journals sat in a pile beside his desk that was almost as high as the desk itself, all unopened, still in their plastic wrappers. It was a look that I thought wouldn't necessarily fill patients with confidence.

'Your hospital discharge plan says when you were discharged and what was prescribed.' He continued to study the document even though what he was saying didn't sound complicated. 'You've been taking too many. They should've lasted much longer than this.'

It had been nearly two weeks since I'd been discharged from the hospital. I thought that seemed like long enough.

'Okay, but I've been in a lot of pain. You don't understand. I've been under a lot of pressure.' Having to speak to Sam Godfrey on a daily basis was part of the problem. He'd spent nearly two hours in my office that afternoon, hammering me about witness statements. I'd expected we'd be done by half past two, but no. It went on so long I'd had to take a toilet break to take my mid-afternoon dose of Vicodin, since I didn't want him to see I was struggling.

'Just because you're under pressure doesn't mean you can pop a pill to make it all better.'

It dawned on me I may have a problem with my GP.

'I'm not popping pills to deal with pressure, honestly,' I said, backpedalling like mad. 'I'm in pain. It's just as bad as it was. It hasn't eased off. If you don't help me, I'm going to be in agony. It would be torture, doc. You can't do that to a man.'

The doctor looked unimpressed. 'Four. Per. Day.' He pressed a few keys and his printer produced a script. 'And this is the last prescription you're going to get. It's got no repeats. Once this one is over, you're onto paracetamol every four hours.'

'I get it, no worries doc. Thanks very much for that.' I glanced down at the page he'd handed me. It had his name on it. *Dr Peter A. George.* 'Yeah, thanks Pete,' I went on. 'Thanks a million.'

The doctor winced. 'Try not to push yourself so hard if you don't want to be in pain. You shouldn't be back at work to start with. Try lying down a bit more. Rest during the day.'

'Got it, thanks doc,' I continued. 'I'll catch you later.'

I flogged the XD round to the late-night chemist and filled my script. They gave me a bottle with only a few tablets in it.

'I'm sorry,' said the pharmacist. 'That's all that's been prescribed. It should last you a couple of days. Do you need to talk about alternative –'

I turned away from her and swallowed four pills on my way from the checkout to the car. Halfway home the pain started to finally ebb.

~

I had a call from the office on the way home, but with no Bluetooth I let it go to message bank. I checked it when I got home. It was Matthew.

Andrew, call me urgently.

I rang his mobile.

'Shit, Andrew,' he opened with. 'You need to get down here.'

'Why?' It was half past seven on a Friday night. We did work long hours as a general rule but usually nothing was deathly urgent at that time of night.

'The place is swarming with cops. You're in the shit.'

'Why?' I repeated.

'I don't know for sure, but the rumour is they've found child exploitation material on your computer. Photographs of under-aged girls.'

That was a relief. I hadn't been looking forward to another stoush with the cops. 'Yeah, that doesn't surprise me. Was it, perchance, hidden in a secret file labelled "Evidence in the Schneider Case"?'

Matthew sounded like he was on the verge of freaking out. 'IT found some unauthorised emails, Andrew. You sent that shit to your home email address.'

My heart gave a single artery-bursting thud, before stopping completely. 'Fucking bullshit I did.'

'That's what they're saying –'

Oh, man. *Oh man*, I was *screwed*. I had – who would have thought it could happen – become a bit too cocky, thinking I was winning the war with Sam Godfrey. I wasn't winning. He was.

I was in deep shit.

'Am I breaking the law by warning you about this?' Matthew asked, as if it was the first time this possibility had occurred to him.

'Well, I'm hardly going to do a runner, am I?' I said, although I was seriously thinking about it. Sam Godfrey had me by the balls. Now it was clear why he'd taken on Schneider, why he wasn't remotely troubled to have lost the argument at the directions hearing. He'd planned this little attack against me from the start. By representing Schneider, by insisting on the directions hearing, he'd somehow given himself the opportunity to send those emails from my computer.

Fuck. I sunk into the nearest dining chair. *Fuck*. I'd be out of Vicodin again in a few hours, Sam Godfrey was on the offensive, and the cops would be coming around any minute to arrest me. I wondered if things could get any worse. I needed time to think what to do.

I needed to get out of here.

I changed in lightning time and got back in my car. It wouldn't start. I remembered in a sickening flash that the ignition had dropped out a couple of times on the way home from the chemist as I had hurtled down the freeway. On each occasion I'd just waited for a bit until it kicked in again. It'd crossed my mind I might need to give the ignition switch a clean, but I hadn't known I was going to need the bloody thing to work so badly, so soon. *Shit. Shit.* I sprinted back the way I'd come and, as the lift lumbered upwards, I tried to think how to fix it. Inside my unit, I grabbed a pocket knife from the top of the fridge and the power cable from my desktop computer, cut off each end and stripped off some black plastic and the ends of one of the wires while I ran back to the lift.

Please no cops. Please no cops.

In the car park I used the hotwire to connect the positive terminal of the battery to the positive terminal of the coil, slammed the bonnet down, climbed over to the driver's seat and turned the key.

The engine kicked into life.

The fact I'd need to pop the lid every time I needed to switch off the engine seemed like the least of my problems. I floored it out to the street.

CHAPTER 16

I parked the XD on the fourth level of a car park in the city. I got out, lifted the bonnet, killed the engine, slammed the bonnet, got back in and stared at the steering wheel. I could see my fingers shaking in the dim light as they rested against the Ford-themed steering wheel cover which the seller had thrown in to double the value of the vehicle. I contemplated my own breath for a few minutes.

Fact number 1.

My desktop computer at home was probably full to the brim of illegal pornography, hidden in files which I had never seen and would never have stumbled across, but which the cops would right now be finding by the bucketload. I should have brought it with me when I left home, but I didn't think of it at the time, even as I grabbed its power cable to get the XD started. Matthew had given me a priceless warning, but I'd blown it.

Fact number 2.

I would not be a popular guy if I were to wind up in jail, even for one night. It was Friday, which meant if I was arrested tonight and refused bail by the cops, I wouldn't be up before a magistrate on the question of bail until Monday morning. That meant three nights in custody, which was plenty of time for someone to get to me. If Jessy was mad enough to ensure that I was refused bail, I could expect she wouldn't be asking for protection for me in prison. And even if she asked for it, that would be no guarantee it would happen.

Fact number 3.

Jessy was going to be mad.

Even if she accepted that I'd been set up, she would not forgive me for getting myself into such a ridiculous situation. I understood exactly how she felt. If I were her, I would want a boyfriend I could introduce to my family and friends without having to explain why he was in trouble with the law and didn't actually in a technical sense have his liberty, as such. The odds of her agreeing to us getting back together were looking slimmer by the minute.

I dug around in the glove box of the XD and found a parking ticket and a heavily chewed pencil. It wasn't me that'd chewed it, but I tried not to get too distracted by that. I wrote: *what I have.*

I looked at the page. I couldn't see the words because they were written in pencil on top of faded printing, and it was dark, but I forged on regardless.

    1. the possibility of a relationship with Jessy, after all this is over.

    2. my job.

    3. my freedom.

    4. some assets.

I hesitated, then added another item.

    5. an addiction to opiate-based prescription painkillers.

I scratched out 1 and 2. They were both gone already. If I went on the run, I had a chance of retaining my freedom, but it was an enormous risk to take. If I was subsequently caught, I would be refused bail as I was a flight risk and would have to spend months in jail awaiting trial. If I turned myself in now, it was in all likelihood only going to be three days at worst, albeit three fairly unpleasant days. At least I would be free until I went to trial. If I was convicted, I could be spending fourteen years behind bars.

Dr George had explained, just in case I didn't understand, that the features of modern computers meant that I couldn't just go and see another doctor and get another prescription for Vicodin without them knowing that Dr George had already knocked me back. I had to deal with my addiction. He gave me a bunch of pamphlets. I planned to deal with my addiction alright. By finding someone on the street I could buy the stuff from.

If I went to jail, my chances of getting Vicodin were non-existent. I didn't know how I could cope without the drug. Even for three nights. The thought of going without Vicodin for three hours was enough to fill me with dread.

I scratched around in the darkness for my mobile phone.

The head of IT at the DPP was a middle-aged foreigner named Malcolm. I never actually got around to asking him what country he was from. I thought Malcolm was a pretty good bloke. A couple of months ago he'd agreed to help me fix my home computer which was bleating error messages every time I tried to do anything with it, and he'd given me his mobile number to arrange a rendezvous. As we sat in my living room while he tinkered with the offending machine, he told me conversationally that he'd been a fighter in some mercenary army in his home country and had been responsible for torturing people. However, he explained, I didn't need to feel too bad, as most of the time he didn't actually need to torture people. Usually just giving them the impression that he was going to torture them had the desired effect.

'Hello?' The voice at the other end of the phone was gruff, heavily accented. Maybe he was Eastern European. Or South African.

'Malcolm, it's Andrew.'

'Right.' He sounded cautious.

'I want to know what's happened.'

'Well, we found some unauthorised sent emails. As per policy we advised management and management called the police.'

'How could this happen?'

'Well, you press send.'

'Don't fuck with me, Malcolm. You know as well as I do, I didn't send those emails. I want to know how it's possible that someone else could've sent them. Has someone hacked into my email account?'

'It's basically impossible to hack into your email account. Any new device requires two-factor authentication. And no one could have picked up those photos from outside the building even if they did hack into your email.'

'But couldn't someone hack into my computer? Then they could send emails from my email account without needing to log in on a different device, right? And attach whatever my computer has access to?'

'Your roaming profile is password protected, Andrew,' said Malcolm patiently. 'You might recall you enter a password into it every morning, and whenever it's been unattended for two minutes. It's practically impossible to hack into your computer from outside the network.'

'But possible from inside the building? Could you get past that password?'

'I suppose with a bit of effort I could.'

'So, anyone in the whole building could log into my roaming profile?'

'It wouldn't be easy. But not impossible.'

'I've been set up, Malcolm. Someone's hacked into my computer and sent those bloody things. I don't know how but I'm going to find out,' I said, before hanging up. After all, I'd seen enough movies to know that it was important to hang up before the cops knew which car park I was in.

I stared at the phone. I wanted to talk to Jessy. I wasn't sure if I dared to ring her.

Maybe she didn't know about the emails yet. Maybe I could just ring her, and everything would be normal.

'Hey, Jess.'

'Where the fuck are you?' Her voice was cold.

I shuddered. 'Out. Are you at my place?'

'Yes. With Richard.'

'I didn't do it, Jess. He's set me up.'

'Don't start this shit, Andrew.' She sounded unimpressed. 'Just get your arse back here.'

'Will you release me on bail tonight?'

'We don't negotiate with fugitives. Get your arse back here. I mean it.'

'Listen, I mean it too, Jess. I can't go to jail.'

She hesitated, as if she couldn't quite believe I was contemplating doing a runner. Her police training kicked in. 'Andrew, everything will be fine if you come back now,' she said. 'We'll do everything we can to –'

I hung up.

My heart beat hard in my chest. Maybe what I should do was go around to Sam Godfrey's place and stab him to death with the pocketknife that constituted the only thing I'd managed to bring with me when I left my place. It probably wouldn't help me much in the scheme of things, but it would cheer me up.

I had about a hundred thousand dollars in the bank, largely thanks to the insurance payout which had arrived, as well as some shares and a couple of investment properties. The properties were fairly illiquid unfortunately. I could hardly go through the process of a property sale and settlement while on the run. But the cash was obviously very accessible, provided I went to the bank and got it out before Jessy got around to freezing my account.

Could I disappear with a hundred thousand dollars? I wasn't sure. I doubted that would get me overseas without the passport I'd left on the top shelf of the walk-in wardrobe in my bedroom, and I knew I had to do it properly if I was going to do it at all.

I stared out through the front window of the XD at the lifeless concrete of my surroundings. I thought about Rod and Ellen and what a downer it would be on their new life together if I pulled a stunt like going on the run. It would be bad enough if and when I was charged with a serious offence. But at least if I was in jail they'd know where I was.

My phone buzzed. I just about hit the roof of my car. Shit, my nerves were lined up on a knife's edge.

It was a text. From Jessy.

Please come back.

A knot started to wind up in my chest.

'*What do you do for a living, Andrew? You're all dressed up in a big, flash suit like a kid at his mother's wedding.*'

Why did he kill you?

'*My brother-in-law's a lawyer, and he's a total arsehole.*'

Lil, please. What did you do to him?

You're messing with a man who is too powerful.

Did you threaten him?

He's too powerful. He'll take everything you have. He'll destroy you.

I smacked my left hand and my right plaster cast down, in unison, onto the steering wheel. I was about to lose everything, whichever decision I made.

CHAPTER 17

In the dim light I forced my way through the crowded bar of The Den.

'I'm due for a break in twenty minutes,' Angie shouted above the head-crushing music. 'Can you wait?'

'Of course.' I had all night.

She nodded, then her attention was demanded by a good-looking young bloke in a suit, collar dragged open as if he'd come straight from the office. He flashed her a wide smile, then leaned towards her to order. Angie laughed, flirting with him as she cracked two beers, reminding me of Lil that night. The last night of her life.

Ordinarily, I would've loved to get up and dance, pulling my moves and flirting with the hot ladies. That wasn't an option anymore. Everything I did caused pain. There were bugger-all pills in Dr George's final script. I was going to need more drugs by the morning. I needed more now, but I was saving the last two to have any chance of getting to sleep.

I stood at the edge of the dancefloor and felt the beat of the music resonate in my body, speeding my heart up to its rate. A middle-aged woman had once described to me the feeling of nightclub music as reminiscent of African beats, the way it calmed and centred her. That was just before she was assaulted by a couple of bouncers and thrown down the stairs.

But I couldn't stand for long, so walked out onto the street to sit down on the curb. Outside were the usual shenanigans of the nightclub departure process. Drunk women in platform stilettos and tiny sleeveless dresses shivering in the cool night air as they contemplated getting in Ubers with men their friends should be warning them against even talking to. Men my age or younger with product in their hair and wearing tight spangly shirts and pointy dress shoes smoking and getting testy with each other. Bouncers having earnest discussions with people who were too smashed, and everything sparkling with artificial light. There were no cops floating around just at that moment, though I knew it was possible they could show up at any time. If they did, I would have to be cool. I doubted anyone would know yet that Jessy and Richard wanted to speak to me. It was just a matter of smiling, being polite, moving if they wanted me to move, making myself the least of their problems on a Friday evening.

Angie sat down beside me.

'Did the cops talk to Godfrey again?' I asked her.

She shook her head. 'They don't think what I told them changes anything. It doesn't give him any motive to kill Lil. It would be different if they knew she contacted him and threatened him somehow. But I don't know if she did or she didn't.'

'The conversation I overheard was far from civil.'

'She would've been pretty dark on him by then, given what I'd told her. But the cops say without any evidence that she actually confronted him on it, there's nothing they can do.'

'Nothing they're inclined to do, more like it.'

'The old fat one, he reckons my statement has actually convinced him Sam wasn't the killer. They now know Lil wasn't having an affair with Sam, and they know the exact date she found out about what he was doing to me. He has an alibi for the time of the killing, and they know that no lump sums came out of any of Sam's accounts after that date, so he didn't pay a hitman.' She shrugged. 'They said they'd keep it in mind in case it turns out to be relevant as the investigation progresses.'

'What does that mean?'

'I don't know.'

My phone buzzed in my pocket. I looked down at it. The caller was unknown. Hesitantly, I answered it, struggling to get to my feet from having been sitting almost at ground level, and walking away from Angie.

'Andrew, it's Jessy.'

'Are you still at the cop shop?'

'I'm on the street. Turns out these payphones are quite handy for private conversations.'

My stomach churned. 'Jess, I'm so sorry.'

She sounded anxious. 'Listen, I know it's not your fault. We need to meet.'

'Tonight?'

'Yes, tonight.'

'Are you going to arrest me?'

'No. Not if you meet with me.'

'How do I know that?'

'I promise, Andrew. I need to see you. I'm so worried ... I'm worried you're going to do something stupid.'

I knew I would be a total idiot to trust her.

'Jess, I'm sorry. I can't. Not until I've thought a few things through.'

'I know you didn't send those emails.'

'We both know if there's enough evidence for a charge, you have to charge me. It's up to me to put up my defence in a court of law in twelve months time. You *have* to charge me.'

'No –'

'What if I was a paedophile?'

'But you're not.'

'That's not for you to decide, Jess, don't you remember going over this stuff at your last refresher course?' These were types of problems we had with the cops all the time. The finer points of not promoting themselves to judge, jury and executioner were often lost on them.

'Yeah, I remember that stuff.' She seemed more worried than annoyed, which only went to show how worried she was.

'I can't go to jail, Jessy, not even for the weekend. I can't trust them to keep me safe. I've just about run out of Vicodin and I need to have a think about what I'm going to do.'

'You don't have a choice. If you run now, Richard and I will find you and then you'll stay in prison until this thing goes to trial.'

'I know, Jess. Listen, I gotta go. I really would love to see you, but I can't right now. I'm not running, okay? I'm just out.'

'Out?'

'Out for the night. I'm sure if you and Richard come back in the morning, you'll find me tucked up in my bed like a well-behaved boy.'

'No, Andrew. That's not good enough.'

'The IT guy reckons it's possible to hack into my computer from inside the building.'

'I'm sure it is. But since Sam Godfrey doesn't work in your office, that's going to add a whole new layer of complexity if you're convinced he did this. It would mean there has to be yet another person involved. First the hit man, then the thugs that beat you up, now this new guy. How many people would a really smart guy like Sam Godfrey draw into an operation like this?'

'He *was* there, Jess. He was in my office today.'

'Does he know your password?'

'Maybe he does, somehow.'

I could tell she was getting distressed. 'Okay, as you rightly pointed out, Drew, we have to charge you, based on what we know. We're doing it tonight, and since you're *out*, and you're refusing to meet with me, Richard will probably issue a warrant for your arrest.'

I nodded, only vaguely conscious of the fact she couldn't see me. Three days. Three days in the company of men I'd prosecuted and, with the assistance of a jury, condemned to imprisonment. Three days of sitting around doing nothing while Godfrey went merrily about his daily business. Three days without painkillers.

'Jess, I gotta go,' I said. 'I'm really sorry.'

'Drew, please don't –'

I hung up, resolving this time we wouldn't be speaking again. Not until I'd sorted out a few things.

~

'I need to get out of here,' I said to Angie. 'I think the cops might be looking for me.'

Her eyes widened. 'What did you do?'

'Nothing. Your arsehole brother-in-law has framed me for a crime I didn't commit, and he's done a good job of it. I need to go some place where I can think.'

'What crime?'

'He's managed to email child exploitation material from my work computer to my home email address. That's obviously illegal. I mean, it's quite normal for me to have it at work, because I prosecute these kinds of cases and it's ... you know, it's evidence. We have all sorts of evidence on the work server, security-camera footage, video records of interview, crime-scene photos and so on. But if I send it to myself, I'm distributing it and I'm possessing it outside of the course of my official duties. They're very serious crimes.'

Angie stared at me for a long moment. 'Was it photos that he emailed?' she said eventually.

I wondered what she was thinking. 'Yeah, photos. Why?'

She shrugged. 'That's pretty full-on. So, he used your own email address to attach files from the DPP server and email them to you.'

'He must've, as otherwise he'd leave me with a defence of the emails being unsolicited.'

'In that case he must've hacked into their network and targeted your computer. That's not easy, you know. Practically the only ways he could do it would be with a phished website which is a lot of hassle to set up for just one target or, more likely, he's infected you with a keylogger or some kind of Trojan sending him your cookies or typed information. Did he have cause to send you any emails, especially ones with attachments, in the past few weeks?'

I stared at her. 'How do you know this stuff?'

She frowned. 'It's what I do.'

'What do you mean? You're a barmaid.'

'I work as a barmaid. I study IT. I'm a student. It's not that unusual for students to work as barmaids, Drew. Didn't you have a job when you were at uni? Or did Mummy and Daddy pay for your whole education?'

'He's had cause to send me emails, yes,' I said, hardly registering the insult. 'We've had to liaise on a case recently. He's sent me letters and submissions and court documents as attachments. About a directions hearing.'

'Does your computer remember your email password automatically?'

'My private webmail address, yes.'

'That's a cookie.'

'Oh man.' I couldn't believe it. 'I don't know if the photos were attached to an email from my work account or my private one.'

'It doesn't matter. If it was your private one, he's got the cookie; if it's work, he'll have picked up your work computer login details from you typing them in, using a keylogger. Then it's just a matter of logging in while he's near your computer, maybe while you're out of the room. Then he'd attach the file off the server to a new email from either of your addresses and send it off, and then hibernate your computer again. He might even have removed his infected email and the keylogger beforehand, if he had time.'

I felt sick. Not only had he been in my office earlier today, wanting me to consent to the defence not calling a bunch of witnesses on the basis that there was no need for them to be cross-examined, and their statements being tendered as evidence in their absence, but I'd left him alone with my computer when I went off to the toilet to take more Vicodin. It was locked, I remembered noting before I left, but that obviously wasn't enough, because he knew the password. He'd gleaned it from something attached to an email he'd sent me days earlier, that recorded every stroke I pressed on my crappy twenty-dollar keyboard.

He'd suggested I go to his office, knowing I would insist on him coming to me in a desperate attempt to retain some dignity. *You can attend on me*, I'd said to him haughtily.

I just couldn't believe it.

'Where would a lawyer get access to keylogging software?'

'You can download it off the internet. With a bit of practice, it wouldn't be that difficult, even for a non-techhead.'

'I can't see how our firewall would've let the keylogger through in the first place.'

'It's not impossible.'

I didn't want to scare her, but I felt like flipping my lid. It wasn't helping that I didn't have the drugs I needed. I noticed my hands were shaking.

'Angie, I have to go.'

She nodded, her eyes dark and round, her brow furrowed.

I left the club and walked briskly down the street, pulling the collar of my shirt up around my neck. It had started to rain. *That's not rain*, my dad would have said. *It's just a bit of mist*. But the bitumen and pavement began to glisten with moisture. More than cold I felt vulnerable, away from the anonymity of the nightclub. There, it was possible to feel as though you could never be found. As though you could hide forever among the dancing, sweating bodies and the deafening rhythms. I supposed that was a large part of its appeal even when you weren't on the run from the law.

I'd parked in the city, so it was a bit of a walk back from Northbridge to the car park. As I entered the car park foyer, my phone rang again, sending my heart to my throat. Car parks made me jumpy.

Give it up, Jess.

I pulled the phone from my pocket. I didn't recognise it, but there was a number there this time. Maybe it wasn't Jessy after all.

'Hello?'

There was no answer for a moment. Eventually, a male voice spoke. 'Mr Deacon.'

I recognised Sam Godfrey instantly.

'What do you want?' I hissed, fishing around in my pocket for the keys to the XD as the lift jerked upwards towards Level 4.

'I just wanted to congratulate you on your win today,' he said smoothly. 'It was well deserved.'

'Yes, congratulations are in order all round,' I snapped. 'You've done a great job of fitting me up for something I didn't do.'

'Thank you, Mr Deacon. I'm glad you appreciate my work.' He sounded satisfied.

'The cops know I didn't do it.'

Godfrey laughed. 'But that doesn't help you, does it? The police are searching your home computer as we speak. They have to charge you because, happily, we don't live in a country where the police get to decide what they do and don't bring to court, and once their evidence goes before a jury, the good folk on that jury will convict you, just like they convict every piece of pond scum who keeps filth on their computer and claims they've no idea where it came from.'

I didn't really need Godfrey to spell out the reality of my situation. I'd been around the block a couple of times.

'Why are you doing this to me?'

It was a dumb question and I regretted it. I stepped out of the lift and strode across the concrete towards my car, which I could see parked between a Prius and a tidy white Jaguar XJ6 on the far side of the level.

'Do you really need to ask, Mr Deacon? I know you met with my sister-in-law, Angela, even after I made it very clear your intrusion into my family matters was not appreciated. I gave you every chance to avoid this situation by simply minding your own business. You ignored my warnings. You started this, Andrew. You brought this on yourself.'

Near my car, a man stepped out from behind a pillar. I froze.

'Now, I believe you've been continuing to communicate with Angela. I have to say, your constant intermeddling in my family affairs is starting to upset my wife.'

I couldn't really make out the man's features, but I doubted it would be anyone I would recognise. There was maybe twenty metres between us. He stood facing me with his legs apart, resting slightly against the boot of my car, his meaty arms folded across his chest.

'I mean business you know,' Godfrey murmured, his disembodied voice seeming only barely audible in my left ear.

I turned and walked back towards the lifts, hanging up on Godfrey and dropping my phone into my pocket. I pressed the button but wasn't minded to wait. I ran towards the sign for the stairs, dragged the door open and descended three steps at a time, hearing someone enter the stairwell above me as I yanked open the door at the bottom.

I whacked my plaster cast against the doorframe as I lurched out into the foyer. I ran past a couple of people paying their tickets and onto the street and, lowering my head, slowed to a fast walk as I headed back towards Northbridge. I crossed the bridge over the railway line and joined the busy night-time throng of revellers once more. I glanced over my shoulder a couple of times.

No one was following me.

CHAPTER 18

I sat down at an alfresco table outside a Greek restaurant and ordered a lamb moussaka. I could see the Constantines' restaurant from where I sat, only three or four doors down the same street.

Was the man in the car park waiting for me? Maybe not, but it didn't matter. If a warrant had been issued for my arrest, the cops would've procured my rego in five seconds flat and they'd be looking for the XD. It wasn't safe to drive it. I was safer on foot. I liked the XD, but it was for the best that I'd been forced to abandon it. I didn't like to consider how it would fare in a police chase, should it come to that. The rings were so worn it had the horsepower of a lawnmower and things went wrong with it on a daily basis. I hadn't paid a lot for it, so I knew it was likely to break down. But I wondered whether I'd done that as some sort of weird internal need to punish myself, like self-flagellation. Flagellation by Falcon. I hadn't really needed to buy such a crap car. I could have bought a nice BA Fairmont for only three grand, which still would've left me with plenty of money for drugs and other necessities.

I turned my mind back to that particular priority.

Rod, I knew, could get me Vicodin if I asked him to. He was recently back from his honeymoon. But I wasn't ready, just yet, to ring up my little brother and hit him up for illicit, career-destroying favours.

The next person to come to mind in connection with the need to source some more opiate-based painkillers was Mr Aaron Thomas Urquhart. Urquhart was a Mr Big, a huge coup for the state in its ongoing fight against the distribution of methamphetamines and other illicit drugs on our streets. Millions of dollars worth of meth, ecstasy and prescription drugs had been seized and destroyed in the course of that operation and, in the end, Urquhart had gone down for twenty-seven years. He was currently serving his sentence in a maximum-security facility.

To get him, though, a few concessions had been required. A number of small-time pushers had been offered immunity in exchange for their testimony against him. They'd been put into witness protection pending the trial, but after that many of them had returned to their old homes and, presumably, their old lifestyles. One, a man in his mid-twenties by the name of Darren Ashwin, had been living near the city, in North Perth. Ashwin's dad had abandoned the family when he was three, and his mum was a heroin addict who left Ashwin and his brother to pretty much fend for themselves. Over the years she brought home a parade of boyfriends, more than one of whom helped themselves to her sons when she passed out on the lounge room floor, as she frequently did. At school Ashwin was diagnosed with ADHD and anger-management issues, both of which the underfunded public school he occasionally attended if his mum was capable of getting him there was ill-equipped to deal with. By the age of eleven he'd stopped attending school completely, was functionally illiterate and was pinching his mum's drugs when she was comatose. When he was twelve, he wound up before the Children's Court on a charge of assault occasioning bodily harm, arising out of an incident at the local shopping centre where he'd taken to spending his days, and it culminated in him being locked up at a juvenile detention facility with fourteen- and fifteen-year-old boys, who alternated between abusing him themselves and teaching him everything he needed to know about surviving on your own in the big wide world. His mother overdosed and died before he was released and, when he did get out, he moved in with the uncle of a friend he'd made in juvenile detention, a drug dealer by the name of Michael Allan Frazer. From there he was introduced to Frazer's boss, a man who worked for Mr Urquhart, and all of a sudden at the age of thirteen, Darren Ashwin had himself a day job.

After the sting, Ashwin had been looking at some serious jail time for his role in the whole thing, but he'd been willing to cooperate with some evidence in exchange for retaining his freedom, as he wasn't keen to return to prison. He was skinny and looked a little effeminate if you were squinting hard enough. I'd proofed him one time after getting him round to our office. He was the only one I'd personally spoken to. The other prosecution witnesses had been proofed by Matthew and Rufus. I'd been informed he was in reception and as I walked out to greet him, he stared at me out of bloodshot eyes, lolling back in the luxurious leather couch, and grinned.

'Nice office, man,' he'd commented. 'Lucky you.'

I wasn't sure he'd still be living in Frazer's house, since I was pretty sure I'd heard Frazer had been murdered shortly after he left witness protection over a dispute with another drug dealer that was unrelated to the Urquhart trial. I thought it was worth a crack, though, so to speak.

A waitress delivered my meal. Three doors down, Mrs Constantine placed two steaming bowls of pasta in front of a young couple. The man seemed unhappy and Lil's mum gave an apologetic nod before taking one bowl back towards the kitchen. She looked tired.

I finished the moussaka and headed down the street. It wasn't hard to find Darren Ashwin's place. It was a dingy inner-city shitbox a short walk from the nightclub precinct and I'd been there before. It was the middle of the night, but that was unlikely to matter much to Ashwin.

Darren Ashwin answered the door wearing nothing but a towel around his waist. His scrawny upper body was marked with red bruises and tracks in his skeletal arms. He was continuing to use too much of his own merchandise, that much was clear. Still, it was good, for my purposes at least, to see that he was still alive.

'What the fuck...' he opened with when he registered who I was, then rolled his eyes in the style of a naughty schoolboy. 'I haven't done anything wrong. Why are you guys giving me a hard time? This is fucking bullshit, man.'

'Darren, I'm not here to give you a hard time,' I explained quickly. *I'm not a cop, you fucking idiot.* 'I need your help.'

'I've already given you my help. I've done what we agreed.'

'No, not that kind of –'

'Fuck off, man.'

'Darren, I need drugs. Vicodin, in particular. I need it tonight. Can you please help me? I've got cash.'

Ashwin eyed me dubiously. I knew for all his learning problems and lack of education, Darren Ashwin could read people. It was a skill he'd been forced to acquire in bringing himself up and surviving juvenile detention. Something in my face told him I was serious.

'I don't have any Vicodin,' he muttered. 'Can get you some but not until Wednesday.'

I fought to stay calm. 'I need it tonight, Darren. You don't understand.'

He laughed then. 'Trust me, Mr Deacon, I understand. But I can't do anything more than I can do. I got no phone number for my contact. He isn't coming till Wednesday. You just got to wait.'

'Isn't there someone you could ask?'

'Maybe. Tomorrow.'

I stared at his gaunt, pockmarked face with its backyard piercings and fungal sores around his mouth and nose. Ashwin and I were around the same age. We'd come from very different backgrounds but what we had in common was that we'd both done what we could to make the best of our lives. And the differences between us were less vast than they had been this time last year. Now we were both slaves to our addictions. Maybe our worlds would continue to converge, if I let this thing play out, if I did nothing to save myself. Maybe I had to act now if I didn't want to become the man I now faced. Go cold turkey. Sweat it out in a hotel room somewhere. Regain control over my disintegrating life.

In between running from the cops and finding the evidence I needed to prove Godfrey killed Lil and framed me for a crime I didn't commit.

'I'll come back in the morning,' I said. 'First thing.'

Ashwin nodded, and slammed the door shut without another word.

I turned around and found myself face to face with Detective Jessy Parkin.

CHAPTER 19

We stared at each other. Neither of us moved.

I cursed myself for my stupidity. I'd told her on the phone I was out of drugs. She knew that would be my first priority. It was a simple matter of considering what she knew about my recent cases to work out where I'd go, following the same thought process as I did. Most of the people I'd come across of recent times who were drug dealers were in jail. A prosecution witness who'd been given immunity was the logical choice. She'd worked with me on Urquhart; she knew of Ashwin.

Idiot.

I glanced behind her. Her car was parked on the verge, but there was no sign of Richard or anyone in the passenger seat. She'd come alone. Why, I had no idea, but I knew I couldn't afford to stick around to find out.

I turned and sprinted down the pavement in the direction of the nightclubs again.

She shouted after me to stop, then followed me on foot.

I leapt across the storm drainage gutter and flew down the street, striding out as I raced along the black, shiny road. There were practically no cars but quite a few people around, mostly young people, pissed and holding each other up, starting fights, arguing over rides. I didn't fancy a discussion with the cops patrolling in the city over why I was leading Jessy on a race through the crowds, not when a warrant had probably by now been issued for my arrest, so I shot down a back lane heading back out of the city. I could hear her behind me as I ran down a pedestrian access onto the next street, and another one onto the next street after that. I wasn't sure if she was gaining on me. I was fast, usually. But right now, I was still healing from some pretty bad injuries, unfit and unbalanced by the weight of the cast, and she could well outlast me. My ribs were already screaming from the pressure I was putting them under by exerting my lungs.

The thing was, I couldn't afford to let her catch me. I didn't know if she was carrying a gun or, even less palatably, a taser, but if she caught me, and she was unarmed, I wouldn't use force against her. I couldn't do that. That meant I had to outrun her. I imagined Russ striding out beside me through the streets. I missed that bastard already.

You got this.

At least, that's what I liked to imagine he'd say as I ran for my freedom. More realistically, he'd say: 'Drew, you couldn't outrun a determined three-year-old on a scooter at the moment. I can't believe you're even attempting this. And people reckon *I'm* deluded.'

I dashed down another laneway and found myself at a dead end, with the lane blocked by a six-foot-high mesh fence. I launched myself at it and scrambled up one-handed, firing up my ribs as I rolled over the top to a pain level beyond what I would once have thought I could bear.

I groaned as I landed on the other side, stumbling to my knees. I was convinced one of my ribs had re-broken with the jolt.

'Drew, please wait,' Jessy shouted again as she followed me over the fence. By the time I was able to drag myself back to my feet, she'd run past me in the laneway. I looked up to find myself between her and the fence, and she stood breathlessly still in the centre of the laneway with her revolver trained at my head.

I closed my eyes.

'Drew, I'm sorry,' she whispered. 'I'm sorry to have caused you more pain.'

I looked at her to see her hands were shaking as she aimed the weapon at me. Her eyes filled with tears while I watched her.

'Are you really going to shoot me?' I enquired, wincing as I lowered myself gingerly back to the ground, the gun following me down.

'I don't mean to sound petulant, but I really don't think I deserve that. Granted, the sex was a bit lousy towards the end there and I accept full responsibility for that –'

'Drew, shut up, please.' She released one hand from her weapon and wiped furiously at her eyes with the back of her hand. 'I'm here because I don't want you to make a terrible mistake. It would be a mistake to go on the run.'

'Jessy, seriously. You're not my girlfriend. You don't care if I make a mistake.'

'I do care. I'm your friend.'

'If you do you shouldn't. I mean, look at me. I'm a drug addict, I'm up on criminal charges, particularly despicable ones, I'm about to lose my job. I'm not the sort of person you want to be associated with.'

'I know the drugs are a problem. If you come back with me now, I'll do everything I can to convince Richard to bail you tonight, and then we'll come back here in the morning to see Ashwin. You'll be okay.'

'What if you can't convince Richard to bail me?'

'Then I'll see Ashwin myself, and I'll get the drugs to you.'

I stared at her. 'Jessy, can you hear what you're saying? You're a *cop*. You're offering to smuggle illicit drugs into a prison. That's a serious offence. It would make you a drug dealer, just to start with. You'd be lucky to stay out of jail yourself if you got caught and your career would be over before you'd even been convicted.'

She bit her lip. 'I know, Drew. I know all that.'

I stood again slowly and walked over to her. Her eyes flashed as I approached her, but she didn't ask me to stop. Eventually I was close enough to touch her. She lowered the gun down beside her body as I took her face in my hands and leaned down to kiss her mouth, salty from her tears. 'No way can I let you do that for me, Jessy,' I whispered into her lips.

Then I turned and continued down the laneway, walking with some difficulty but staying on my feet.

'Andrew Deacon, stop. You're under arrest. You're under arrest, dammit.'

I kept walking, half expecting to feel a bullet tear into my back or, if I was lucky, my shoulder or the back of my thigh.

But she didn't do it. And she didn't follow me.

I turned into a busy street and spotted a taxi rank at the end. I got into the back seat of the first cab in the line, and realised I had no idea where I should say I wanted to go.

I leaned my head back against the headrest. 'Somewhere I can have a sleep,' I said. 'Somewhere in the suburbs. Thanks.'

~

I dropped my wallet on the bench in my motel room, turned off my phone to save its battery, and sat down on the corner of the bed to attempt the delicate process of leaning over my ribcage to remove my shoes. The motel seemed from the street to be suitably austere, the sort of place that wouldn't be needing a credit card imprint for the mini bar. I'd paid for three nights' accommodation with cash and the bloke didn't seem to bat an eyelid. He'd just been a little pissed off about being woken at one o'clock in the morning.

The mini bar comprised two little plastic pods of UHT milk. I drank them both, and resolved I'd go back to see Ashwin again in the morning. Jessy may well have him staked out by then, but it was a chance I had to take. My only other choice was to go to the chemist and buy cough medicine to drink, which didn't seem attractive at this stage, although doubtless it would eventually.

Half an hour and my last two Vicodins later, I lay down to attempt to sleep. I just had to make it through the night.

~

I stared at the ceiling.

It was four o'clock in the morning. I lay awake on the hard, bowl-shaped bed, sweating into the linen sheets. The bed was practically a lump of concrete. My ribs felt like someone was kneeling over me with a jackhammer. I knew I hadn't had enough painkillers and needed more.

I thought about Jessy. About how I'd walked away from her. Her eyes, her tears, that foxy way she'd pointed her weapon at me and told me I was under arrest. I'd wanted nothing more than to go back to her and let her cuff me and call for backup. But I couldn't turn around.

Not while I had unfinished business with Sam Godfrey SC.

CHAPTER 20

In the morning, I climbed out of bed and dragged my jeans over my twenty-four-hour-old jocks. I could've rinsed them the previous night but didn't think of it. Trying to ignore the pain, I pulled my socks and shoes on, and stuffed my wallet into my jeans pocket.

Twenty minutes later I took a seat on a bus, in the second last row. I hadn't used public transport since I was at university, and the bus driver had been quite rude about the fact that I wasn't across the latest technology when it came to paying for my berth. Last I'd known, cash could get you anywhere.

I was assured the bus was headed to the city. From there I would walk to Ashwin's place.

In the hard light of a fresh autumn day, it did not seem a brilliant idea to be going back to Ashwin's. Jessy knew that was where I was going. There was every chance she'd tell Richard about what had happened last night, if she hadn't already, since he would know for sure by now that I wasn't just 'out', and he'd be wanting my guts for garters again. But I had no choice. I was in pain from my injuries, and the fact that I wasn't getting enough of the drug made for some even less pleasant symptoms, like shaking and sweating and panicking, and lying awake all fucking night. I had to just pray she'd cut me some slack.

I turned on my phone and listened to my messages. There was one, a frantic call from Rod.

I mustered some courage, then called him back.

'Drew, if it's not too much trouble,' said my brother, sounding unimpressed, 'would you mind telling me what is going on? The police have been around here looking for you. Ellen's very upset. She's ... we don't need this kind of stress at the moment, Drew.'

'I understand. I can explain.'

'Explain away.'

'I've been framed.'

'Really? How surprising.'

'Well –'

He didn't let me go on. 'Who could have imagined that badgering this lawyer despite numerous warnings could have led to such an outcome?'

'Listen, Rod –'

'You know I'm not necessarily the world's most honourable character, but when I make a promise, I mean it, Drew. You, on the other hand ... do your promises mean anything to you?'

'Yes, of course they do.'

'No, seriously. I mean, you made a promise. To me. Your own brother. Your flesh and blood.'

'Rod, I can keep my promises. I made a promise to Lil, and I'm keeping that.'

Rod sounded annoyed. 'We've been through this. She was a root.'

'She was a *human being*.' I smacked my plastered hand hard against my forehead, just about knocking myself out. '*Fuck*. This is just fucking bullshit.'

Rod said nothing for a long moment. Then he said: 'Okay, I understand.'

Then he hung up.

An old lady sitting opposite me looked at me oddly, as if she'd never in her life seen anything out of the ordinary. I found myself feeling jealous of her. I wanted to explain to her that what she just heard, what she could see, it wasn't really the real me. Really, I was a pillar of society. I was just like her. Instinctively I knew that the more I tried to explain it, the less she would believe me.

Rod called again five minutes later.

'I've got you a car,' he said. 'The cops won't trace it because it belongs to a friend of Ellen's who left it with her to look after while she's on holidays.'

'What if I trash it?'

'If you trash it, I'll just have to pay.'

I felt something inside my chest, something I hadn't even realised until now was coiled like a spring, begin marginally to unwind.

'Hey, thanks Rod. Can you get a phone charger too and leave it in the car? So we can stay in touch, you know.'

'Sure, anything else you need?'

I hesitated. *Yes.*

'No.'

'Jessy says there might be.'

'You're talking to Jessy?'

Rod snorted. 'You make it sound like they give you some choice in the matter. The cops have been all over me. That's why I had to hang up on you earlier. I just about got sprung having a natter with you when that grumpy old fat one walked in the room.'

'How are you going to get the car to me? They'll follow you.'

'I've got a plan. You'll find the car at His Majesty's. I reckon I can get it there by nine. The keys will be in the passenger side suspension. It's a bit of a hot rod, an EL GT, maroon.'

'Should sort out the police Commodores in a car chase.'

Rod didn't reply. I could tell he was worried about me. There wasn't much I could say to ease his fears. I too was worried about me.

'Yeah,' he said eventually. 'All it needs is nitrous and a nine-inch diff.'

'Listen, thanks for this, bro. I really appreciate ... I mean, I really need help right now. Team Drew is kind of a small group. Or at least it feels like it.'

'I think it's got more members than you realise,' said Rod. 'Listen, I'm going to leave some Vicodin in the car for you. But it won't be much. I'm sorry Drew, but I just don't trust you to ration your own supplies.'

'Yeah, you're not the only one.'

'You've got to promise me you'll try to cut down. Try to stretch it out.'

I laughed. It came out more like a cough. 'I'm going to have to, aren't I?' I felt grateful to be able to delay going back to Ashwin's for the time being. More grateful than I sounded.

'Yeah. And listen, I think you should get rid of this phone. They'll track you down in a heartbeat once they decide to get serious. I'll leave a prepaid in the car.'

CHAPTER 21

The GT Falcon was a mighty beast. Whoever owned it no doubt loved it a lot, but a quick glance under the bonnet revealed that there weren't too many after-market mods. Shouldn't be too hard to replace if it came to that. Well, it would cost a lot, but it wasn't like the car was unique. After finding and quaffing a fair bit of the Vicodin in the centre console, I turned on the engine, anxious to get out of the car park.

The cavernous building amplified the burble of the GT's five-litre Windsor V8 as I circled down to ground level. I pulled up there and used the ticket Rod had left for me to negotiate my exit. I passed the boom gates then idled forward to the street and stopped to wait for a gap in the traffic.

That was about when the two back doors opened simultaneously and suddenly I had a full car.

I swore.

'That's not very nice,' Rod observed. 'I expected a more appreciative response to the procurement of a particularly decent set of wheels.'

I turned around and my eyes met Jessy's, in the other seat. She was in civvies – jeans and a fluffy jumper. I had to take that as a good sign. But she was giving me the full intensity of her green-eyed glare.

'It would have been better if they didn't come with a member of the constabulary in the back seat,' I informed him, without looking away from Jessy. 'Did I forget to mention that on the phone?'

'Just drive,' said Jessy. 'We'll get out of the city then find somewhere to pull over.'

'You know I didn't do this, right Jess?' I said as I drove down Wellington Street towards the freeway.

'Of course I know that,' she said.

'What does Richard think?'

'According to the techies, the emails you sent from work that flagged all this were sent at just after half past three in the afternoon on the third of May. Your Outlook calendar showed an appointment with Sam Godfrey at two. In the visitor register at the front desk, Godfrey had noted his departure time as three o'clock, but one of the receptionists recalled him leaving well after that, at closer to four. She remembered him because he was rude. If she's right, it means you sent the emails while you were still with Godfrey. Even Richard had to admit that it was a bit unusual. Often meetings can be boring, especially meetings with lawyers, but when there's just the two of you, you don't usually get away with firing off a few private pornographic emails during the course of the discussion. He agreed it was worth asking Godfrey about it, so we pulled him in. He denies having anything to do with it, of course. He reckons he left your office at three. Pitting his credibility against the receptionist's. Though there's likely to be surveillance footage. We're getting hold of that soon. Richard isn't impressed.'

'Pretty sloppy work by Godfrey.'

'Yeah, it's incredible that he would go to all the trouble to hack your computer and send the emails, but not worry about the fact that there could be evidence putting him in a meeting with you at your office at the time the emails were sent.'

'I guess he doesn't care. Even if his presence in my office at the time ultimately amounts to reasonable doubt, he figures I'll probably still be charged and tried and maybe jailed pending the trial and, in any event, my reputation would be permanently trashed. That'd be enough to make his point.'

I stared out the window at the clogged traffic on the freeway. Beside us was a young man, a university student judging by his UWA parking permit, in a clapped-out Gemini with a coathanger for an aerial and odd coloured panels suggesting numerous small accidents over its lifetime. Just in front and to the left, a lady in a people mover with stick figures on her back window symbolising her family. Husband, wife, a boy and a girl and a baby, two dogs, four chickens. Three quarters of said family was in the back seat of the people mover, fighting.

'Yeah, well it seems he's right about that,' said Jessy. 'In my opinion, there's no reasonable prospect of conviction, but the word from upstairs is that we're to arrest and charge you. They are insisting these are matters for a jury.'

'Super.'

'It'd help with your bail app., though. That's why I wanted to talk to you, tell you what happened.'

'Drew,' Rod interjected, 'if they give you bail, it doesn't matter what the surety is, we're good for it. Dad says he'll remortgage the farm.'

I nodded, changing gear as the traffic finally began to move. I didn't trust myself to respond to that. Family Lady moved across in front of me into my lane. We sped up to eighty.

'There's still the matter of my home computer,' I said. I sensed that Jessy already knew this was going to be a problem. 'How bad is that?' My suspicion was confirmed when her eyes skipped away from mine in the rear-view mirror.

'Yeah, it's ... not good. There's pictures. A lot of them make our Mr Schneider look like a model citizen.'

I tried not to react, in case she looked in the mirror again. I didn't want her to see me losing it. I wanted her to think I was strong.

'Has someone been in my unit?' I said, hoping my voice wasn't shaking too badly.

'Well, maybe.'

My heart started to race.

'Your home doesn't have any security to speak of, Drew,' Rod observed. 'Not like your office. Any crook with half a brain could just walk in there and do what he liked while you were at work and no one would ever know he'd been there.'

'There's a swiper.'

'Where do you keep it during the day, while you're at work? Not in your decrepit heap of a car that any halfwit could unlock with a piece of bent fencing wire, I hope.'

I swallowed a large mouthful of air. 'Yeah. I was framed. I just can't wait to give that one a run before a jury. It's always gone so well for every punter who's tried it over the course of my career. And there have been a lot.' I was starting to feel sweaty, and it didn't feel like the drugs. 'There's no evidence that he framed me. Just because someone had the opportunity to frame a person doesn't mean that they did. Did he delete the email he sent me that was infected with the keylogger? Have your guys been able to find that?'

Jessy dodged the question. 'Listen, don't get upset –'

'Sorry, but I am upset,' I rasped. 'I'm upset because my getaway car has been hijacked, and you two are trying to convince me to give myself up when you both know there's a fuckload of illegal porn on my home computer that a magistrate on a bail application is going to have even less sympathy about than a jury at a trial. So, I can't see how I can be convinced. If you two have some kind of plan to *make* me do what you think is in my best interests, then I don't know ...' I glanced from Jessy to Rod in the mirror. 'I don't know what I'm going to do because I cannot go to jail with or without my fucking drugs. They'll kill me in there. You know they will.'

'Just keep driving, Drew,' Rod said quietly. 'Don't get worked up.'

'Stop saying that.' I changed lanes recklessly and for no reason, since we weren't going anywhere in particular anyway, leading to a chorus of indignant honking. The reality of the situation with my home computer had rattled me. I felt like losing it, like just freaking out and screaming and crying. I felt like there was a wild animal inside me that wanted to do just that, to scream like a monkey until all this horror went away, until I regained some semblance of control over my life.

'Okay, pull over,' Jessy ordered. 'You'll kill us all driving like a lunatic.'

'Fine by me,' I sulked, effecting a country lane change across three lanes of traffic and swinging the GT into the emergency lane on the far left of the freeway.

'There was an emergency lane right next to you,' Rod observed as we skidded to a halt and the GT stalled. I had momentarily forgotten it was not an automatic.

'Whatever.' I was not in the mood for being told how to drive.

'Leave your seatbelt on,' Jessy instructed me.

I sensed they wanted to say something to me. I braced myself. Eventually Rod came out with it.

'Drew, maybe some time in jail wouldn't be such a bad thing.'

I let my head sink to the steering wheel. *God save me.*

'You can get clean there,' my brother went on. 'And you'll be safe from Sam Godfrey. And you might not get yourself killed, which is where you'll be heading if you're planning on living on the streets and hanging out with drug dealers. I'd have thought the streets would be just as dangerous for you as jail. There's plenty of people out here who've got family you put away.'

'I don't plan to live on the streets,' I informed him. 'I have a car and I have some money.'

Rod didn't reply. When I turned around, I could see he was starting to look a bit choked up. That was a bit of a shock.

'Drew, I can't ...' His voice was breaking in a way I had never heard it do before. 'I can't have my brother living like this.'

'It's temporary,' I assured him, which was no doubt true, whether I liked it or not. I just had to pray I could find a way to prove myself innocent and Sam Godfrey guilty before time ran out on my freedom. 'If you can find that keylogger, that would help a lot,' I said. 'I would've saved the email and its attachments to the file, you know. Maybe he forgot to delete it from there too, or maybe he couldn't. There's a secondary password to get into the file management system. If it's still there you'll be able to access it from any computer, not just mine. See what you can find out, Jess, if you would. The name of the file is Schneider.'

'Drew, he'd have needed the password to the file management software in order to attach the photos,' said Jessy quietly. 'He already has that.'

Shit. Of course.

'Listen, I'm really sorry, but I need to tell you that Richard is with the senior sergeant on this. He's determined you're not going to make a fool of him. He wants to bring you in. You can't assume he won't do what it takes to find you. If you're on the run and he catches you, you won't get bail in a million years.'

'Yeah, I know.'

'Be careful, Drew.'

CHAPTER 22

I got away with staying in the motel for the remainder of the weekend, but I wasn't confident it was a great idea to keep risking it. I had ditched my smartphone, as Rod had suggested, before I left the city on Saturday. The cops probably wouldn't even need to bother checking which towers it was pinging on since in more carefree times I'd given it all sorts of permissions to track my movements and the police could probably access all of that. The prepaid Rod left for me, almost certainly without having let Jessy know he was doing so, didn't have internet access (who knew you could even buy such a thing?) so I was restricted to buying the daily paper for news on my wanted status, which was a bit of an unacceptable time lag. I knew also there was plenty the police could do without going to the media, as such. They could send my picture to every accommodation provider in the state if they wanted to. And they'd most certainly given my picture to every patrol cop in the state. Jessy had given me the heads up that Richard was going to go all out to find me. It was up to me now not to blow it.

As far as I was aware, my face wasn't in the news yet. I didn't know if Richard would actually do that to me, when he knew I was innocent. It would no doubt be a spectacular and permanent destruction of my personal reputation, even though really these accusations were already unlikely to do my career much good in the long-term. I just didn't know if Richard gave enough of a shit about me and my personal reputation to hold back for even a moment on going public. The offences they wanted to arrest me for were so vile, the community would expect nothing less than a one hundred per cent effort by the police to track me down. They could not judge me innocent.

I reasoned that if the cops did decide to up the heat, I didn't want to be caught short for money, and I didn't like the idea of them tracking my movements through my use of ATMs. I firmed up a plan to pull all my money out in cash. I did it with a two-stage approach, driving to David Jones in Claremont on Sunday to buy a new suit, shirt, shoes and tie, and a briefcase with my credit card, then checking out of the motel and heading to a branch at Booragoon to withdraw my cash first thing Monday morning. Of course, it was my money, and they had to give it to me however I was dressed, but I didn't want to draw unnecessary attention to myself with such a large withdrawal, and I knew the suit and a matching swagger would be the best way to minimise the chance of that. And it went well. There might be an anti-money laundering and counter-terrorism financing report to AUSTRAC on account of the size of the withdrawal, but not – at least in the short-term – a police one.

I drove to Baldivis and parked at a small complex featuring an independent bottle shop, a second-hand furniture store with crap spilling out onto the pavement and a permanently closed Chinese restaurant. There, I took some more of the drugs Rod had given me, and panicked.

I felt like I wasn't going to be able to do anything at all about Sam Godfrey until I'd shored up my own position. Despite being a bit of a smartarse on most dinner party topics of conversation, I knew nothing about going on the run and remaining undetected. I felt that moving around was a good idea, but I couldn't afford to get recognised by anyone, because once I was associated with this purple hot rod, the game was up. I guessed that meant not getting videoed, which meant not buying fuel. Which meant not moving around. Staying still in a car for too long might also attract unwanted police attention. I wondered if the best option for me was to get out of the city, to go back to where I'd grown up. Not literally, of course, since my parents' farm was probably staked out, but well, back to what I knew. The country. Where there was a chance there may be petrol stations without CCTV. I knew how things worked, at least around Esperance and the Great Southern. I knew where I could hide out there, where I could bunker down and have a good hard think about becoming the fucker rather than the fuckee in my dysfunctional relationship with Sam Godfrey.

The problem was, there were limited routes out of the city. The highways were always infested with cops. They often set up random breath-testing stations at the side of the road, where they would check your rego at the same time, and sometimes ask for your driver's licence. If they saw my vehicle was registered in the name of a woman, would that be enough to prompt a licence check? I had no idea how they made these kinds of decisions.

The other thing was, I needed to get Vicodin. I had no known supplier in the country. I might know my way around, but I had no knowledge of the illicit drug marketplace there. It was not something that I'd ever felt inclined to participate in when I was a fresh-faced country lad.

At least in the city, I knew people who could help me with that particular issue. I had Darren Ashwin, who may not look like the sort of guy I would usually hang out with at Ascot on a sunny Saturday afternoon, but who had recently become my best and most helpful friend.

Rod had given me enough drugs to last maybe two more days at the rate I was getting through them. I suspected Ashwin would sell me a lot more. Maybe as much as I wanted. Perhaps I could buy a huge stash of them and then go bush, rationing them out carefully to ensure I didn't need to return to the city before Sam Godfrey was behind bars for Lil's murder and had confessed to framing me.

That sounded, even to my screwed-up mind, like a plan with some obvious problems.

I thought about friends. Was there someone I could ask to let me stay at their home? Someone no one could link me to? Someone who would never betray me to the cops?

Russ was the most obvious choice. Yep, Russ would help me out, for sure. Cindy might not be thrilled about harbouring an accused paedophile in her home with two small children, but Russ would no doubt explain I wasn't actually a paedophile. Having said that, he could be put off by the prospect of his front door being kicked in at midnight and everyone getting guns pointed at their heads, leading to post-traumatic stress issues for his children over and above any mental conditions they might be destined to inherit anyway.

No one else sprung to mind.

I'd lost touch with most of my friends from uni over the past few years while I worked long hours to advance my career. I wasn't too sure how much I would trust any of them anyway. Many had glittering careers in the justice system like the one I'd recently enjoyed. Harbouring a fugitive was probably not something they would countenance. Matt was my closest friend at the DPP but he'd rat me out in a heartbeat. He'd never had the nerve for veering even incrementally from the straight and narrow.

I thought of my childhood friends. We were a tight-knit bunch and played a lot of sport together. We had each other's backs then, but that was a long time ago.

I turned my mind instead to thinking of a place where I could get away with parking and sleeping the night. In the end I decided that the side of the road in the leafy streets of a well-heeled suburb like Mosman Park or Cottesloe was my best bet, one where the owners parked on the street. I could park in front of a vacant block to avoid stressing out the owners of any particular property. If I stayed horizontal on the back seat of the car it was likely no one would notice me at all. I would move on with the sunrise and not spend two nights in the one street.

I did that, and the exact same thing the next night. I did make an effort to cut down on the painkillers, but it didn't last for long. Until I took more, my heart raced with anxiety, everything hurting, even bits that hadn't been injured in the first place: my muscles, my guts. For the most part I lay awake on the back seat of Ellen's friend's car, the cramped conditions compounding my discomfort, making zero progress on solving any of my problems.

Then the drugs ran out, and I was back at Darren Ashwin's house in North Perth on Wednesday. This time he opened the door clothed, which was a relief. He wore skinny black jeans and a black vintage Iron Maiden singlet that revealed scraggy armpit hair. His feet were bare. The calluses beneath his flaky skin suggested he went barefoot a lot.

'Thought you must've found someone else,' he said when he saw me.

I shook my head. 'Can you help me?'

He threw me a grin punctuated with only a smattering of teeth. 'Sure, Mr Deacon. You got cash?'

I waved an appropriately sized wad, then pocketed it again.

'Come in.'

I followed Ashwin into Frazer's house. The house was seventies-era with peeling wallpaper, brown laminate benchtops and an asbestos roof. The carpet had clearly been there since it was built, and the smells of cigarettes and cats vied for ascendancy. Both were bad enough to make my throat constrict.

'I was just about to have a beer,' said Ashwin. 'Want one?'

It was ten o'clock in the morning. 'Sure.'

Ashwin handed me a can of Emu Export. He opened his own and then flopped into the centre of an orange vinyl two-seater lounge that sagged badly in the middle since its guts were spewing out onto the floor beneath it. I took a seat on a matching armchair. I sensed dried sweat coating the vinyl. I tried not to think about it.

Ashwin looked at me through red-veiny eyes. I remembered seeing him at my office, talking across my shiny desk about who he was and what he had to offer me that could help with nailing Urquhart. Only time separated this hardbitten drug dealer, angry, remorseless, at times violent, from the five-year-old boy no one had protected, but I couldn't have cared less about Darren Ashwin's past. That was probably appropriate, given I was a state prosecutor, but I'd noticed at the time his lawyer hadn't seemed to care about it anymore than I did. That had suited Ashwin just fine, though, because he didn't want to talk about it either. The last thing he wanted was for the cops, or the lawyers, or the judge, or anyone else in the courtroom or the world to know his mother's boyfriends had raped him regularly as a little boy. He'd rather go to jail.

'How come you still live here? Isn't Michael Frazer dead?' I realised after I'd said it, I probably could have been a bit more sensitive. Ashwin had moved in with Frazer when he, Ashwin, was only just a teenager. He was perhaps a father figure. The only one Ashwin had ever really had. Or, alternatively, he could have made Ashwin pay for his board and lodgings with head jobs. Both possibilities were equally likely, I supposed.

Ashwin didn't look too troubled by my question. 'Yeah, he's dead. But someone's got to look after Millie.'

He glanced up towards an adjacent dining room, where a very overweight old lady sat motionless in an ancient brown velvet armchair. She'd obviously been there the whole time, but I hadn't noticed her.

'Mick's mum. It's her house.'

'Hi Millie.' I waved politely. Millie stared at me, her face crumpled by toothless gums. 'That's a lovely name. Is it short for Millicent?'

'Mildred,' she said, her voice low and gravelly. 'How about you just buy your drugs and then fuck off?' She lit up a cigarette.

'Don't worry about her,' Ashwin said. 'She doesn't approve of my line of business.'

'Got my boy killed,' sulked Millie.

Ashwin swigged the first half of his beer. 'Sort of.'

'What do you mean *sort of*?' I took a sip of beer myself and decided it was actually not too bad, despite the hour. 'I thought I heard Mick Frazer was murdered by another dealer.'

'That's what the cops reckoned. But it wasn't. He went to see this buyer he was trying to squeeze, then they found him in a skip bin.'

'Why did the police think it was a rival then?'

Ashwin shrugged. 'I guess that's what they always say when they can't work it out.'

'Didn't you tell them what happened?'

'No. Why would I?'

I shook my head in disbelief. 'Oh, I don't know … because Mick was your mate? If I had a mate and he went to threaten someone and never came back, I'd tell the cops about it.'

Ashwin seemed confused. 'I seen him but I dunno who he was. Mick only knew the guy 'cause his girlfriend bought coke off us.'

'Yeah, I figured that.'

'Anyway, the bloke the cops liked for it was no mate of ours. Mick would've been stoked to see that prick go down for murder. Shame he got off in the end. Got a fancy-talking lawyer. Some arsehole like you.'

'Yep. Listen, Darren, thanks for the beer and everything, but can we talk about Vicodin, please? Do you have some?'

'Keep your shirt on.' Ashwin finished his beer in three long gulps, then got to his feet. 'I got a shitload of it, just for you. Was worried you weren't coming back.'

A shitload of it. I felt myself start to get excited and tried to calm down.

Darren pulled out a plastic ziplock bag filled with pills. I handed over a hefty wad of cash, which Darren sat and counted laboriously for three minutes or more. Finally, the deal was done.

Yep, Andrew Deacon had just purchased illicit drugs from a bona fide drug dealer. Darren threw me a grin and wrote down his mobile phone number, which I pocketed.

'You're a good man to do business with, Mr Deacon. You come back any time.'

~

Compared to trying to seduce Dr George into parting with a precious script, or putting Rod's career into perilous jeopardy, buying drugs off Darren Ashwin was easy. Too easy. I could see myself churning through a hundred grand like this, lying in my car night after night, week after week, taking more and more of these drugs, permanently wrecking my liver and kidneys, maybe even killing myself.

I had to do something about my life.

I'd learnt over the past few days that sleeping and stewing in my car was not helping, overly. Yes, it was entirely Sam Godfrey's fault that I was hurt, it was entirely his fault that I was addicted. It was entirely his fault that I was wanted over serious criminal charges and had abandoned my job and my life to become a fugitive. And that my beautiful Beamer was a charred wreck. But identifying blame for the disintegration of my life was not a matter of particularly complex logical deduction. It was Sam Godfrey's fault, but the only one who was going to fix it was me.

The only way I was going to do that was to prove Godfrey guilty, and myself innocent, with or without the assistance of the police.

I decided to put some distance between me and my illicit drug deal. I took the Polly Pipe east in the direction of the scarp, towards Midland. It was one of Perth's outer suburban zones, and a suburb where the GT would fit right in. As I popped out of the tunnel and into daylight, then guided the powerful machine onto Great Eastern Highway at not a hair's breadth above the speed limit, the pills I'd popped in the car out the front of Ashwin's place started to work their way into my bloodstream and my pain eased. Since I wasn't going anywhere, there would be no point in pursuing my usual course of weaving in and out of lanes to avoid Transperth buses and cars turning right. Instead I just pottered along in the left lane and while waiting for people to climb on their bus I slipped the car into neutral and thought about what I knew as a result of the investigative crumbs the police had thrown my way.

I knew Godfrey had hired a hit man to kill Lil. I strongly suspected it was because she said something to him after she found out what he was doing to Angie. She must have confronted him, threatened to tell someone or even report him to the cops. And he murdered her for it. If we knew who the hit man was, there was a decent chance we could find out how Godfrey paid him. Likewise, if we knew how Godfrey paid him, there was a decent chance we could find out who he was. At the moment, of course, we knew neither, and the cops weren't interested in finding out either, because they were convinced that Godfrey could not have been the killer because he didn't withdraw money out of a bank account in the last two days of Lil's life. In my opinion there were still a few ways Godfrey could have been behind the hit, even though he had no beef with Lil until two days before her death. One, Richard and I had discussed, being the possibility that he'd been hiding money in anticipation of divorce, and he used that to pay the killer.

A second possibility, as I tried to gather my thoughts for the first time in days, was shaping up to be even more horrifying, as it suggested a much greater level of premeditation for murder.

A couple of young guys looked at me in disbelief as they pulled out to overtake both me and the bus I'd been following. I guessed they were expecting to see someone's grandad behind the wheel of the GT.

I hoped they weren't friends of Ellen's friend. Other than that, I didn't care what they thought.

The bus lumbered back into motion and I reviewed the facts as I knew them.

After investigating the Constantine family's finances, Godfrey learns Angie has been stealing from her parents. Not being one to let an opportunity pass by, he contacts her privately and tells her he knows what she's been doing. He explains to her in no uncertain terms that he will show her parents all the evidence he holds unless she agrees to satisfy some of his more depraved desires. He gives her the prepaid so he can contact her at his convenience. He tells her not to tell anyone about their arrangement or he'll tell her family what she did to them. He thinks he's got everything covered. But it's not going exactly to plan. He thought she'd get used to their arrangement, but he can see Angie is getting more distressed each time they meet. She's started begging him to stop what he's doing to her, in a way that smacks worryingly of total desperation. He realises that even if he does stop, even if he promises to keep her secret forever, she could still tell someone all about his abuse of her, or she could take her own life and leave an ugly detailed note. He realises the risk of her telling someone about this is one risk he can't afford to take. Angie is so obviously distraught he knows she'll be believed. He'd be guaranteed of losing his marriage, which will be costly, and if the police start sniffing around over questions of consent, his career will be at risk too, and he could very well go to jail. He decides he needs to get her bumped. He had been planning the hit for some time. But he'd been planning it against Angie. He had the hit all planned and paid for and his alibi squared away, but just before it was due to take place, Lil contacted him and threatened him, and she became the bigger immediate problem and he decided to transfer the hit to her.

The biggest problem with this idea was that Godfrey would not be keen to murder Lil and leave Angie alive. Angie knew everything. She might even have sat with Lil and listened to her sister telling him in no uncertain terms what she was going to do to his life. There'd be no doubt Angie would finger him as the killer. She might keep their secrets for a short time, but eventually she'd confide in someone. To one of the many police officers who'd be interviewing her regularly over Lil's death, tempting her to spill her guts with their soft, understanding voices and gentle hand pats. People he couldn't keep her away from without drawing attention to himself. She couldn't hold out for long. She was already a basket-case and he knew it.

That's to say nothing of whether Godfrey would be dumb enough to give a hit man the key to the apartment that Angie had given him, if he intended to kill Lil. In the absence of forced entry, Angie would know instantly who the killer was. The man she'd given a key to. Or someone he hired.

Neither problem was a big enough deal to put me off the idea that Godfrey had been secreting cash for quite a while, whether for the purpose of divorce or paying for a hit on Angie, and that the cash had been used by him, ultimately, to get a hit on Lil. Maybe he felt he had no choice but to pit his credibility against Angie's. Lil had to die, after all, and whilst Angie's knowledge would be a problem, it was evidence as to a possible motive only. A motive with no other evidence of guilt could not amount to a conviction. And there would be no other evidence.

That was certainly how it was looking so far. The killer had left no DNA, murder weapon or other forensic evidence, so finding the hit man and working out from there how he was paid would be impossible. The only option was first to work out how he was paid and, from there, work out who he was. And then, once we knew who he was, get him to roll on Mr Sam Godfrey SC.

If Godfrey was accumulating cash, how did he get it in the first place, and where was he keeping it? How did barristers get paid? Barristers, as Richard had reminded me, never dealt with a punter direct. Their dealings were with solicitors, who the punter engaged. The solicitor was liable for the barrister's bill, so solicitors did not engage barristers unless they had one hundred per cent of the anticipated fee in their trust account. Expenditure from trust accounts was very strictly regulated for solicitors, who were at risk of losing their practice certificates over even a minor irregularity. If a client was to pay a barrister's fees by funds which were not intended to be deposited into the solicitor's trust account, the solicitor was still required to record it in their trust records as having passed through their office. If a client paid a solicitor cash for a barrister's bill, the cash would just go straight into the trust account, and a trust cheque would then go to the barrister.

It just wasn't a cash business. I didn't know how he would see a cent of cash in his line of work. And as Richard had pointed out, he would've needed a fair bit of it to get the level of reliability he needed in a hit man.

I slowed down for some roadworks and, as a sign held by a woman in hi-vis at the side of the road was rotated to 'stop', I brought the GT to a halt and slipped it out of gear.

So how would a hit man want to be paid? Cash would be the big one. But maybe a hit man would accept something other than cash, something with near-cash value. Bitcoin or some other digital currency? Maybe, but I'd no idea about who bought what with Bitcoin. I'd have to ask the cops about that. Drugs, yes, if of known purity. Weapons. Jewellery or gems, or gold, maybe, but I wasn't so sure a gun for hire would want to take a risk on something he didn't know much about. Perhaps Godfrey could've taken jewellery to a pawn shop and got cash for it to give to the hit man? But he'd only get a fraction of its value, and then there would be an evidence trail. Amanda could say what was missing from their home. The police could visit all the pawn shops in town and find it, getting a description of Godfrey or even security-camera footage in the process. Anything he sold to anyone would mean there'd be evidence against him out there, somewhere. No, I felt he would've avoided this risk. He gave the hit man something he had, something the hit man wanted. Cash, drugs, weapons, an asset of known value possibly. Cash seemed unlikely since I didn't know where he could have got it, as did the idea that he'd have drugs or weapons sitting around at home. What else would a hit man want? What would I ask for in payment for my services, if I was to kill someone for a client? Technically, the exchange had to be one of only three possibilities. Cash or some other currency for services, goods for services, or services for services.

Services for services.

Then I remembered in a flash how pissed off Godfrey had seemed at the conclusion of Schneider's directions hearing, when I suggested he would accept kiddie porn in exchange for legal representation.

I had it.

The name of Lil's killer, I knew, was just one quick internet search away.

CHAPTER 23

After an interminable period, the woman at the side of the road rotated her sign back around to 'slow', and I accelerated away from the roadworks. Due to the lack of internet access on my phone, I would need to visit a public library and to even find that I needed a street directory, which of course necessitated a trip to a service station. Everything was hard these days. I didn't know how people got anywhere or did anything before smartphones. I wasn't super keen about going to either the servo or the library, due to the possibility of surveillance cameras, but I didn't have too many options.

Half an hour later I arrived at the Midland Public Library. Within twenty minutes I'd secured membership of the library by promising to follow the rules and sought and gained permission to use a public computer. Because I hadn't utilised the automated PC reservation system (surely if I had the ability to use the internet to reserve the computer, I wouldn't need the computer?), I had to wait for someone to finish. Users were entitled to a maximum period of two hours.

One hour and forty-seven minutes later, a rake-thin, six-foot tall teenaged boy with long brown hair and pants with the crotch hanging down near his knees shuffled out, and I was cleared to begin my search.

I was looking for newspaper articles. Specifically, I was searching for news reports on anyone in the past year – since Sam began blackmailing Angie – that Sam Godfrey had represented on a murder charge and got an acquittal for. It had to be a murder charge, because Sam had to be confident that the guy had what it took to do the job. For the same reason, the accused had to be probably guilty, though he had to have been acquitted or otherwise he'd be in jail.

Within ten minutes I had my results.

The search for accused murderers represented by Sam Godfrey had yielded three people. All three were acquitted. One was a man accused of murdering his wife, and the second was a woman accused of murdering her newborn baby. Neither of them was the person I was looking for. What Godfrey would be needing was a cold-blooded killer. Someone who would knife a stranger to death without a shred of remorse. You'd think the guy who was charged after punching his wife in the stomach, lacerating her liver and failing to call an ambulance would be a possibility, but over the years I'd learnt blokes who do that kind of thing are generally appalled by the suggestion they might be the violent type.

There was only one other person represented by Godfrey in the past year on a murder charge.

And with this guy I hit the jackpot. The article was dated March 21.

Leon Charles Robilliard was yesterday cleared of a charge of wilful murder over the death of convicted drug trafficker Michael Allan Frazer, who was shot three times in the head in August last year. Over the course of a three-week trial the 35-year-old fitness centre owner was accused of the wilful murder of Mr Frazer.

'The evidence against my client was so scant as to be embarrassing for the State,' Robilliard's barrister Samuel Godfrey SC said on the doorsteps of the courthouse after a three-hour deliberation by the twelve-person jury returned a 'not guilty' verdict. 'They had no evidence whatsoever other than that a gun found in Mr Robilliard's home was the gun used to shoot Mr Frazer. That is true, but the fingerprints on the gun were not Mr Robilliard's and not a single solitary person was able to identify Mr Robilliard as the killer. There is no doubt he was framed. That gun, which my client had never seen before – never even touched – was placed in his home for the police to find, which they did after a convenient anonymous tip-off.'

The State had alleged that Robilliard had executed Mr Frazer at very close range in an unknown location, then dumped his body in a skip bin.

'There's no question that whoever it was who killed Mr Frazer was a savage, ruthless assassin,' Mr Godfrey said. 'However, as has been proven today, my client was not involved in that killing.'

It annoyed me whenever crooks announced they had been 'proven innocent'. The State being unable to prove guilt beyond a reasonable doubt – a very high standard of proof – was not the same thing as being proven innocent. It was a distinction of which I was quite confident Mr Godfrey was well aware. He liked to play the media game, though; that much was apparent. He was confident he was clever enough to handle them.

I printed the article, paid twenty cents to retrieve it and folded the page. I spent another ten minutes carrying out a couple more searches, including one of my own name (which mercifully turned up nothing too fresh) and hotfooted it out of the library. The lady behind the counter looked up at me as I went past her, but I didn't make eye contact a second time.

I walked down the street to where I'd parked the GT out of sight of the library's car park security surveillance. I pulled my phone out of the centre console and dialled Jessy's mobile. She didn't answer, so I called her work number.

It took ages to be put through to her. I didn't want to spend too long on the phone, and it didn't have a lot of battery life left in it either. I knew spots to use my charger were scarce, yet somehow I'd still overlooked plugging it in for the three hours I was at the library.

The whole phone thing was unacceptably stressful.

Finally, Jessy picked up the transferred call.

'This is Detective Parkin.'

'Jess, listen, I know the name of Lil's killer.'

'Drew, is that you?' She sounded shocked to hear from me.

'Of course it's me.' I imagined her right at that moment snapping her fingers at the hordes of uniforms loitering in her office. *Turn on the tapes, trace this call!* Maybe I'd watched too many movies, but still, it wasn't a nice feeling to visualise it. 'Listen, I know how he paid for someone to carry out a hit without any money changing hands.'

'How?'

'He represented this guy on a wilful murder charge. For free.'

'If Lil said anything to him at all, it would only have been two days before the hit, remember?'

'I reckon he might've been planning the hit for Angie but transferred it to Lil at the last minute.'

When she didn't reply right away, I knew I'd got her interest. 'What's the name?'

'Leon Charles Robilliard.'

'How do you know it's him?'

'I searched the *West*'s online archive. All you have to do is subscribe and pay a fee of eight bucks and you can get full access back to 2004.'

'I'm familiar with how the newspaper's online archive works, thanks Andrew. So, what did you search for?'

'I searched for people Sam Godfrey had represented in the past year who would be capable of doing that to Lil and were likely not in prison when she was murdered. There were three people he'd got off a murder rap in that time. Robilliard was one of them, acquitted a week before Lil's death of shooting a drug dealer in the head at point blank range last August. Our mate Ashwin's buddy Michael Frazer, in fact. Remember he was murdered soon after Urquhart's trial?'

'Yeah. What about the other two?'

'Not hit-man material. Domestic violence and infanticide. Robilliard sounds to me like a perfect fit.'

'So, you think Godfrey proposed a deal. *I'll get you off this charge, and all you have to do is another hit, this time for me.* The payment was extinguishment of a debt.'

'Exactly. The thing is, I'm pretty sure I remember Ashwin saying he reckoned Robilliard might've been innocent of the Frazer murder, which I would take with a grain of salt, but could you search your database to be on the safe side?'

I listened to the tapping of keys on her keyboard.

'He's got a lot of drug stuff...' she said slowly. 'Possession, sell or supply... a lot of sell or supply... but yes, he has got a record of violence. He's done time for assaults, grievous bodily harm, an unlawful wounding... hello, there's even a manslaughter charge here he only got two years for.'

'Perfect.' Of course, the jury wouldn't have known about any of that, enabling Godfrey to get an acquittal on the big one. But Godfrey knew all about it, and knew that whether or not Robilliard killed Frazer, he had the man for the job.

'So, you think he was planning to kill Angie, and that's why he was organising everything with Robilliard. Right when he was ready to go, Angie told Lil what was going on. Lil made Angie call Godfrey and tell him his abuse of her was to end. Lil promised she wouldn't contact Godfrey herself, but she did. She went straight home and called Godfrey and threatened to reveal all to Amanda or the police or both, and Godfrey decided to transfer the hit to Lil.'

'Yes. That is what I think.'

'Why would he leave Angie alive when Angie would be able to tell the police she'd given him a key to the apartment?'

'I don't know. That's one thing I can't work out.'

I could hear the cogs turning over in her mind.

'You need to get a warrant for Godfrey's business records,' I pressed. 'If I'm right, there'll be nothing in his bank statements showing any payment from Leon Robilliard or his solicitors. His financial records will show either a big debt in Robilliard's solicitor's name which has not been paid at all, and which he plans to write off when the heat dies down, or alternatively absolutely no mention of Leon Robilliard at all, as if he never existed. But the paper confirms he did exist, and the court transcript will back it up.'

'Drew –'

'Godfrey is going to have a lot of explaining to do to justify spending three weeks in court with no pay. I had a look at the Law Society's eligibility requirements for pro bono assistance while I was in the library. In criminal matters, they only offer assistance for vulnerable applicants, even if they're convinced the applicant is innocent. You know, people who have some disability or they're homeless or something – possibly not a bloke who is successfully running his own fitness centre. That's assuming Godfrey is even on their pro bono database. That'd be interesting to find out.'

'Drew, just ... listen for a minute, will you?'

This did not sound good. 'Sure. Sorry.'

'I know what you're saying. I do. But I don't know how I'm going to get a warrant for Godfrey's financial records on the strength of this. To even have a chance of getting a warrant for the records of a criminal barrister, in the face of legal professional privilege and all that, we'd need evidence implicating Robilliard in Lil's murder. And I don't think I could, on the strength of this article, get a warrant even to search Robilliard's house for forensic evidence.'

She let this sink in, obviously confident that if I gave it some thought I too would have no choice but to accept the facts. But I wasn't in the mood for thinking rationally.

'Drew, we've no evidence linking either Godfrey or Robilliard to this crime. We've no grounds even to *suspect* either of them may have been involved. What you've found, at best, connects Godfrey and Robilliard with *each other*. But we can't get any warrants without something linking either of them back to Lil's death. Do you understand? That article establishes that *if* Godfrey had wanted to kill someone, he might have had a way to do it. That's all. Your article is not evidence. It's just a theory as to how he could have done it.'

'A hypothesis,' I said almost noiselessly.

'Whatever. It's just an idea. And it's not an idea I can do anything with.'

I leaned my head back onto the GT's black leather headrest and stared at the roof of the car. It was only inches away. Like the walls of a prison cell. What I'd hoped was that the hit man, now we knew who he was, would provide the police with another whole avenue of investigation. If they couldn't find anything on Godfrey, they could pursue Robilliard instead and work back to Godfrey from there. But everything Jessy was saying sounded depressingly correct. Without a witness statement or any forensic evidence against him, all the cops could really do to Robilliard would be to give him a ring and ask if he wouldn't mind voluntarily popping down to the cop shop and rolling on Godfrey.

Getting a witness statement required a witness, of which there just weren't any. Getting forensic evidence required a warrant. Reg Thompson, I knew, would be less than impressed to see *Andrew Deacon's intuition* as the whole and sole grounds for the application. He was filthy with me after the Schneider directions hearing, concluding that it was my fault his integrity had been called into question, and I knew he was going to be doubly gun-shy from now on. And all the other JPs around town knew that we usually asked Reg to sign the warrants. If we were trying to dupe one of them into it to avoid the scrutiny Reg inevitably applied, they'd know.

'Yes, I understand.'

'Drew, I'm sorry –'

'Jess, was it you who interviewed Godfrey?'

'Yes.'

'Do you believe he did this? I mean, when you interviewed him, did you smell a killer?'

She hesitated, and I expected she was preparing to blow me off.

'Jessy –'

'Andrew, yes. Okay? I looked into his eyes, just as you did, and I felt the same way you did. I felt that he was capable of doing this. But our gut feelings count for nothing. Our opinions count for nothing. You know what counts is evidence. Of which we have none.'

'Where does Robilliard live?'

'I'm not going to tell you that. Don't ask me to do illegal shit.'

'I'm trying to get us evidence, Jessy. That's what you want, isn't it?'

'If you're going to confront Leon Robilliard, you better be careful, Drew. His record makes it clear he'd just as easy slit your throat and bury you in the backyard as make himself a coffee in the morning.

And if he does make a habit of doing Godfrey's dirty work, he could have been one of the men who bashed you. He might –'

My phone ran out of battery. I cursed and threw it on the passenger side floor. It didn't matter. I knew what she was going to say.

He might know exactly who you are.

CHAPTER 24

I could appreciate that when it came to getting forensic evidence pointing to Leon Robilliard's involvement in Lil's murder, the cops' hands were tied.

I, on the other hand, had a little more room to move.

But not much more. Yes, I could stake out Leon Robilliard's place of work, which was helpfully practically identified by the newspaper article. I could follow him home, wait until he was next at work, break in, seize the bloodstained clothing still sitting in the laundry basket and the murder weapon resting snugly in the kitchen drawer, then take them round to the cops and tell them to run their tests.

However, there was one major problem with all that. The courts had a very unfortunate tendency to refuse to allow a jury to consider what they termed *improperly or illegally obtained evidence*. The cops might argue it wasn't their fault. After all, they never asked me to break into the suspect's house. But there was still a real risk the courts would consider it appropriate to exclude the evidence, even if it meant letting a killer walk free, in order to send a clear message that the police must without exception ensure that every aspect of a criminal investigation is one hundred per cent above board.

Which did not leave me with a lot of options. In fact, after half an hour of what Matthew liked to refer to as 'deep thinking', I had come up with only one.

There was no forensic evidence putting Robilliard at the scene. That is, he didn't leave his DNA at Lil's place. In order to get a warrant to search Robilliard's home to look for further forensic evidence – that is, to see if Lil's DNA had wound up at *his* place – what the police needed was a witness statement.

What would be ideal would be a statement from someone to say they witnessed a man they could identify as Leon Charles Robilliard perpetrating a violent crime, from which police could deduce to Reg's satisfaction that there may be evidence of such activity splattered across Robilliard's clothes and other possessions.

That crime need not be Lil's murder. Any such crime, against any victim, would enable the police to get that warrant. If they happened to find Lil's DNA as well as that of the other victim, well, that would be just tops. They'd solve two crimes in one day.

Trickily, though, in order to give their statement to police that would then lead to a warrant to search Robilliard's home, the victim needed to actually survive the assault.

~

I lay awake stretched, to a certain extent, across the back seat of the car parked in a cul-de-sac in the quiet beachside suburb of Ocean Reef. It'd been after ten o'clock when I'd parked, and the good people of Ocean Reef were asleep. I would wake before sunrise, no later than half past five, which was unavoidable when sleeping in a car, and be gone by the time any of them had cause to peer into my windows in the morning.

I knew it wouldn't be too hard to convince Leon Robilliard to beat me up. After all, brutality was his way of life. The trick would be ensuring he didn't kill me. This would be a delicate balancing act, requiring some thought and careful preparation.

I thought about whether I really wanted to do this. My parents would be pretty distressed if I was to get hurt any worse than I already had been, but I just couldn't see that I had any choice. I'd be caught eventually if I kept loitering around the city. Ellen's friend would soon return from her holiday and demand to know where her car was. She would likely report me to the police even if she promised

Ellen that she wouldn't. I knew that was what I'd do in her situation.

That was all the time I had. Until Ellen's friend returned from her holiday, whenever that was.

So my only option was to push on. Go after Robilliard. Go after Godfrey.

I woke at first light, and as soon as I was conscious, I moved into the driver's seat. I elected to drive south along the coast, just for the hell of it. The sun was rising over the land, at my left shoulder, so the water was cool and blue.

I stopped at a convenience store and gave the kid behind the counter fifty bucks to let me charge my phone and use the internet.

The imaginatively named Robifit Fitness Centre, run by Leon Robilliard, was situated at Mirrabooka, a working-class suburb twelve kays north of Perth. I quickly secured a street address and took a good look at a low-quality photograph advertising the joint that purported to include the impressively unappetising face of its proprietor. Before closing my tab, I did a quick Landgate search but it seemed Robilliard didn't own his own house. He wasn't listed in the White Pages either.

~

I parked on the street a block away from Robifit Fitness Centre. I didn't want to drive past as I was pretty sure Robilliard, like most serious drug dealers, would have the exterior of his premises under surveillance. Richard would be able to seize and study the footage of before and after whatever went down here this morning.

I shoved my hands in my pockets and walked up the street towards where the Yellow Pages online had told me the place would be. I could feel my heart, already under enough pressure as it was from my lifestyle, beating hard in my chest. I knew there was a chance that evidence linking Robilliard to Lil's murder would be on these premises, but it was more likely, I thought, that it was to be found at his home. If I got myself assaulted here it would almost certainly be a bit of a waste. But introducing myself to Robilliard here would hopefully minimise the chance of getting killed, as opposed to merely assaulted, at his house later. People could be a bit touchy about strangers showing up at their home.

The exposure of Robilliard's business to the street comprised one reinforced steel door with a sign above it reading 'To Robifit Fitness Centre – open 24 hrs' and an arrow pointing down. For a trendy tapas bar aiming for underground cred it would not have been a bad shopfront. In the case of Robilliard's so-called fitness centre slash illegal drug trade headquarters, it was just seedy.

I swallowed a shot of bile as I descended along a narrow flight of stairs lit only by ambient light from the street. At the base I walked through a kind of open broom closet with stacks of toilet paper rolls on a shelf and a couple of sets of car keys hanging from a hook on the wall. One was for a vintage Holden Torana, the other for an old Jaguar. They obviously appreciated their classic wheels at the Robifit Fitness Centre.

There was no reception desk as such. The stairs led straight into an artificially lit dojo with cushioned mats on the floors, punching bags suspended from the low ceiling and two broad-shouldered brutes sparring in the far corner. When I entered the room, they lowered their fists and backed away from each other before one, the taller of the two, walked towards me.

I recognised Leon Robilliard from the photo. He was a big man. He'd have towered over Lil by at least a foot. He was built like a phone booth but not in a hardworking, sunburnt, ploughman's lunch kind of way. More in a steroid-fuelled gym junkie kind of way. He had pasty white skin and his veins stood out on his arms like rivers. His face, which I knew to be that of a thirty-five-year-old man, was scarred from acne many years earlier, weathered from steroid abuse and oversized. It was far too big ever to have been attractive, even without the scarring. He stared at me with an expression that made goosebumps stand up on my only available forearm, folding his own muscular arms across his broad chest.

'What're you doing here?'

I pretended he hadn't just indicated he knew me. 'Hi,' I said. 'I am looking for a Mr Robilliard? Leon Robilliard? I was told he works here.'

Robilliard narrowed his wolverine eyes. While I hadn't got a good look at the facial features of the man standing in front of the XD the day I'd abandoned it in the car park, Robilliard's build was certainly a match for that bloke too. I remembered the Jag parked next to my car that day. It was a white one.

He said: 'I'm the owner.'

'Oh, okay. Do you know him then?'

He stared at me for a long time, like no matter how hard he concentrated, he couldn't formulate a functional thought. Finally, he drew the conclusion I was going for. That I didn't know who he was.

'What do you want with Leon Robilliard?' he asked.

'He was recommended to me. I'm actually – I'm in the market for Vicodin. I was told Mr Robilliard might be able to help me. I got beaten up a few weeks ago, you see, and I'm still in a lot of pain, but the doctors won't give me any more drugs.'

Robilliard was still while he digested this. My heart seemed about to beat out of my chest as I faced the man who I was almost certain had been one of my assailants, and I felt suddenly like throwing up. I thought about Lil, waking to the sight of this monster in her bedroom. She would've begged him not to hurt her, but nothing she could have said would've made the slightest difference to him. Business was business, after all. I wondered at what point she knew she would die. The police had said there was nothing to suggest he'd struck her head, knocked her out. He'd just held her down with one hand and begun to stab with the other, and kept going until she was dead. So, she'd have known. She'd have looked up at this emotionless face I now observed, and she'd have known that was it for her.

Not surprisingly, it seemed he found my story plausible. 'Who sent you?'

I decided it would not be kind to mention the name of anyone living. 'Well, the man who recommended Mr Robilliard is dead now.

Mick Frazer was his name.'

'Mick Frazer would not have sent anyone to see me.'

'Oh, okay, so you're Mr Robilliard.' I tried to smile. 'I guess it wasn't so much a referral as an attempt to rat on you. I used to work for the DPP, you see. I was talking to Mick at one point and now that I need some drugs ... well, I remembered Mick had mentioned you.'

Robilliard's top lip curled up as if he had smelt something bad. I knew that whatever drugs he was on personally could well make him paranoid, and his paranoia was clearly just about to kick in with gusto.

'If now is not a good time ...'

'Are you a cop? I thought you –'

'I'm a prosecutor,' I interrupted before Robilliard had time to moronically admit to knowing who I was. I didn't particularly want to give him the opportunity to admit to assaulting me, then decide he needed to kill me to shut me up. 'Not a cop.' The difference, though seeming vast to us, would probably be lost on Robilliard. 'Or at least, I used to be. I lost my job recently.'

He glanced towards the other man, who hovered nearby, then back at me. 'Fuck off.'

'Sure. I just wanted the drugs, man. But if you can't help me –'

'I can't help you. Fuck. Off.'

I nodded. 'Sure. Sorry to waste your time.'

I backed away from him for a few paces before turning and scooting up the stairs. I burst out into the sunlight and drew a relieved breath of fresh air.

I noted a white XJ6 Jaguar parked on the street, right in front of the gym, and committed its rego to memory before hoofing it back down the pavement to the relative safety of the GT.

~

Robilliard didn't leave the Robifit Fitness Centre until after midnight. He was probably on some drugs that obviated the need for sleep, but I'd been awake since before dawn and I was exhausted. I set the air-conditioning in the GT to freezing to try to keep myself alert, then followed the white Jag through the streets, taking care to stay at least four cars behind at all times. If he appreciated cars at all, it was possible he would spot the GT in his rear-vision mirror. Though functional, she wasn't exactly stealthy. The Jag, on the other hand, was not easy to keep my eye on, due to its nondescript colour. Only its distinctive silhouette, low-slung and long like a cigar, enabled me to spot it out of the corner of my eye each time I thought I'd lost it.

Finally, he turned into a tree-lined driveway in the guts of East Fremantle. The car disappeared from view as it continued to the rear unit of a battle-axe block. I brought the GT to a stop a hundred or so metres before the driveway.

It was half past one on Friday morning.

I thought about what my parents would think about what I was about to do. It felt worse than reckless. It felt idiotic, like I was throwing back in their face all the effort they'd gone to over the years to keep me alive. I knew I could drive away now but if I did I would have nowhere to go except down to the nearest police station where I would turn myself in. I would then go directly to jail and I would stay there for months until I could give *I was framed, you don't understand* a run in the District Court. My family would have me back, but as an accused and ultimately maybe even convicted felon. I could easily spend the next seven years in jail. Meanwhile, Lil's murder would remain unsolved and Sam Godfrey and Leon Robilliard would never pay for what they did to her and to her family. There was nothing attractive about that option at all. I'd be better off being beaten up by Leon Robilliard.

I started the car again and idled up to just before the end of Robilliard's driveway.

Robilliard had already taken off his shoes and shirt and lit a joint by the time I knocked on his front door. He looked anything but pleased to see me as he blew marijuana fumes in my face.

'What the fuck're you doing here?'

'Listen, I'm really sorry, Mr Robilliard. But I really need the drugs. I don't think I got to explain to you earlier just how –'

'How do you know where I live?'

'Mick Frazer told me. You see, I'm in a lot of pain –'

'Mick Frazer was dead before I moved here,' Robilliard hissed, taking a step towards me. His eyes flitted momentarily towards the next-door neighbour's windows overlooking his front porch. He didn't want to mess me up while there was a possibility of anything being witnessed. Wise, I thought.

'Okay, look, I admit I followed you here. I just really wanted to ask you again about the Vicodin. I'm willing to pay. I've got money.'

Robilliard was half a head taller than I was, and probably, right about now, about twice my weight.

'Listen, I know who you are,' he hissed. 'I don't know why you're hanging around me but you're an annoying prick and I'm going to knock your head off if you don't get the fuck out of here and stay away from me.'

Well, that seemed encouraging, though a little more extreme, physically, than I was hoping would be the outcome of today's efforts. A woman appeared at the doorway, behind Robilliard. She was very young, maybe only in her late teens or early twenties, with a fake tan and enormous fake boobs. I wondered what sort of a surgeon would operate on her at that age. She peered around Robilliard's enormous frame to see who he was talking to.

'Don't suppose I could use your toilet before I go?' I asked.

Robilliard stared at me for a long moment before, ominously, deciding to agree. He stepped aside and so did the woman. I walked into his house. Now we were out of sight of anyone who happened to be looking through their bedroom window. I actually wouldn't have minded using the toilet, but I doubted I would make it that far. And I was right. As I stepped onto the carpet of Robilliard's pleasantly furnished living room, he laid a strong hand on my shoulder and spun me effortlessly to face him.

'Oh, Leon, let me put down some sheets,' the woman said quickly.

'It took me forever to get the stains out of the carpet last time. Just ...' she looked around herself. 'Just hang on a second. I'll just be a second.'

Robilliard and I stared at each other while he waited patiently for his girlfriend to return. Thirty seconds later she was back, clutching a pile of linen. Robilliard reached out and grabbed me around the neck, pushing me hard and cracking the back of my head against the wall. As I struggled to breathe, I was aware of his girlfriend on her hands and knees near my feet, shuffling as she pushed sheets around my legs. I could've kicked her in the head, but that didn't seem like a sensible course of action if I wanted to live.

Robilliard leaned in close to my face. 'Listen carefully, Andrew Deacon,' he said, his thick fingers crushing my neck. 'I don't know what the fuck you're doing here, but you and I have no business with each other. Do you understand me?'

I nodded. 'Sure,' I rasped.

He let go of my neck and gave me a short, sharp thwack to the head with his open hand, breaking my nose again. Blood started pissing out of my face and down my shirtfront.

'Listen, I don't want to have to mess you up, man.'

Again, I nodded, while Robilliard's girlfriend moved sheets at my feet to try to catch the rivers of blood that were now making it all the way to the floor. I was pretty sure I got a few drops into the carpet, despite her efforts.

'Stay out of my way,' snarled Robilliard.

'Yes, I will. I'm sorry.'

~

'Jessy isn't available,' Richard informed me coldly over the phone later that morning. 'Are you turning yourself in?'

'No, I'm not. I want to make a complaint about an assault. A man by the name of Leon Robilliard. I was at his house earlier and he hit me in the face. A woman who was there mopped up most of my blood, but some of it will be on the floor, and the sheets she used might still be there. You need to get a warrant and search the place for evidence that he assaulted me.'

Richard seemed unimpressed. 'Sure thing, Andrew. Just come down to the station and I'll take your statement.'

'Over the phone.'

'Not possible I'm afraid. We have protocols. You need to be identified. You need to personally sign your statement.'

My nose hadn't really stopped bleeding since Robilliard had smacked me in the face. When I lay down on the back seat of my car, it kind of slowed, but soon I'd start to feel like I couldn't breathe, and I'd sit up and a big clotty lump would come out of me, followed by a flood of fresh blood. I wasn't exactly sure how fast my body could make fresh blood, but I assumed it was keeping up, on account of me still being alive. I hung up on Richard. From experience I knew there was nothing to be gained by arguing with him.

You need to personally sign your statement.

Yes, of course I did.

I took three Vicodin and went to sleep with my head against the steering wheel of my car so the blood could drain into a used hot-chip box on the floor. The sun was high in the sky.

~

I slept for a while. If you could call it sleeping. I woke every ten minutes or so to panic, then slept again once I'd rationalised there was nothing immediate to panic about. That went on for about two hours. Then I decided to give up on sleep and drove the car to the smallest independent petrol station I could find at the outskirts of the city, to buy fuel with cash.

As I waited in the queue, a dirty t-shirt pressed to my still-bleeding nose, I thought about all the big promises I'd made to myself and to others.

I've been set up, Malcolm. Someone's hacked into my email account and sent those bloody things. I don't know how but I'm going to find out.

But I didn't find out. I did nothing that might have begun to help me to find out.

I had to do it properly if I was going to do it at all. That's what I said to myself about going on the run in the first place. I'd thought about going to the country. I'd thought about going overseas. Yet here I still was, driving aimlessly around the goddam city of Perth, a level of pathetic beyond what I'd ever considered myself capable of. I'd gone on the run, but I hadn't even *attempted* to do it properly.

I will protect you, I'd told Angie.

To Rod, I'd promised I would stay out of Sam Godfrey's life. After I breached that promise, I told him I'd make an effort to cut down my Vicodin use.

And that was nothing compared to the promises I'd made to Lil and broken.

With a full tank of fuel, I drove around until I found a good spot to park. It was a wrecker's yard which had a sign on the front door saying it was *closed due to family emergency until Friday*. I didn't know if they meant today or next Friday, but the doors were locked, and the sign looked pretty fresh. There were cars parked in the yard, in the driveway and spilling out onto the verge. It was a shame I didn't have the XD any longer. I could have lived in it for weeks parked on the verge in front of this place, and no one would have noticed or cared, not even the owners probably. But I hoped I would be alright here for the next two days anyway. Parked here, people would be more likely to want to break into this car than report it to the police, but once they saw me in the back, they hopefully wouldn't bother trying to steal it.

CHAPTER 25

The prepaid rang and I pressed it to my ear. It was Monday morning and I was back at the fuel station where I'd last filled up, figuring it was as good a place as any to get some food. I hadn't eaten since Saturday and although I didn't feel hungry now, I was conscious of the fact I should eat something or I might die.

The place was like a throwback to the eighties. Even the ice-creams were old-fashioned. No flash Magnums here, oh no, it was a Giant Sandwich, Golden Gaytime or nothing, thanks very much. The proprietor had gone to fill another traveller's car with fuel, which was consistent with the numerous signs outside warning people not to dream of attempting to do it themselves. I was alone in the shop.

'We've decided you're coming in,' said Richard.

I laughed. 'Ah, negative.' I grabbed a couple of bags of salt-and-vinegar flavoured potato chips off a rack at the front counter and fished around in my pockets for some cash.

'You need to lodge your complaint over the assault by Mr Robilliard.'

'I've decided not to proceed with that.'

'And we need you for the Schneider trial.'

'Are you mad?' I thought perhaps he was. Either he was losing it, or I was. Actually, now that I thought about it, the latter was more likely.

'Look, Andrew, we've got nothing on this Constantine murder. Nothing. And Jessy really seems to think you've found the hit man. So, I'm going to give you the benefit of the doubt. You're coming in, you're going to make your complaint and I'll get the warrant. But let me tell you, you better not be making this up. If I don't find evidence you were assaulted there, and some fucking defence lawyer starts suggesting you and I conspired to get a warrant based on a false complaint, I'm going to throw the fucking book at you so hard that cricket bat's going to feel like a lover's caress.'

Richard is determined you're not going to make a fool of him, I remembered Jessy telling me. I had no doubt he meant what he said. I was impressed by his spectacular lack of sensitivity on the subject of my bashing, though. I could only aspire to become such an arsehole.

'I really was assaulted there,' I said. 'There was a lot of blood. Some ended up in the carpet. It was quite traumatic.'

'Okay, good. So on Thursday we'll execute the warrant at Robilliard's place and bring him in for questioning on your assault. If we find anything at his place to scare him with, we'll ask him a few questions on the Constantine matter while he's there.'

That all sounded perfect, except for the fact that I'd be in custody from the moment I walked into the police station.

'What does Schneider have to do with it?'

'Schneider is listed for this Thursday and Friday. Godfrey's doing the trial. You're going to prosecute. It's all cleared with Rufus and the sergeant who charged him. The longest session on Thursday will be from half past ten to one, when they'll break for lunch. You're going to ensure the jury is empanelled before morning tea, then time your witnesses to make sure Godfrey is unable to check his phone between ten thirty and one. At ten thirty we'll execute the warrant. Meanwhile, you're going to make sure there are no fucking toilet breaks all morning, and no adjournments and no substitutions of legal counsel all day. See if you can convince the court to cut lunch to half an hour and if he says he has a family emergency, once he finds out what's going on, you're to call bullshit on it. You'll have all the drugs you need to keep you going all day.'

No, Richard was the one who was crazy after all. That was a bit of a relief. 'If I come in now, I'll be arrested,' I pointed out.

'Not if you're in the course of assisting the police with a sting.'

'Oh.' I wasn't sure what to make of that. His use of the word 'sting' seemed slightly melodramatic. It wasn't exactly a sting as such. More a tactic for reducing the amount of effort the police would need to expend in order to do their job.

'I've got it all organised. It's cleared with the Commander.'

'Isn't that a bit improper, denying Robilliard his right to a lawyer?' I knew Richard would be unimpressed with my question.

'No, it's fucking not.'

'I mean –'

'This is exactly the sort of bullshit I'm expecting from your colleagues, Andrew, which is why only you can help us with this. We're not doing anything wrong. We just need to get a clear run at Robilliard. We're not denying him the right to a lawyer. He can have a lawyer if he wants. Just not that particular lawyer.' He sighed. 'Look, if Robilliard gets the chance, he'll say he wants Godfrey. The legal argument about whether we are entitled to refuse him permission to speak to a particular lawyer purely on the basis that we suspect they will collude is not one that I want to be having in the course of Godfrey's murder trial.'

Godfrey's murder trial. That sure did have a nice ring to it.

'Richard, can you put Jessy on? I need to find out if you're telling me the truth or not.'

~

In the disabled cubicle of the service station toilet, a place so grotty that even the sign saying 'Please advise management if this area needs attention' appeared to be smeared with shit, I stood in front of the mirror and stared at my reflection. The mirror itself was thinner than I was, the edges of it deteriorating to a patchy grey, like it was being consumed by some disease. It cut my reflection off across the centre of my forehead, and the dim anti-drug-injecting light in the centre of the ceiling cast a blue hue over everything, but I could get a general impression. I'd put on my good suit, the one I'd worn to the bank to take out all my money, because I would be seeing Jessy again, and I wanted to look my best. But even though it was only a week since I'd worn it to the bank, the suit didn't seem to fit me anymore. I looked a bit like the mirror. Kind of thin, grey and patchy. Like I too was being consumed from the outside in.

I ditched the suit and pulled on my jeans and a dirty grey polo shirt. They too hung off me but there was nothing I could do about that. At least without the suit I looked a bit more like a grungy teenager and less like a homeless guy.

I drove into the city and parked a couple of streets from the cop shop. Despite that precaution, I still half expected a dozen police officers to wrestle me to the ground as I stepped out of the GT, but there was no one. There were a few people about when I walked into the foyer. A young woman paying for a police clearance. Someone arguing about their right to bear arms, even though there was no such thing in Australia. I stood in the queue and waited until I was called.

'I'm here to see Richard Simms,' I told the young constable behind the desk.

'Name?' she barked.

It always annoyed me when people asked me questions without using complete sentences. *Do you want to know my name or yours?* I would have asked in any normal circumstances. But I didn't have the energy for my usual wanker routine. 'Andrew Deacon,' I told her. 'The prosecutor with the warrant out for his arrest.'

She narrowed her eyes in my direction, as if she half suspected I wasn't really Andrew Deacon, even though I looked – and smelled, at the moment – a lot like the missing desperado they'd all been told to keep an eye out for. It didn't matter to her, anyway. If I'd come to turn myself in, Richard Simms could handle it. She telephoned him, and then informed me that he was on his way down.

'Take a seat,' she told me, a directive I always viewed as an invitation to do the opposite in the interests of being contrary.

A door opened behind me a minute later. I turned and saw Jessy standing in the doorway. I knew to her I would look a bit ordinary. A bit dishevelled. Skinny. Unshaven. A bit drug-fucked, maybe. Not so much that I stood out greatly from all the other clientele hanging around in the foyer of the police station. But still, enough to make her look at me with a slightly alarmed expression. She didn't speak, but stepped aside, indicating for me to enter the room she'd come from.

I did that, hoping as the electronic door clicked closed behind me that this wasn't all a trick. There was still a decent chance it was all a trick. That nothing was approved by the Commander and they weren't really going after Leon Robilliard after all. That they'd seen an opportunity to lure me in by pretending they were finally taking me seriously, knowing that I would take the chance, even if it was a small chance, that they were genuine about questioning the man I believed to be the hit man. And really, I would. Even if they'd told me there was only a twenty per cent chance they weren't bullshitting me, I'd have considered it a chance worth taking. I really needed Sam Godfrey to be brought to justice.

The room was small. It was just the two of us.

'Hey, Drew,' Jessy whispered.

I smiled, as best I could. 'I've missed you.'

'I've –' She stopped and swallowed. 'I'm glad you came.'

I wanted to touch her. I wanted to hug her. But I wasn't totally sure I wouldn't get pepper-sprayed and tasered if I went anywhere near her, and I really didn't feel up to that. 'Still good for Thursday?'

'Oh yes.' She nodded. 'All good. We don't want to make a fuss at this stage, so you won't be going back to work just yet or getting electronic access. Rufus has given us a hard copy of the file for you to prepare for the trial. You can do that at home. There's been no major developments. The cops produced some extra photos and they were disclosed to Godfrey but your guys have now decided not to proceed with them.'

'Great, I'll get stuck into it then. I'll need to borrow a laptop if that's okay.'

~

My first stop on my way back to my real life had been the police station. Now, armed with a pile of witness statements for the Schneider trial and a borrowed police-issue laptop computer, I stood out the front of my apartment. I had not been arrested. I would not be arrested, it seemed, until at least Thursday. What was going to happen after Thursday, I wasn't sure, but for now I had some kind of amnesty, a get-out-of-jail-free card I was at liberty to play for the next couple of days. I used the key to enter my apartment and walked down the familiar hallway, past the lounge room and spare bedroom. I stopped at the room I'd called my home office. My computer, of course, had not been returned. I could see the police had been there. There was fingerprint dust everywhere, which was a surprise. It meant they'd been trying to find a sign of an intruder.

The apartment felt cold. Or maybe I'd just lost a bit of body fat. Either way it was quiet. I went into the kitchen and put the files and computer down on the bench there. The flowers I'd put in the vase the day before the Schneider directions hearing were dead.

I walked through to the laundry and stripped naked. I flipped open my prepaid phone as I shoved everything into the washing machine with one hand, even though the suit was probably dry-clean only.

'Hey Rod,' I said when he answered. 'You free?'

Rod panicked instantly, as he had taken to doing every time I called. 'Holy shit, bro, are you okay? What's happening? Where are you?'

'I'm at my place,' I said as I piled in twice my usual amount of washing powder. 'I can't tell you why, but I've got a presidential pardon until Thursday. I want you to take me to Esperance tonight. You can call in sick tomorrow. I'll just have a shower and a shave then I'll meet you at yours to return this car for Ellen's friend.'

'Okay, sure.'

'Can you get hold of some plaster cutters or whatever you people use to get this cast off my arm?'

'I guess. It's only been on for ... what ... three weeks?'

'Three and a half weeks. But I've had enough of it.'

'Okay. I don't know what I'm doing but I'll have a crack.'

~

Rod pulled Ellen's friend's cheap silver car-cover over the boot of the GT and, kneeling on the front lawn of his and Ellen's place in the posh part of Willetton, tied the straps together beneath the car. We'd just spent half an hour washing and detailing it, and both of us were sweating. 'Wouldn't want a bird to shit on it,' he remarked, standing. 'I quite like this car, actually.'

'It's going to come to an end soon,' I told him. 'One way or the other. They've brought me in to help them interview a witness, but once that's over, they'll probably arrest me. I mean, I can't imagine they're going to close their eyes and count to a hundred before they come after me.'

'So why'd you come in?'

'There's a chance it'll work. There's a chance we can get him. I had to take it.'

The drive to Esperance took about seven hours. We arrived at one o'clock on Tuesday morning. For large chunks of the trip, Rod and I sat in companionable silence. It felt good that he was in charge. He was younger than me by two years. In the past, I'd looked after him. I'd been the first to do everything. The first to go out at night on my own, the first to have a girlfriend. I'd lost my virginity three years before he did. I was the first to live on my own, and when he'd moved to the city to study I'd shown him the ropes, introduced him to new friends, made sure he was okay. He was more than capable of looking after himself, though, and it wasn't long before he started overtaking me with the firsts and now he was the first to marry, and likely would be the first to have a family too. He was strong, smart and dependable. Now, I was the older brother but I was all over the shop, and Rod was looking after me. That my brother had an enormous capacity to take care of those he loved, and was unconditionally willing to do so for me, made me feel ridiculously calm. I leaned back in the passenger seat of his treasured survivor XB GT coupe and closed my eyes.

Rod was driving. Rod was in charge and even if the XB broke down in the next ten minutes leaving us stranded on the side of the Albany Highway, Rod would be able to fix it with a couple of tools and a few spare parts from the boot.

'I got you more drugs,' he said. 'You don't need to go back to the drug dealer.'

A stab of guilt like a knife to my lungs drained them fully. 'Thanks Rod.' I sucked in a fresh lungful, squashing the unsavoury emotion. 'That's going to come to an end soon too.'

He nodded. 'I know.'

~

I lowered my body into the lake's dirty water. It was almost mid-May, so although the days were still mostly sunny, the nights were starting to cool off. Usually, just two or three cold nights in a row with the change of season would cool the water right down. The coolness seemed to settle straight to my core, in the absence of my usual layer of fat, but of course I didn't complain, as that was not the done thing in the company of one's little brother.

The sun was low in the sky and setting sunlight lay on the water, bright and uncomfortable. Squinting without my sunglasses, I was suspended, motionless, my head and just the tops of my shoulders above the water's surface. My left foot was snug in the boot, my right foot jammed into the kicker, my knees between my elbows. My right arm, now free of the plaster, was kind of white and shrivelled. I told myself it felt strong enough for this, but I knew water-skiing did require a fair bit of forearm strength. Rod hadn't commented, probably figuring I didn't really need a doctor's advice on the subject.

'Righto,' I shouted in the traditional way, then took a quick breath before Rod threw the boat into gear and spun the engine up to three thousand revs to drag me out of the water. I tucked up my body until I slid out onto the surface. Then I was skimming across the water, the hiss of the ski beneath me as loud to me as the engine of the boat fifteen metres ahead. I bent my knees, pressing my right into the crook of my left, pulled my shoulders back and pushed my hips forward, switched from a shopping trolley to an opposing grip on the handle, swung out to the left then turned, slamming into a hard cut across the wake, through the gate and out towards the first buoy, a tiny orange orb suspended in white light.

In the course I didn't feel the breeze or the spray which usually burned my legs. I thought only about the buoys, about what it would take to get there and beyond with the rope length I had, and all I felt was determined. And alive.

I made six good turns, getting out well in advance and skimming the edge of each buoy on my return towards the centre of the course. Getting the gate from number six was easy.

'Bloody hell, Drew,' said Rod, idling up to where I rested in the water. 'That was awesome. You smashed it at thirty-two off. You going again?'

'Yeah, I'll go again.' I decided to shorten the rope. 'Let's try thirty-five off.'

Mum and Dad sat in the shade of some yates on a couple of folding chairs at the end of the lake. They hadn't said much to me about the Lil-and-Sam affair, which was good. Rod had updated them about the deal with the police, and now they were trusting me to handle it from here. I hadn't done much to convince anyone so far that I was capable of handling it. But nevertheless, they trusted me.

After the next pass I signalled to Rod to drop me off. Dad stood as he saw the boat approaching and walked towards the jetty he'd taken most of one winter to build for us twenty years earlier. Rod turned the boat at speed at the top of the lake, and I let go of the rope, continuing tangentially and sinking into the water just a couple of metres shy of where Dad now stood at the end of the jetty. I slipped out of my ski and handed it up to him. I clambered up onto the slimy wooden platform. My arm had held together. I was stronger than I felt.

At dinner that night I told them all that I would handle it. I would not let them down any more than I already had. All three of them looked like they believed me. Or, at least, as if they wanted to believe me.

Rod and I drove back to Perth first thing Wednesday morning. We arrived late in the afternoon and went straight to the police station, where the cops, after payment of a reasonable ransom, authorised the release of the XD from the impounding yard.

Rod and I spent the rest of the evening together, disassembling, cleaning, relubricating and reinstalling the flaky ignition switch.

CHAPTER 26

I hardly slept that night. This was not that unusual for the night before a big trial, but for once I wasn't even thinking about the accused. The directions hearing which, in Schneider's case, was effectively an entire trial but without the jury, had ensured I was, like the witnesses, fully prepared. I knew the evidence like the back of my hand. All I could think about was how the cops would handle their move on Robilliard. If either the questioning or the execution of the warrant at Robilliard's place went well, it would hopefully lead to warrants for Godfrey's business records and those of Robilliard's solicitor. If the lawyer didn't get funds upfront into trust – a cardinal rule when dealing with crooks – they would need to be explaining why not. But over the course of the day and a bit I'd spent with my family on the farm at Esperance eating Mum's home-cooked meals and not preparing for the Schneider trial, I found myself starting to get worried about whether any number of warrants against Godfrey and Robilliard's lawyers were really going to help us. The reality was, there would be no debt in respect of Robilliard, and every single one of them – Robilliard, his solicitors and Sam Godfrey – would claim that Godfrey had agreed to do the trial pro bono. Despite the fact Robilliard wasn't a woman who'd shot her spouse after eight years of emotional, physical and sexual abuse. Or a man who beat his father to death for sexually molesting his children. According to the statement of material facts, he'd just popped a fellow drug dealer who was threatening to muscle in on his turf, but that didn't mean it was inconceivable Godfrey would conclude he was innocent of the charges levelled against him. That in the interests of justice he should get the best representation possible despite his limited financial means.

What that meant was, there was still only one way to prove Godfrey ordered the hit on Lil. We would need to convince Robilliard to roll on Godfrey. I really hoped he would, but I knew the plan would be for everyone to keep their mouths shut. If the cops searching Robilliard's place found some forensic evidence conclusively incriminating him, he might consider looking to shift blame to Godfrey. But if not, well, I didn't know exactly how the police would persuade him to be the first to deal.

~

Sam Godfrey SC looked like he had, to use a cliché, seen a ghost.

'What're you doing here?'

'Working,' I said, putting my briefcase and files down on my side of the bar table and adjusting the Velcro on the white-collared bib we lawyers wore around our necks and referred to imperiously as a *jabot*. 'What're you doing here?'

He seemed to be having trouble with this concept. 'You're a wanted fugitive,' he said, eventually.

I waved one hand dismissively. 'Oh, that. It's sorted.'

I wished.

Godfrey stared at me.

'Insufficient evidence,' I went on. 'They're not going to proceed. So, you know ... back to work. No rest for the wicked, as they say.'

I wondered if he would work out that someone was up to something, and ask for an adjournment straight up. But an adjournment was not going to be easy to get with eighty members of the public queued up outside for the jury empanelling. I wasn't too worried.

Eventually, he closed his mouth and turned to speak to Schneider, who'd been trying to get his attention for the past minute or so.

There was no adjournment request, and at ten o'clock, the jury, which I'd ensured had been fully empanelled by morning tea, filed out to the claustrophobic jury room to enjoy their ham and cheese and curried egg sandwiches. Godfrey scurried off to take the only available interview room to chat with Schneider and his lawyer about how he would play the jury we had. I sat down in the empty courtroom to pore, once again, over the newspaper article I'd printed at the library.

> *'They had no evidence whatsoever other than that a gun found in Mr Robilliard's home was the gun used to shoot Mr Frazer. That is true, but the fingerprints on the gun were not Mr Robilliard's and not a single solitary person was able to identify Mr Robilliard as the killer. There is no doubt he was framed. That gun, which my client had never seen before – never even touched – was placed in his home for the police to find, which they did after a convenient anonymous tip-off.'*

I texted Jessy. *All set?*

There was no response. I wondered whether the cops were secretly pleased I was tied up in a trial all day, as much as they were pleased that Godfrey was.

I thought of Darren Ashwin and what he'd told me about Frazer's death. *He went to see this buyer he was trying to squeeze.*

To be bothering to blackmail him, Mick must've known this customer had money. And he must have thought he had something over this wealthy customer, something he could do something with without needing to involve the cops, which was probably an unnecessary complication if you were a drug dealer. Could it be, perhaps, that Mick found out the buyer was married, and figured his wife would not likely be pleased to learn about an attractive girlfriend? I smiled to myself. Yeah, the buyer was, no doubt, Sam Godfrey, the girlfriend Angie Constantine. Godfrey was probably responsible for everyone killed in the whole city in the past year and a half. Settle down, Drew. One murder charge will be quite enough.

Mick only knew the guy 'cause his girlfriend bought coke off us.

I struggled to focus on the trial. I owed it to the victims to do everything I could to object to the outrageously objectionable questions Godfrey was putting to the witnesses, and I really tried. But I struggled. Meanwhile, Sam Godfrey SC was at the top of his game, blissfully unaware of the fact his knuckleheaded mate was at this very moment being questioned about their dealings with each other.

By one o'clock I was desperate to know what was happening with Robilliard and the warrant. But instead, I launched into a discussion with the judge about our rate of progress and the number of witnesses still to be called, eventually persuading the court we'd do best to take a short lunchbreak. Godfrey agreed to my request, which no doubt seemed innocuous enough to him at the time. At ten past one the court went into recess and, like everyone else, Godfrey turned to check his phone for messages. I watched as he dialled into his message bank. Seconds later, he hung up, his expression revealing more fury than fear. He stared at the phone for a moment, before launching into a new phone call. He turned his back on both me and Schneider's lawyer as he did so.

I rang Jessy's mobile.

'What's happening?' I hissed. 'Have you got Robilliard?'

'Found him selling ecstasy to a bunch of schoolkids, would you believe? We've booked him for that. We'll probably have to bail him tonight.'

'Is he talking?'

'Not really. He tried to get Godfrey straight up, but of course he had to leave a message. After that he decided to talk, though he's not admitting anything. Well, he admitted that Godfrey did the Frazer trial for him pro bono. But he says that was because he was innocent, and Godfrey was the only one who understood that.'

'Right.'

'He's denied killing Lil.'

'Does he have an alibi?'

'No.'

I preferred it when the punters had alibis. That generated the possibility of cracking them wide open.

'The thing is, they did find some things with that warrant. Some bloodstained clothes, stashed in the boot of his car. Tracksuit pants. According to the forensic guys the blood seemed a fair bit older than the blood that was presumably yours on the sheets in the wheelie bin at his place.'

'That older blood could belong to any of a number of victims. Of assaults, not necessarily murders. Or it could be his from a dust-up.'

'True. But the tracky pants were wrapped up in a plastic bag, which is a bit suss. They've gone off for DNA testing. We can only hope.'

'Good work, Jessy.'

'Thanks Drew, your approval means a lot,' she said, leaving me in no doubt that my approval didn't mean anything. 'How's your trial going?'

I wasn't really sure. 'Good. I think.'

'This is important, Drew. Schneider has to go down.'

'I'm pretty sure he will.'

She gave an exasperated sigh. 'Drew, Godfrey will walk all over you if you aren't on the ball with this. You know you're up against one of the best defence lawyers in the country.'

'Yeah, yeah, I know. Our evidence is pretty strong. I think we'll be okay.'

'I hope so, for your sake. How's your pain?'

'Okay. Under control.'

'Good.' She paused, then changed tack. 'Richard's on the phone to Godfrey right now. He's going off his rocker.'

'Richard?' I found that hard to believe.

'Godfrey. He's insisting that we release his client immediately, he's not to be interviewed further et cetera.'

I glanced over at Godfrey's still hunched figure. 'I bet he wants Robilliard out of there. Where he can't blab.'

'Yeah, well, Richard's told him he's most welcome to come down and speak to his client or send another lawyer if he wants to. But at the moment Mr Robilliard has been advised of his rights and he hasn't refused to speak to us.'

'We reconvene in twenty-five minutes. He can't get to you and back in that time. But he'll be down there immediately court winds up.'

'We've only got another few hours, I know. You have to drag it out for as long as possible. Text me the moment you finish for the day, okay? Then I'll know I'll have half an hour before Godfrey can get here, assuming he travels at the speed of light, which he will.'

'I will. Good luck with it Jess.'

'Thanks. See you later on.'

'Hey, listen, before you go –'

'Make it fast, Drew.'

'Okay, okay.' I pinched my forehead with my good hand. 'I wanted to ask you – do you think it's enough?'

'What?'

'The tracky pants. Do you think that'll be enough to persuade Robilliard to tell us Godfrey hired him to carry out a hit on Lil?'

Jessy gave it some thought. 'Depends. Only Robilliard knows if they were the pants he was wearing when he killed her. If they weren't, I guess he won't be too worried. And he certainly hasn't cracked yet.'

'Yeah.' It didn't sound too hopeful. 'I reckon we need more.'

'You got any ideas?'

'Maybe.' I tried to organise my thoughts. There was something in the back of my mind that made sense, but I couldn't bring it into focus. 'I don't know if you have time – but it might … it might be worth talking to Angie again –'

'Listen, Drew, Richard's just finished with Godfrey. I've got to go. I'll talk to you about this later, okay? I'll call you as soon as I can.'

'Sure.' I hung up the phone and tried to switch my mind back to the matter of Rocco Schneider.

It'd been anticipated that the trial would run for two days. However, following lunch, Sam Godfrey SC didn't seem interested in continuing with the extensive cross-examination of police witnesses he'd been indulging in prior to the break. He probably could have tried to fake a family emergency, but he knew I would be insisting he first go on oath about exactly what that emergency was and where he was going as a result of it, and he clearly didn't fancy an unnecessary perjury conviction. Instead, he did his *Browne v Dunn* duties by putting to the police witnesses an appallingly short version of whatever Schneider had concocted by way of a defence, then sat down. He didn't call his own client to give evidence or any witnesses on behalf of the defence, and by three o'clock the whole trial was over bar the final submissions. His took a minute and a half.

Mine was a rambling discourse of musings, observations and dubious analogies that meandered on for over three quarters of an hour, at least fifteen minutes of which was taken up with Godfrey complaining about how long they were taking (a point I indignantly took great issue with). Eventually the judge gave me a serve and a time limit, and I had to wrap it up. By four o'clock the jury had retired to consider its verdict. They stayed in the jury room for long enough to eat the free sandwiches, then delivered a verdict of guilty on all charges. Godfrey asked for a pre-sentence report and a psychological assessment and the judge adjourned sentencing for a couple of months, remanding Mr Schneider in custody.

'Damn shame,' Godfrey tossed in the direction of Schneider's lawyer before striding for the door. I followed him to the nearby car park, another dimly lit, multistorey edifice. Earlier, I'd parked the XD five inches from his Lexus, which I'd located after a short search, leaving no space for him to get in through the driver's side door. It meant I had to leave my own car unlocked and get in via the back door on the driver's side, and I knew it wouldn't make much difference to his movements since all his doors presumably worked quite well, but it had amused me to do it.

'It's too late, you know,' I shouted at him as he jumped into the passenger's side of the Lexus without missing a beat and scrambled over the centre console, probably not an easy feat for a man of his size given he wasn't practised at it like I was. 'Robilliard's already spilled his guts.' I sincerely hoped he had by now, but I was far less confident than I was making out. Jessy hadn't called me back, which meant that she'd been tied up in the interview all afternoon. The matter I'd tried to raise with her had been on my mind all through the trial. During the three and a half minutes the jury was out, I decided I was going to have to do something about it myself.

The window of the Lexus lowered, and Godfrey glared at me. 'I've no idea what you're talking about,' he hissed.

'You don't remember Mr Robilliard?' I said. 'The hit man you hired to kill Lily Constantine?'

Godfrey ignored me, irritated beyond his own generally impressive ability to verbalise. He pressed a button and the starter motor of his Lexus obediently sprung to life, dedicating a valiant effort to the starting of his car. Unfortunately, it was destined never to succeed beyond the first couple of splutters. That was because I'd used a tapered reamer from the hardware store, which conveniently opened at seven in the morning, to pierce the fuel tank on my way into court, figuring that *would* indeed slow him down a fair bit. He would have to wait ten minutes or more for a ride and then he would have to accept that the driver would convey him only as fast as the driver was prepared to go which would, I expected, depend on how many demerit points the driver had accumulated. Ah, paralysing his car. I knew it was clichéd, but it was effective.

Godfrey realised straight away that there was no way he was going to get the Lexus going. I expected him to reach into his briefcase, pull out his mobile and order an Uber or call a taxi, but he did something I hadn't quite expected at all.

He reached into his briefcase and pulled out a gun.

CHAPTER 27

Holy shit.

Clutching the weapon with a degree of care that suggested it was loaded, Godfrey scrambled back across the passenger seat of his car and climbed out. As he skirted around his car, I leapt into the XD and while still in the back seat activated the central locking. In the XD this involved slamming the driver's side knobs down with two fists and then throwing my body across the seat to do the same on the passenger side. I couldn't believe he'd been *carrying* in the fucking District Court. Was there no limit to the laws this guy was prepared to flout?

I wriggled into the front and started the car – *thanks be to God* – and then reversed out of the park at a rate of knots. I knew he could be behind me but it was a chance I had to take. Mercifully, I didn't hear any thud. The last thing I needed was to have to remove a defence lawyer wedged under the diff before I could get on the road. Of course, the lack of thud meant one thing. He was probably standing next to my car pointing the gun at my head as I engaged drive.

Oh man. I so did not want to look up and see that.

I came as close to actually shitting myself as I would ever want to be when the tempered glass window not a foot from my head shattered into a million pieces. Within a fraction of a second, my brain had processed the ragged hole in the passenger side seat that suggested a bullet had torn into it and concluded without a shadow of a doubt that he'd *taken a shot* at me.

I wasn't going to stick around to discuss it with him. The XD emitted a series of ominous crunches as I swung the steering wheel to its limit and burned down the ramp with all the thrust of a whoopee cushion. In the rear-view mirror, I saw him take a couple more shots at my car, standing there on the concrete looking like James Bond with his legs apart, two hands on the weapon, in a goddamn *suit*.

It didn't sound, or feel, like either of them had hit me or my vehicle and he disappeared from my line of sight.

My breath escaped in a slow shudder as I reached for my mobile phone. I found Jessy's number and pressed to dial it as I emerged from the car park.

'Schneider's finished,' I said when she answered. I could hear a tremor in my voice. Geez, I hadn't heard my voice tremble like that since I was a graduate lawyer standing up in court for the first time.

'We need more time.' She didn't sound happy. 'We're still interviewing Robilliard. He doesn't want to crack.'

Geez, some women were hard to please. 'I did the best I could,' I snapped. 'He's been held up by car trouble, but he won't be too far away I'm sure. Please Jess, make sure they check him for weapons at the front.'

'Thanks Drew. I'll let you know how it –'

'I'm coming too, of course, but I've got to go and see a couple of people first. I'm going to try to get something you can use. Don't let Robilliard go until I get there.'

'It's fine, Drew, really, we can handle –'

I hung up. I wondered if Godfrey would be old-fashioned enough to still use taxis. On the off-chance, I started dialling all the taxi companies I could think of, until one of them confirmed the booking under Godfrey from St Georges Terrace was now cancelled and thanked me for letting them know. Again, it wasn't a long-term solution, but it would slow him down. By the time I'd finished with that I'd pulled up at Angie Constantine's apartment.

I rapped on the door. 'Angie, it's Drew,' I yelled.

She opened the door. Barefoot, she wore a short black skirt and white cotton shirt, her thick hair piled up on top of her head and held in place with a single clip. She looked like she was getting ready for work. 'You're back.' She smiled.

'Angie, we need to talk.' Without intending to, I glanced around her apartment, searching, this time, for any sign she was a cocaine user. I wasn't sure what I expected. Used syringes sticking out of the flowerpots, perhaps, or maybe some lines of white powder on the kitchen bench?

'Sure, sit down. Are you still running from the cops?'

I shook my head. 'Listen, I'm sorry, but I don't have time to sit down. I need you to tell me the truth. It's really important, Angie. For Lil.'

'What's going on?'

'The cops are speaking to a man who they think may have carried out the hit on your sister.'

She let out a small whimper.

'His name is Leon Robilliard. He's someone Sam represented recently and got off a murder charge.'

'Sam hired this man to kill Lil?'

I hesitated. 'That's what it looks like.'

'Her last – the last thing she saw was some hit man?'

'Listen, Angie, Sam's heading straight down to the police station now to try to stop the cops from interviewing this bloke. We don't have much time. I need to know a few things from you.'

She looked at me then as she had outside the cemetery, as if she was afraid of me. I didn't know whether she was afraid of what I was going to ask her, or whether she was afraid of me physically. I had kind of muscled my way in, and now I was standing over her, looking and sounding a bit freaky. I decided I would sit down after all.

'I've got a mate,' I said, watching her face carefully as she perched tentatively on the edge of a kitchen chair. 'His name is Darren Ashwin. He's mates with a bloke by the name of Michael Frazer. Do you know them?'

She wound her fingers together in her lap but didn't speak.

'I'm serious, Angie. I need you to tell me the truth. Darren Ashwin reckons that one of Michael Frazer's customers, a few months back, was a woman with a bit of a coke problem. And he says that particular woman had a boyfriend who it sounds like must have been wealthy.'

Angie looked up at me. I could see she was shaking.

'It's not about the drugs, Angie. It's about Lil. I need to know if that woman could have been you. If that wealthy boyfriend could have been Sam.'

When she spoke, I could barely hear her. 'Yes,' she whispered. 'Maybe.'

'You know them?'

'Yes, I know them. Because of ... how you said.'

'Did Godfrey know them?'

'Yes. We'd go there together.'

'He uses coke?'

'No, he doesn't. My first boyfriend got me on it and after we broke up, it really spiralled out of control. That's why I was stealing from my family. After Sam saved the restaurant I decided I had to get clean, and I moved in with Lil and she was trying to help me. But Sam made it impossible. He took me to Frazer and he paid for it all. It wasn't just because he was threatening me that I let him do to me what he did. It was because he was feeding my addiction too.' She looked like she was about to burst into tears. 'What does this have to do with Lil?'

'Frazer was trying to blackmail this wealthy customer. That's what got him killed, according to Darren.'

She shook her head. 'If Sam killed Michael Frazer, I knew nothing about that. I knew nothing about any blackmail. Drew, I swear –'

I got to my feet and left, slamming the door behind me. I had what I needed from Angie Constantine.

'Jessy,' I said to her voicemail as I belted down the street in the direction of Ashwin's place. 'Please call me. Please – it's urgent. Don't let Robilliard go. And call me.'

I pulled up at Ashwin's thirteen minutes later.

'Darren, I need you to help me,' I told him as I stood on his front doorstep. I could tell by the look on his face he didn't like what I was wearing. 'I need you to come down to the cop shop with me and identify someone.'

'Fuck off, man,' said Ashwin. I was pretty sure the only reason he hadn't whacked me already was because he was a tiny bit amused by my idiotic request. He seemed pretty mellow, actually. I wondered if he was high or coming down. His pupils were kind of small. He avoided my eyes and seemed to be focusing on a spot behind me and some distance away.

'Darren, please listen. That buyer you were talking about, the guy you reckoned shot Mick Frazer. I need you to have a look at a bunch of photos – a photo board, we call it – and tell me which one was that guy. It's important.'

Ashwin slammed the door in my face.

'I've got cash,' I shouted at the closed door, knowing there wasn't any other option at this point.

It opened again slowly.

'Of course, you'd be paid for your time.' I smiled weakly.

'How do I know you're not setting me up so the cops can pinch me?'

'Darren, I'm asking you to do this for your friend. Frazer was your friend, wasn't he?'

Ashwin said nothing.

'Did he hurt you?' I asked, far from sure it was a good move.

Ashwin's eyes flashed, and he actually looked at me. 'Mick *never* hurt me,' he hissed. 'He was the only one who didn't. He was the only one who gave a shit about me, ever. When he got killed ...' He stopped himself. I knew he didn't want to be talking about this shit, not with me, or anyone.

'Wouldn't you like to see the guy who killed him pay for his death?'

'Will he, though?' Ashwin looked up at me, his face screwed up against the fading light. 'Will anything I do make any difference? I mean, the photo board's not the end of it, is it? Don't I still have to go in there and give evidence in court and say that's the guy, that's the guy Mick went to see that day?'

'Yes, but –'

'Aren't they going to say, hey, you're just a fucked-up fucking useless junkie pusher? This dude, he's rich, right? He's somebody important.'

'Maybe.' I shook my head. 'Alright, fuck – yes, probably. It won't be easy. But at least you can say you've done it. You can go to Mick's grave and tell him you tried.'

Ashwin looked at me like he thought I was dribbling shit which, let's face it, I was.

'Darren, I swear, if you come in and identify this guy, and it is who I think it is, I swear, I will prosecute the fuck out of him for Mick's murder, I promise you. It won't be just you trying to get him. It'll be me too, because I'll believe you.'

Ashwin cocked his head to the side. 'You're a junkie too,' he pointed out.

'Well, yes, but I will soon turn my life around and retrieve my reputation and become one of the people you hate again very shortly. Did I mention you have to do this soon? As in, right now?'

Ashwin narrowed his eyes. 'Where's the cash?'

I handed over a thousand bucks. I was pretty sure that would do the trick. 'Don't bother mentioning that to the police,' I said. 'It'll only complicate things.'

I was confident Ashwin could keep a secret.

He nodded. 'Let's go.'

~

Jessy returned my call as I was fanging the XD down to the cop shop with Darren Ashwin in the passenger seat.

'Has he cracked?' I demanded as I answered the call.

'No, he hasn't. But Godfrey isn't here yet, so we're still trying. Drew, I can hardly hear you. Do you have the window down?'

'Listen, Jessy, I need you to sort out a photo board, fast. You've got to trust me on this. I've got a witness, and we'll be there in a few minutes.'

'A witness for what?'

'He can identify the last person to see Michael Frazer alive.'

'Michael Frazer? Are you serious?' Mercifully, she paused, then took her voice down a couple of octaves and into my audible range. 'I've got a few things on at the moment, Drew. Perhaps we could look at solving Michael Frazer's murder, say, next week?'

'Please Jess. I can't explain it now because I've got my witness with me in the car. Please trust me. Can you just put together the photo board? Make them males, middle-aged and clean cut. Men who would pass for rich. I need one person in particular. I can't mention his name. But you know who I'm talking about. Do the photo board, and my witness will look at it when we get there.'

'Do you mean Godfrey? We don't have a photo of him.'

'You need to get one off the internet. He'll have one on the website for –' I stopped. It was important this witness was not contaminated in any way. 'Just make sure you get it photoshopped first, so it looks like the others.'

'Yes, thanks for telling me how to do a photo board, Drew.'

'Just sayin'. Mistakes have been made in the past.'

'How far away are you?'

'I'll be there in about ten minutes, I reckon.'

'Alright, I'll have it done by then.' She gave an exasperated sigh. '*Photoshopping* and all.'

CHAPTER 28

A photo board was much the same concept as a line-up, but a lot cheaper and less time-consuming. That suited the police, who were always trying to keep within their budget. There were a lot of rules imposed by the court about how a photo board was to look, usually in response to the cops ballsing it up. For example, you couldn't have one scatty-looking punter with long hair and facial tattoos, and twenty-three clean-shaven police officers in civvies with AJ hairdos and a superior expression, because that would give the witness a clue. The witness can't be given any clues. What was worrying me was that if Godfrey happened to be in the foyer when we got there, it'd be curtains on the photo board, because if Ashwin subsequently picked Godfrey out of the board, he could be argued to have been influenced by the presence of the same dude in the foyer before he got started. *That must be the bloke the cops are interested in*, he would be presumed, at a directions hearing, to have concluded. *I'll be helpful by picking him out.*

Hopefully Jessy would've already realised this and would be onto the job of making sure it didn't happen.

As the electronic doors of the cop shop slid closed behind Ashwin and me, there was no sign of Godfrey, but his wife Amanda was sitting in the waiting area. I remembered her from the funeral. She was about Lil's height, with long, dark hair just the same as Lil and Angie, but she carried the particular harried lines of a woman who had raised children.

I'd no idea why she would be there.

'Hey,' she threw at me as we scurried past. 'What're you doing here?'

I ignored her and pushed Ashwin through the door Jessy had opened for us. She showed Ashwin to an interview room and sat him down with instructions to wait for her to return.

'Now,' said Jessy, when we were alone in the corridor. 'Tell me what this is all about.'

'What it's about is that I think Sam Godfrey killed Michael Frazer.'

'Yes, I figured that's what you think.'

'And I don't think Leon Robilliard is going to be one bit happy about that.'

Jessy stared at me. She opened her mouth to speak, then closed it again.

'Look, I don't know for sure he did it,' I went on. 'All I know for sure is that Sam and Angie were two of Frazer's customers, and Frazer was planning to or trying to blackmail some customer of his. And that Frazer had headed off to see the guy when he was killed. I don't know if that customer was Sam. Not until you do that photo board.'

There was no time to tell her more. She disappeared into the interview room to go through the photo board procedure with Ashwin. About three minutes later, the dulcet tones of Amanda Godfrey going off her brain in the foyer settled over me. I was still waiting in the corridor; I glanced through a tiny vertical window in the door to observe the reception area, to see her standing in the artificial light. Jessy had interviewed her briefly earlier in the afternoon, I'd been informed by a loitering cop, to suss if she knew anything about what Sam was doing to Angie. She didn't. It hadn't been pretty.

'You told me you didn't do this, Sam,' she screeched, her body trembling as she glared at her husband, who was in the process of being searched for weapons by two uniforms. 'You told me they were pissing in the wind.'

'They are,' hissed Godfrey, his arms stretched out from each side of his body. 'Keep your voice down.'

'Do you think I'm a total idiot? I found out today what you've been doing to Angie. If you'd been having an affair with her, it would've been better. But you've been *assaulting* my sister for months. And they think you hired a hit man to kill Lil. They've got proof you defended that scumbag in there for free, and he killed her for you.'

'No. They've got nothing.' The uniforms finished the search – he'd left the gun in the car, thankfully – and Godfrey stepped towards his wife. Despite her obvious reluctance he pulled her into his chest. 'Amanda, I would never do anything to hurt Angie. She's just … I know it's not her fault. I'm sorry to tell you this, but she's a drug addict. That's why the restaurant nearly went bust. I would never hurt her, and I would never hurt Lil. And I would never hurt you. They've got no leads on Lil and they're just making shit up. I promise you.'

She managed to push him away. 'Why the fuck would you defend that man for free?'

I turned from the unfolding drama in the waiting room to see Jessy stepping out of the interview room then closing the door behind her. She held a manila folder in her hands.

'All good?'

'Yes,' she said. 'We've got the ID. Straight up, no hesitation. We put a nice pic of Robilliard in there too and not even the presence of the man actually charged with the murder put him off.'

'I knew it.'

'I'll get someone to run Ashwin home. You can come with me. We'll see how Richard's going. Did I hear Godfrey arrive?'

'He's out the front arguing with his missus.'

'Shit.' She took off back down the corridor, and I scampered after her.

'Robilliard talked to us all afternoon,' she explained as we walked. 'I think I told you he tried to get hold of Godfrey first up, but when he had to leave a message, he decided to back his own ability to outsmart us and agreed to be interviewed. But he hasn't made any admissions, just denied everything. This –' she shook the manila folder in her hands, 'is going to be our last hope.'

I handed her the printout from the newspaper archive and she read it quickly, before slipping it into her folder. We entered the main observation room at the end of the corridor, where two young police officers were watching, through the glass, Richard continuing to interview Robilliard.

'Come on, Leon,' Richard snapped. 'How long are you going to sit here and tell me bald-faced lies? No jury is ever going to believe that Sam Godfrey SC was so moved by the injustice of your situation that he offered to do a trial worth north of a hundred thousand dollars for you for free as part of his service to the community. Trust me, if I don't believe it, a jury isn't going to believe it. And if they don't believe it, you're going down. You can't just pull an identification swifty on this one, Leon.'

'How did you say she was killed again?' Robilliard asked, as if he didn't know.

'I told you fifty times. She was stabbed. I've shown you the photos.'

'Yeah, yeah. Well, *if* I was guilty, as you seem to be suggesting I am, of the Frazer hit, then wouldn't *shooting* be my MO, or whatever you people call it?'

Richard leaned across the desk and grinned at him. 'One,' he sneered, 'you've been watching too much Criminal Minds. Two, by asking me that question, on the video tape, you've demonstrated you're capable of considering this issue and therefore capable of altering your behaviour to put the police off the track.'

I'd have expected an average crim to be rattled by an exchange like that, but Robilliard's face showed he wasn't troubled at all. He just shrugged. He was hardcore.

'Why do you think Godfrey's not here, Leon? Hey? He's had all day to get his sorry arse down here to see you, to respond to that desperate message you left on his phone this morning. But the reality is, you've served your purpose for him, haven't you? You did his dirty work for him, and now he's done with you. He'd rather play golf with his buddies and have long lunches on the Terrace than waste any more of his precious time on you. You're on your own now. We're all over you and Godfrey's nowhere to be seen.'

Robilliard said nothing.

'Those tracksuit pants we found at your place are going to have

Lily Constantine's DNA all over them,' Richard persisted. 'And when we have the results back, we're going to have a chat to Mr Godfrey. We're going to tell him we've found Lily's killer: one Mr Leon Charles Robilliard.'

Robilliard's eyes narrowed, but still he didn't speak.

'What do you think he's going to say, Leon?' Richard demanded. 'What's he going to say about that? Oh, don't give Leon a hard time, he was just following orders? Or will he say *thank goodness you've found the killer. I hope you lock him up and throw away the key?*'

'I'm tipping the latter,' Jessy commented under her breath.

Robilliard just gritted his teeth.

'I bet he's got a plan for how he's going to ensure you're the only one implicated in all this,' Richard continued, undaunted. 'He's going to feed us a story about how Lily visited his office one day to drop off something for Amanda and as she was leaving you turned up to speak to him, and you commented how much you'd like to have a piece of her. Godfrey's going to hang you out to dry, Leon. The best thing you can do for yourself is talk to us first. There'll be a deal on the table for you Leon. You can count on it.'

Jessy left the observation room and entered the interview room. She handed the file to Richard, who opened it and read for a short moment, before letting out his breath slowly, leaning back in his chair and closing the file. He glanced up at Jessy, deferring to her.

Jessy sized up Robilliard, her gaze focused.

'I just heard my colleague rudely allege you got off the Frazer charge by confusing the jury on identification,' she said quietly. 'The thing is, Mr Robilliard, I don't think you were guilty of the Frazer hit. I agree with you. You were framed. Did you know that?'

'I know I didn't do it.'

Jessy nodded. 'And do you know who framed you?'

For the first time, Robilliard seemed unsure how to respond. He was confused by the change of subject, and couldn't work out where this was going, if it was a trap. My heart was in my throat.

'Would you like to know who framed you?' Jessy persisted. 'I can tell you right now if you'd like to know. I've just had a witness pick the real killer from a photoboard, not five minutes ago.'

His arms still crossed across his broad chest, Robilliard flexed his biceps. Trap or not, Jessy's offer was tempting him. And she wasn't even asking for anything in return.

'Yes,' he said. 'I would like to know.' The look on his face suggested that later on this evening, once he'd finished up here, signed some paperwork and been bailed, whoever it was who'd framed him for Frazer's murder would be a dead man.

Jessy sat down next to Richard. 'A woman was buying drugs from Michael Frazer, and Frazer thought he'd make a few extra quid when he found out just how rich her married boyfriend was.' She stared at Robilliard, who was now sitting forward in his seat. 'The boyfriend was Sam Godfrey, Leon. Godfrey was the one who shot Frazer, because he didn't want to pay up. Godfrey framed you, as a fairly easy target, a former client I assume but, in any case, a known crook with known form. And Godfrey then offered to get you off the charge he'd framed you for in the first place.'

A vein on the side of Robilliard's head was pulsing with his heartbeat, which was evidently fairly rapid.

'Those unidentified fingerprints that gave you reasonable doubt, actually belonged to *Godfrey*.' Jessy waited for the news to sink in. 'They weren't in any forensic database, and Godfrey knew that. So, he gleefully built a case that poor Mr Robilliard had been framed, pointed over and over again to these unknown fingerprints, the prints of the *real killer*, knowing all along that *he* was the one who'd framed you, that they were *his own prints*.'

Richard grinned. 'Boy, was he laughing at you, Leon. You thought you owed him something. You thought he *saved* you from a murder rap. He's the whole and sole reason you were in the shit in the first place. He's tricked you into killing someone for him, for *nothing*. Now, thanks to those tracky pants, you're going to jail. For life. For him. For *nothing*!'

A bang on the door of the interview room made me jump, though it didn't seem to have any such effect on Richard and Jessy. I watched as Godfrey burst in and demanded to speak to his client in private.

The two uniforms in the room with me tensed.

Robilliard turned to look at Godfrey. Controlled rage lurked in Robilliard's steady gaze. 'I don't need a lawyer,' he said.

Godfrey's eyes widened. 'Leon, we need to speak. We need to discuss ...'

Robilliard shook his head.

Godfrey froze. Robilliard couldn't have made it clearer that he was ready to deal if he'd announced it via Twitter to a hundred thousand followers. Richard stood. He was going to make the call, on the strength of Robilliard's five words, to arrest Godfrey. He knew that later on this evening he'd have the evidence he needed to charge him with Lil's murder.

One of the officers in the room with me left without a word.

Jessy glared at Godfrey as Richard approached him. 'You heard the man, Mr Godfrey. You're not needed here. Now let's keep this civilised.'

Godfrey stared at her for a moment, before turning his attention to Robilliard and lifting one hand to point at him. 'You shut up,' Godfrey barked as his pointing finger was dragged behind his back by the combined efforts of Richard and the uniformed cop who'd just walk in the door. 'You shut the fuck up, Leon.'

Robilliard seemed unmoved. He observed dispassionately as Godfrey was dragged from the room, as if lack of impulse control by one's acquaintances was an everyday occurrence in his life. The racket of Godfrey's threats woven with Richard's recitation of his arrest spiel faded abruptly as Richard kicked the door shut behind himself.

Robilliard and Jessy faced each other, alone together, in the stark space. I felt anxious for her; she wouldn't have been three quarters his height, probably a third of his weight. I felt like he could snap her before I could get in there to help her. It didn't feel right, as her almost, sort of, well, in-my-fantasies-at-least, boyfriend, to leave her in there alone with that monster.

'Can you go in?' I said to the remaining uniform standing beside me.

He shook his head. 'She'd kill me. He's about to confess to her.'

'Yeah, but –'

'If he moves, I'll be in there in a heartbeat.'

Jessy didn't seem worried. She waited for Robilliard to speak.

Robilliard leaned back in his chair, folded his arms again and said: 'Sam Godfrey did not hire me to kill Lily Constantine.'

'Is that really what you want to tell me, Mr Robilliard?'

Robilliard nodded. Then he smiled at her. It was the sort of smile that'd make you get back in your car and lock all the doors.

'He hired me to kill Angela Constantine. I think I must've made a mistake.'

CHAPTER 29

I watched Jessy pour herself a strong, black coffee from the percolator on the bench. She sat down at the table in the centre of the police station's clinical kitchenette. Richard and I had been nursing our coffees for a couple of minutes, while I told him about what went down in the car park earlier. He had Godfrey safely in custody and was planning to interview him once Jessy had finished with Robilliard, which she'd just done. Robilliard had provided a full confession, so it hadn't taken long. Not even an hour, by my estimation. Richard had only finished processing Godfrey's arrest in the last ten minutes of the interview so he missed most of it. That was not ideal, but Jessy had not been minded to wait in case Robilliard's rage ebbed and he was no longer in a talking mood by the time Richard was ready to go ahead.

'Godfrey intended to off Angie from the start,' Jessy explained. 'Just as Andrew suspected. But he never switched the hit to Lil. Robilliard killed the wrong sister by accident.'

Richard digested this. 'Of course,' he breathed. 'They live together, Angie usually worked late and slept in, but she decided to go out and then spend the night at a friend's place ... Lil was usually up and at work at the florist by nine in the morning, but she decided to call in sick that morning and go back to sleep because she'd been up all night shagging Lover Boy here.' He waved dismissively in my direction. 'Let me guess. Robilliard had directions to the correct bedroom, but when he found Angie's bed untouched and found Lil asleep in another room, he called on all the keen intellectual thrust that'd got him into that line of work in the first place and decided Lil was probably Angie.

They do look alike, especially if you're particularly stupid.'

'Yep, that's pretty much what he said. Except he didn't admit he was stupid.'

'It explains why Godfrey gave Robilliard the key to the apartment. He believed that only Angie knew he had that key, and that Angie would be dead before anyone knew there'd been unforced entry.'

'Yeah, though he didn't plan to take that risk in any case,' said Jessy. 'There was meant to be forced entry. Robilliard told me Godfrey gave him the key so he could make a quiet entry, with the target – Angie – asleep in her bedroom. He was meant to kill her silently, without her seeing it coming. After that he was meant to go outside, lock the door again, break a window to simulate forced entry, and then disappear before anyone had time to investigate the racket.'

'But he didn't do it.'

'He didn't see the point. He thought it was an unnecessary risk.'

Richard rolled his eyes. 'It's hard to get good help these days.'

'But still, Lil must've said something to Sam,' I pointed out. 'Otherwise he wouldn't have called her the night I was with her in the bar.'

Richard frowned. 'There's no way Godfrey would have gone ahead with a hit on Angie if he knew that Angie had told Lil about what he was doing to her. There'd have been no point in silencing Angie if she'd told anyone. He'd have to kill both or neither.'

'Maybe he was ringing Lil to suss whether she knew,' Jessy suggested. 'Maybe he was trying to find out whether he'd left it too late to off Angie, figuring if she told anyone it'd be Lil. Maybe he pushed her hard over the two days after Angie told him she would no longer let him abuse her, annoyed her regularly, so she would snap and let slip what she knew. But she promised Angie she wouldn't say anything, so she didn't.'

'And he concluded he would be in the clear once Angie was gone.' I could recall as if it was yesterday the moment she'd got that call. *I don't know what we have to talk about.* Then she'd described him as someone who couldn't take no for an answer.

Then she'd said: *I am the Queen of the Night.*

And all morning I'd sat at my computer, hoping in the back of my mind she would call me, while in her apartment Leon Robilliard violently drained her of her life.

Jessy's explanation for why Sam had called Lil when I was with her at the bar made sense, but there was still something I didn't like about the whole thing. The idea that the motive for killing Angie was the fact he was blackmailing her into sex ... it just didn't sit right. He'd made that decision himself, he'd thought about it and he'd weighed up the risks and he'd decided to back her so hard into a corner she could never tell anyone what was going on, and never escape from him. And he'd achieved that. She was wracked with guilt and hopelessly hooked on free cocaine. Godfrey didn't seem like the kind of guy to second-guess his decisions. To decide she now needed to be killed to ensure her silence was tantamount to admitting he'd made a mistake in his initial assessment of what would be required to control her.

Was there another reason Angie had to die?

Jessy skolled the second half of her coffee, picked up the file and got to her feet. Richard followed suit; they were ready to interview Godfrey. She glanced back at me from the doorway.

'How'd you go today?'

'With what?'

She looked at me like I had a screw loose. 'Schneider.'

'Oh, yeah.' I'd forgotten about that. 'Convicted on all counts.'

CHAPTER 30

I took another three police-issue Vicodins and sat in the observation area watching Jessy and Richard commence their interview with Godfrey. They introduced themselves, explained the purpose of the video, required him to state his name and address, and delivered, for once, a word-perfect warning to the effect that Godfrey was not required to answer any questions, but that if he did, his answers could be used against him.

His eyes, as he watched them both, were not entirely devoid of emotion. The emotion I saw there was probably best described as *disdain*. Disdain for the two police officers who now sought to interview him, disdain for the process and perhaps for the justice system as a whole.

'Mr Godfrey,' Jessy began. 'Do you understand the warning I've just given you? Can you please repeat it back to me? In your own words.'

Godfrey leaned forward and eyed Jessy with a kind of misogynistic scorn. I sensed that, given the opportunity, he'd have liked to whack her around the head a few times. She didn't seem that fazed. No doubt she'd interviewed a few hard cases over her time, but I'd have thought he'd have to be up there. It was no wonder she'd found interviewing me to be not particularly taxing on her energy levels.

'Detective Parkin,' he almost whispered, his words delivered slowly and deliberately, as if to make it clear he thought he was speaking to a fool. 'Let me make this crystal clear for you. I will not speak to you. I will not answer any of your questions.' He sat back in his chair and looked from one officer to the other. He raised one eyebrow as if to say: *Are we done here?*

Yup. It was starting to look pretty clear this interview wasn't going to be a happening thing. There's a fine line separating talking to the cops being a good idea and a bad idea. Very early in the piece it can be advantageous to appear helpful, to give the police the information they might need to rule you out of their investigation, to put them off the scent. But it's rarely long before it's not to one's advantage to speak to the police. Court, in front of a jury, is generally the best place to explain your story. The more you say to the police beforehand, the more prepared they are for your defence, and the more they can use against you as admissions on relevant facts, or to prove you're a liar. Godfrey was well aware of the position of that line. He was clamming up.

Unfortunately for him, though, there was one little thing he'd forgotten.

Richard smiled as he leaned back in his chair. 'Very wise, Mr Godfrey. I can see you're very familiar with how things go. Best not to say a word to the cops, isn't it? Anything you say could be used against you, might harm your defence. And you do have a defence, of course. That Leon Robilliard acted alone when he murdered your sister-in-law, and now he's trying to deflect blame by pinning everything on you. He's a deadbeat drug dealer. You're a pillar of society. *His* word means nothing. *You* didn't know a thing about it. You never paid him, in services, to kill Lily *or* Angie. You only represented him for free because you thought it was your moral duty to do a bit of pro bono work from time to time. Admirable, really.'

Godfrey's eyes narrowed as he looked at Richard.

'Yes,' Jessy agreed. 'Refusing to speak is definitely a smart move, given it's not a cut-and-dried case. You're still in with a chance of getting off completely. Why cooperate in those circumstances? It'd be a different story if, say, we had evidence that'd be sure to throw you in the bin for life. If that was the case, well, I'd expect you'd be looking to perhaps try to be as helpful as possible, with a view to minimising your sentence and one day experiencing freedom again before you die.'

A scintilla of doubt flickered across Godfrey's face. I knew that Jessy would've noticed it. Noticing stuff was her strong suit.

She got to her feet. 'So, righto, let's just get you charged, identified and bailed and we're done for today.'

Beautiful.

A muscle started to twitch above Godfrey's right eye. He turned away from Jessy, towards Richard, who he obviously viewed as the officer with authority. 'You can't charge me,' he hissed. 'I did not hire anyone to kill anyone.'

'Yes, well, thanks for clearing that up,' said Richard. 'But sadly, we don't believe you. You've said nothing to persuade us otherwise, and we do have evidence. We have Mr Robilliard's statement that you hired him to kill Angela Constantine, and that that was exactly what he attempted to do. That's more than sufficient evidence to persuade me to charge you with Lily's murder. If you're innocent, a jury can sort that out. You've got a pretty good chance of getting off, we agree.' Richard did not reveal a shred of the glee I knew he would – or should – be feeling. He wasn't the type of person to gloat. 'Don't worry, we'll give you bail, just as soon as we're done with the paperwork, you know. And all the procedural stuff.'

I smiled to myself.

Godfrey shook his head. 'No.'

'Come on, Mr Godfrey, you know we need to do our jobs.'

It wasn't really the charging or the paperwork Godfrey was worried about. What he was worried about, belatedly, was the Western Australian *Criminal Investigation (Identifying People) Act*. That handy piece of legislation provided for the forcible collection of a DNA profile and fingerprints, among other things, from a person charged with an offence. And it had done since 2002.

Richard and Jessy waded into the charging process.

'You are requested to consent to an identifying procedure being done on you,' Richard began before launching into a memorised recital of the matters he was required by the act to inform Godfrey of. I watched Godfrey's face as Richard injected as little enthusiasm into his monologue as he possibly could. *Information derived from the procedure may be compared with or put in a forensic database ...*

Godfrey was looking stressed and scatty. His hitherto steely composure was crumbling like a pile of pick-up sticks.

As Richard continued, I thought about Lil, waking from a light sleep to the sight of the behemoth that was Leon Charles Robilliard leaning over her, the knife scraping between her ribs for the first time before she had even the chance to scream. *The procedure may provide evidence that could be used in a court against you ...* She'd have struggled, but he'd have held her down effortlessly with one burly arm, while he used the other to stab until the struggling stopped. *If you do not consent or withdraw your consent to the procedure you may be arrested, and the procedure may be done on you against your will ...*

She'd have run out of strength at some point before she actually died, and she'd have lain there, watching Robilliard as he made sure the job was finished.

Yes, Godfrey was panicking now, I could see it in his eyes. But his trauma was nothing compared to what Lil would've experienced as she felt her life slipping away, her body wracked with unendurable pain.

'Do you understand all this, Mr Godfrey?'

Godfrey's eyes flitted back and forth between the two police officers who faced him. I sensed he was about to lose it. If he still had a gun, he'd be pulling it out right about now.

Slowly, he nodded.

'Are you consenting?'

'Yes.'

They messed around for a while with photographs, swabs and then ink. The swabs and the prints were handed to a uniform who took them away. I wondered just how long it would take for those fingerprints to be *compared with a forensic database*.

Richard looked at Godfrey and sighed. 'Now, Mr Godfrey, I don't want to be a smartarse, and I expect you're probably not in the habit of accepting legal advice from the police, but I'm going to say this anyway. If you're a bit worried your prints might match up to any currently on our database in connection with any unsolved murders –'

'Such as, say, the shooting of a man three times in the head,' offered Jessy.

'Yes, that sort of thing. In those circumstances, well ... you might do best to be helpful. As helpful *generally* as you possibly could be. Your whole defence to the charge of murdering Lily Constantine rests on the fact that you're a model citizen, and your word should be believed over that of Leon Robilliard. Were you to be convicted of another murder –'

'Such as, say, the murder of Michael Allan Frazer.'

Richard nodded. 'Yes, well then your status as a model citizen is going to be under threat, wouldn't you agree?'

Godfrey faced Richard without moving a muscle.

Come on, Mr Godfrey. Just cough. It won't hurt a bit. It looked like he was giving it some thought. The cogs were trying to turn; there was just a question of whether he could pull together some coherent frontal lobe activity while also panicking.

Finally, he made a decision.

'Frazer was threatening *me*,' he hissed.

Yes. I jumped up and did a little dance in the observation room, safe in the knowledge no one could see me.

'Maybe so, Mr Godfrey,' said Jessy without missing a beat. 'But not in a way that would justify the use of deadly force, it would seem. Of course, I don't know, I'm just a cop. But you will recall the killer of Michael Allan Frazer was described by a particular senior barrister in town, on the public record, as *a savage, ruthless assassin*.' She met Godfrey's gaze as he turned to face her. 'Correctly, in my view. And I can safely say from experience that the courts are unlikely to allow that type of a person ever to experience freedom again unless he shows remorse by cooperating with our investigations.' She glared at Godfrey while she let that sink in, then continued. 'Furthermore, there's the matter of the attempted murder of Andrew Deacon in a City of Perth car park a couple of hours ago.' She leaned down to face Godfrey, eye to eye. 'Trust me, I agree with you. Mr Deacon can be *extremely* annoying at times and is often quite persistent in the face of clear instructions to the contrary.'

'But you really ought to know by now, sir.' Richard gave a theatrical sigh. 'CCTV is a thing.'

CHAPTER 31

'I was going to leave a USB in his unit for the police to find. But once I got there, I found he has a desktop computer which he doesn't have password protected at all. So I put everything onto the computer. Once that was done I sent him an email at work which carried a keylogger. When he opened the attachment the keylogger installed itself on his computer and I was able to observe his keystrokes. It wasn't too hard to work out which of them might have been the password to his file management software. Once I had that, I arranged to visit his office to discuss a file. When he went to the toilet I logged on and sent the email, attaching copies of the images from the DPP database.'

'You're a bit of a computer whiz, then?'

Godfrey looked at Jessy like he didn't appreciate the sarcasm, even though I could tell she was trying to minimise it. 'I understand the basics.'

'Just seems like an odd skill for a lawyer to have. I'm sure you can type a letter and reply to an email. But what you're talking about isn't *the basics*, is it? Surely not just any mug could get a keylogger past the DPP's firewall?'

I already knew the guy was a computer whiz. But Jessy was right. The reason why was not clear. I remembered Angie's words, again.

Was it photos that he emailed?

What had she remembered just before she asked me that? What had she seen? Something odd on his computer, something that hadn't meant much the time she first noticed it, but which came back into her mind when she learned what he'd done to me. It answered a question in her mind. Perhaps one she didn't even know was there.

Godfrey leaned back in his chair, crossing the ankle of one pinstriped leg over the knee of the other, his crisply dry-cleaned attire and shiny leather shoes seeming to belie the brutality of the offences Jessy was getting ready to charge him with. 'I'm not just any mug,' he said, his voice low and gravelly.

'What do you use these skills for?'

Godfrey stared at her for a long moment. 'Listen, I'm happy to cooperate, Detective, but how about you try to keep your questions relevant?'

Jessy lowered her head submissively. I suspected her intention was to give him the impression he was in control. In fact, he had precious little control remaining over the course his life would take, but she didn't particularly want him to throw his hands up and ask himself why he was even bothering to talk to her. Not just yet, anyway.

'Sorry,' she said. 'So why did you hire a hit man to kill Angie?'

'Why the hit man? Or why Angie?'

'Both. Let's start with the hit man. You shot Frazer yourself, when he came around to your house and blackmailed you. Why didn't you kill Angie yourself?'

'I shot Frazer because I had to. He was on my property, demanding money, making all sorts of threats, and my wife was due home. It was a matter of necessity that he be dispensed with. I did the world a favour with that one, though I know the constabulary doesn't see it like that, other than when it suits you.'

'You didn't want to kill Angie yourself?'

'Not particularly. I don't *enjoy* killing people, Detective. I'm not a serial killer that does it for fun. I'm a killer by necessity. I've been forced to do it because people won't stop making a nuisance of themselves. It impacts on my enjoyment of life, and that of my family.'

I shivered. If that was all it took to get yourself killed by him, it really was a wonder I was still around. I suspected the real reason he'd hired a killer for Angie was so he could ensure he had an alibi, which meant he had premeditated not only the killing, but his own defence as well. I wasn't surprised he'd chosen not to volunteer that information. It was unlikely to go over well with a sentencing judge.

'So, you convinced Leon Robilliard to do the job for you?'

'Yes.'

'Did you decide to kill her before or after you killed Frazer?'

'I was only dealing with Frazer because of Angie. After the confrontation with him in my *home*, of all places, I felt it was all getting a bit inconvenient and I just ... I felt like she was starting to become more trouble than she was worth.'

Was he lying about his reason for killing her? I stared at him. My ability to pick a liar may indeed be finely honed through years of working in law, but it didn't cope too well with the one per cent of our population who are psychopaths. For an observer to be able to identify a liar there needs to be some degree of awareness on the part of the liar that what they're doing is wrong.

Surely if he was worried about the effect he was having on her mentally, he needed only to tell her he'd decided to stop what he was doing to her. It should have been obvious to him – as it was to me – she'd have got clean with Lil's help and then there'd be every reason to expect she'd keep her mouth shut about the drugs, the theft and the rape for the rest of her life.

I wondered if she'd asked him about whatever she stumbled across on his computer. Had she raised it with him, and in so doing, signed her own death warrant?

'As a junior barrister, years ago, I'd represented Leon Robilliard on a particularly nasty assault charge, and I'd been impressed at the time by his ruthless streak. He was the type of man who would pull limbs off kittens. I decided he would kill Angie for me. I thought the easiest way to do business with him would be to frame him for an offence, so I could get him off it. At that time, of course, the police had no leads on who'd killed poor Mr Frazer, and they weren't trying all that hard to find any, either. So, I planted the gun at Robilliard's house and tipped off the police, so they'd charge him. I needed to be able to get him acquitted, of course, so he would be able to do the job for me that I needed done, and that's not easy when you're claiming to have been framed, so I left my prints on the gun to give me enough room to create reasonable doubt in the minds of the jury.'

'You left your own prints on that gun *deliberately*?'

'Well, I couldn't exactly get someone else to donate their prints, could I?'

Jessy seemed a bit stunned by this. I too was astounded by the arrogance of the man.

'I didn't expect you would ever have my prints on your database.'

CHAPTER 32

Lily Constantine had called in sick the day she was murdered. Because she'd called in sick, she was in bed asleep at the time *the type of man who would pull limbs off kittens* entered her home, and solely as a result of that, she was stabbed to death.

She called in sick as a direct result of the fact that she met me.

I sat down at my kitchen table with a bowl of cornflakes for breakfast. It was nine o'clock in the morning. I'd listened last night to about seven and a half hours of Jessy's interview with Godfrey before I decided I was just too tired and sore and had to go home. As a potential witness – at least in respect of the offences against me – the cops should never have let me observe the interview, but I didn't care if it compromised those cases. I wasn't interested in pursuing them anyway. And I doubted I would ever be called to give evidence about the time I spent with Lil the night before her death. That she received a call from someone I thought she called Sam was not sufficiently probative, and too unreliable, to ever get past a directions hearing and before a jury.

And hopefully there would be no directions hearing or trial. It wasn't uncommon for punters to comprehensively cough, then plead not guilty, but Godfrey wasn't your average punter. I was confident he wouldn't make a mistake, then try to wriggle out of it. If he coughed it was because he knew that, strategically, it was the best thing for him to do. He wasn't likely to change his mind, least of all because it would necessarily mean the brilliant Samuel Godfrey SC had made an error of professional judgment. No, he would do what all lawyers did in the face of an apparent balls-up.

Forge on regardless and pretend it was deliberate.

I left last night without saying anything to Jessy or to Richard; I just had uniforms show me out. I didn't particularly want to give them an excuse to remember about arresting me, though I was pretty hopeful that wouldn't happen given Godfrey's confessions about sending the offending emails from my work computer and breaking into my home.

The dead flowers still sat in the vase in the centre of the table, their petals dry, their stems slimy with decay. I hadn't done anything about them before the Schneider trial and I didn't know if I would do anything about them now. Getting fresh ones would possibly be the best way forward, but the strata manager had installed security cameras to monitor the flowerbeds in my absence and I didn't fancy another brush with the law at this stage, even if it was only for pinching a few hydrangeas. I rested my elbows on the table and let my head fall into my hands.

I'm sorry Lil.

By refusing to admit to Godfrey that she knew anything about what he was doing to Angie, she'd unwittingly taken herself off his hit list. She should have been okay. She would have been, had she not met me. I'd thought I was the only one who could help her – or could at least bring her killer to justice. But I had put Lil in the path of that train in the first place.

I tried to swallow a mouthful of cornflakes, but they'd already gone too soft. The smell of the decayed flowers in front of me limited my tolerance for gluggy cornflakes. I thought about Angie. I hadn't spoken to her since the interview. I knew she'd be a bit of a mess. Lil wouldn't have died were it not for meeting me, but it was also true that she wouldn't have died were it not for Angie's cocaine dependency and the theft. Lil's death had almost cost me my freedom, and I supposed I could be angry at Angie over that, but it seemed hypocritical. She was an addict. She'd have got clean long ago if she hadn't been manipulated by someone determined to see her remain addicted. I was addicted to Vicodin, on the other hand, through my own reckless stupidity. I thought I was clever, popping pills like a real junkie, being the bad-ass I'd never had the chance to be until now. Really, I was nothing more than a spoilt brat, just like Sally had tried to explain to me, with no idea how good I had it and had always had it right from the very start. I'd fucked up my head along with my body without a backwards glance, when people like Russ fought battles all their lives that the likes of people like me couldn't imagine, just to live a normal life. There was no question I'd hurt those I loved, those who trusted me. I may not have stolen from my family, but I wrecked my brother's honeymoon, caused Jessy to do shit that could've got her sacked, and worried both her and my family for weeks. And if anyone ever found out that Rod had supplied me with drugs, and was continuing to do so ... well, then, I'd pretty much fitted him up for a serious criminal charge. Would it make it any better that I'd only wrecked Rod's life after Sam had wrecked mine?

I picked up my new phone and sent Jessy a text: *Is Angie okay?*

I stared at my reflection in the black pool of the phone's glass while I waited for her to reply. Jessy and I hadn't been alone together since I'd gone to the police station on Monday to talk to the cops about Schneider. Even then it was only for a minute, and before that it'd been – well, it felt like it was perhaps in a past life that we'd been intimate on any kind of equal footing. Her pointing a gun at my head in a dark alleyway had certainly been intimate, but not in the kind of way I really wanted.

I didn't think she wanted to be alone with me. I could hardly press the point. I had nothing to offer her. I'd have to have the hide of a rhinoceros to ask her out again now. The old me probably would've had that kind of hide.

She replied within a few minutes: *She will be. She asked the same thing about you.*

I wasn't really sure what to say about that. I was not okay, on any objective measure of the word. My wounds were almost fully healed, but I was not looking good on account of my addiction. I'd been permitted to do the Schneider trial because the cops had somehow, without telling him why, convinced Rufus they needed me. But I doubted that meant Rufus would be willing to give me my job back on any permanent kind of basis. And I couldn't even think about trying to beg for it back, at least not until I'd been to rehab. Rod had woken me with a phone call at quarter to six this morning to tell me that he'd wangled me a spot in a sixty-day inpatient program starting next week. The program was going to cost twenty-five thousand dollars. The first thing that was going to happen was medical personnel were going to help me get through the process of withdrawal with as little pain as possible.

I wasn't looking forward to that. It sounded worse than getting beaten up in a car park.

Amanda wants to talk to you. So do her parents. Do you feel up to it this morning?

I texted back: *Sure. Of course.*

~

I met Amanda, in a kind of perverse déjà vu, in the foyer of the police station. Jessy had asked me to turn up at eleven o'clock and ask for her. Amanda was at the end of the queue as I joined it.

She looked tired. Without makeup, her face appeared sallow, her eyes sunken and dark.

'You look like I feel,' she said.

It was the sort of comment only a lady could get away with, so I refrained from giving her a *right back at you*. I wondered if she'd slept since her husband was arrested.

'Is he out on bail?'

She shook her head. 'No, the police said they were always going to refuse him bail on the Frazer charge, since the evidence was compelling even without the confession. He's going before a magistrate on Monday, but he says he won't get bail then either.'

I nodded. That was a bit of a relief.

'I'm sorry.'

'No, I'm happy about it.' She gave a wan smile. 'It's for the best that he's in custody. I can take the children to visit him, so they're coping okay for the moment. But I need some time together with my family. With Angie and my brothers and my parents. We all love Angie and we're going to be okay, but we need to have some time together to work things out.'

'Sure.'

She turned towards a couple of children who were sharing an iPad on the seats at the far side of the waiting area, and called to them. They came over, a boy and a girl, perhaps seven or eight years of age. The girl looked like her mother, which meant she also looked like her aunt. Like the daughter Lil was never going to have the chance to have.

'This is my daughter Bella, and my son Marco,' said Amanda. 'This is Mr Deacon.'

I gave the kids my best smile, though I knew they were unlikely to be too impressed with me, since I was the man responsible for getting their dad locked up. 'How's it going?' Kids were not usually my area of expertise. 'Looking after your mum?' I enquired, before feeling guilty for making her happiness their responsibility.

'Yes, Mr Deacon,' they both sang, then they took off again. They were good kids, well brought up. Their dad was a murderer. It was unlikely they knew the details of that just yet, but I wondered how screwed up their lives would ultimately be as a result of what he'd done. More victims.

I looked at Amanda's brown eyes, so like Lil's. 'I feel responsible for what happened to Lil,' I told her.

Amanda gave a hollow laugh. 'Andrew, Angie feels responsible, I feel responsible because I'm the one who brought that ... brought him into our family. My parents feel responsible because they could not protect her, as parents always want to do. My brothers feel the same. Sam is the one who ... did this, and he's the only one who doesn't feel anything at all. But you brought him to justice. We will always be grateful to you for that. And so will Lil.'

Right now, Amanda would be trying to hold it together for her children, for her parents, trying to deal with the police, the family lawyers, the media, trying to help Angie while she began to come to terms with what had happened to Lil. Her life right now would be a circus. But it felt like she had spoken to me from her heart.

I knew she was a passionate woman. She had a fiery temper just like Lil. But I knew she wasn't lying when she told me how much she loved Lil. They all loved her desperately, this woman I'd known for less than a day.

'Where are your parents?'

'They're coming. They're just parking.'

'Amanda, can you do me a favour? Can you tell them that I will see them after I've been to rehab? I don't want to see them now. I didn't think it mattered but ... I'm sorry ... now I feel like it does.'

Her eyes were still locked with mine. She nodded. 'I'll go and stop them.' She took one of my hands in hers and gave it a brief squeeze. 'It's okay, Andrew. I am sorry for the way I treated you.'

I smiled, but I felt a bit like I was going to lose it. Meeting Amanda properly had been unexpectedly emotional. I realised I needed some time to prepare for her parents.

When I saw them again, I wanted to look like a man who had, if only for a very short time, been worthy of their daughter.

~

I knocked on Darren Ashwin's front door after lunch for what I knew would be the last time. I didn't need Vicodin. Rod had been keeping me in supplies until now, which was handy, since I'd been going through twenty-five pills a day.

'I'm going to rehab,' I said. 'Do you want to come with me?'

Of all my drug-addicted friends, Angie was the obvious choice to ask to join me on a two-month rehab date. She clearly needed to get her shit together just as much as I did. I wasn't keen to do that for a few reasons. Part of it was that I didn't like the idea of being cooped up with her in a residential facility for any length of time. I felt she would be a distraction. It wasn't like there had been any particular sexual tension between us, perhaps due to us both having other things on our minds, but I'd been attracted to Lil and I was worried I might be attracted to her too and I just ... I could see myself getting sidetracked and running the risk that my life would turn to shit again. And I wanted a simple life.

But the main reason I didn't want to take her with me was that she didn't need me to. Like me, Angie was lucky. If she wanted to get clean, she could do so with the support of her family. They could no doubt cobble together the funds, and they had plenty of love to give her.

Ashwin, on the other hand, had nothing. All his money went up his arm, and he had no one to put their hand in their pocket or give him some moral support, other than maybe Millie. She had a house, but I couldn't see her mortgaging it to put someone who wasn't even her kid through rehabilitation.

'It costs money, dunnit?'

I nodded. 'But I'll pay for you, if you want to come.'

Ashwin stared at me for a short moment. 'Listen, man, thanks. But no.'

'Do you want to think about it? I mean, if you –'

'Mr Deacon, I really appreciate the offer to help me. But the answer's no.'

'If you change your mind ...'

'I'll come see you, man. If I change my mind, I'll come see you. But, you know, I can't read real well. I can't do what you normal people do.'

'Yeah, I know.' I supposed things wouldn't necessarily be straightforward for Darren Ashwin. He might get clean, but what would he do then? Who would give a job to an illiterate ex-junkie with an eye-watering criminal record? And even if they did, it wouldn't last. His anger management problem would mean he couldn't work in a team, and he couldn't work for a supervisor. Adult literacy classes, anger management counselling, vocational training, I supposed it was all possible. And maybe it would all work, if the public purse felt inclined to pay for it all, and Darren ever felt inclined to embark on it.

But at the moment he had a job, and he did it quite well.

'If you need anything in the future,' said Ashwin, 'I'm your man, don't forget.'

Oh, that so wasn't going to be necessary. 'Thanks, Darren.'

He smiled. He'd heard all this shit a million times before. He knew how things went.

I just hoped he was wrong about me.

CHAPTER 33

'Your treatment will follow a standard program,' Nurse Chelsey informed me, her reading glasses shoved to the top of her head through masses of curly blond hair. 'It involves a thorough intake process including assessment of your overall medical and mental condition. After intake is complete, you'll undergo supervised detoxification, then group and individual therapy. You can choose whether or not you want to receive the benefit of support groups. Then you'll be afforded our full aftercare program.'

'Okay,' I said. My father patted me on the shoulder. He'd been doing it a lot ever since the decision was made not to proceed with charges against me on the basis that the chances of conviction were so low it wasn't in the public interest to proceed. Meanwhile, Mum kept squeezing my hand.

'That will normally include continued therapy in a group or individual setting and participation in support groups, if you so choose.'

'Sounds good.'

'It will also address any professional, legal, medical or financial issues that may have arisen due to your Vicodin abuse.'

I nodded. 'That would be handy. There's been a couple of those.'

Chelsey frowned. 'There is a limit to the services we provide.'

I didn't care, really. 'That's cool.'

Dad made a funny noise then. I glanced at him and saw his eyes were brimming with tears. 'You're going to be okay, Andrew,' he whispered. 'Everything's going to be okay. You'll get through this.'

'I know, Dad, it's fine, honestly.' I watched as Mum took his hand too and gripped it just as hard. 'Don't worry about me.'

'You can speak with family and friends any time you like, by phone,' Chelsey confirmed. 'And most times in person too. You just need to make an appointment.'

'See, there you go. I'll stay in touch. It'll be fine, I promise. I'll be back on track before you know it.'

Mum nodded. 'We'll come and see you as often as we can.'

'That'd be great. And I'm sure Rod will visit too.'

'Of course he will,' said Mum. 'And Jessy too I hope.'

'Jessy?' I hadn't expected Mum to remember her name.

'Your friend, the police officer. The nice lady you brought to Rod's wedding.'

'Oh, I remember who she is.' Usually Mum only remembered the names of local lasses, and if she did, it was only their surname, as in "the girl McFarlane". 'I don't know. I'd really like to see her. But I don't know if she'll visit.'

'We could ask her if you like?'

Yikes. 'Thanks Mum, but there's no need.'

Mum nodded again. She was fishing around in her handbag for a tissue for Dad. I remembered he'd been caught short and had used his hanky to check the oil in the ute before we departed for the semi-rural utopia of the rehab centre this morning, so I passed him mine.

'It's great that you still carry a handkerchief,' Chelsey observed as Dad blew his nose. 'Sometimes attention to hygiene tends to suffer in the severely addicted.'

Wow, Chelsey really knew how to compliment a guy. 'No, I'm still pretty good with showering and stuff, as long as I'm not living in my car,' I confirmed.

Chelsey was around my age, and attractive by anyone's standards. Once upon a time I wouldn't have wasted a second in hitting on her. Now I couldn't have cared less about the idea. It wasn't that I didn't want to get laid. Since my wounds had started to heal, I'd found myself feeling more and more like getting that side of my life back on track. But I felt distracted. I wanted Jessy to look at me the way she had the night before Rod's wedding, the night we slept in my childhood bedroom with the Transformers on the wall.

'So, if you can just sign here, thanks, Andrew,' Chelsey finished, pushing a clipboard across the desk in my direction. The forms I had to sign were on the front. A pen was tied to the board with sticky tape wrapped around and around its barrel to prevent unauthorised removal. I picked it up and signed. I wondered how many people had signed before me with that pen, hoping – believing – they were just about to get their life back on track.

CHAPTER 34

Two months later, I wrapped up my final group session, and made my way down towards the reception area, where Rod was meant to be picking me up. I knew Mum and Dad would probably come too. They'd make some kind of celebration out of it, like it was a big special occasion. *Andrew's graduated from rehab! Yay!* I had only a backpack of stuff on me, but I knew my old life, or most of it, was waiting for me. The counsellors had helped negotiate with Rufus for my return to work, which he'd reluctantly permitted. I suspected he figured it was the only way he'd ever get these touchy-feely types to stop coming around to his office for daily collaborative goal-focused dialogue about my future. I had a wardrobe full of suits ready to go, and I was fitting back into most of them again on account of having regained the weight I'd lost. I looked into the mirror before I left my room. My body no longer felt weak or damaged. I'd been taking a long run each morning and hanging out at the gym during the day. I looked good. I *looked* like the old Drew.

Mum and Dad had visited me a lot over the past two months, and so had Rod, and Ellen, who was going to have a baby. Matthew came once. Russ came a few times on weekends and made me participate in runs that made the City to Surf feel like a cool-down jog. Even Richard came around to let me know that Godfrey's prints had matched those on the Frazer weapon and the tracky pants turned out to be splattered with Lil's blood and DNA. On the back of that, both Godfrey and Robilliard had pleaded guilty to Lil's murder and Godfrey had also pleaded guilty to the murder of Michael Frazer. Sentencing was to take place in the coming weeks and Darren Ashwin's testimony wouldn't even be required. Ashwin, I knew, would be pleased about that. Richard asked if I wanted to press charges on the unauthorised entry and transfer to my computer of child exploitation material, which amounted at the very least to burglary and to which Godfrey had also confessed, as well as the attempted murder in the car park though, he confirmed, Godfrey still hadn't coughed on the bashing. Protecting his goons. I said I'd think about it.

Jessy was the only one who didn't visit, and she didn't call either.

I only had myself to blame, but it sucked, nevertheless.

I had a bad feeling from the start that Matthew would ask her out, taking full advantage of my two-month absence. He'd made it clear he was attracted to her. Matthew and I were friends, or at least I thought we were, but he'd never been the type of guy you would rely on in that or any department.

When he actually showed up to visit me, I felt physically sick. He pretended he'd turned up to see how I was, but after three quarters of an hour of painful small talk I decided giving up Vicodin was easier than enduring another minute of this. As I was shuffling him towards the door, he said: 'Oh, also, me and Jessy are together. I hope you don't mind. I knew you guys never really got it together, so ...'

He trailed off as if he was expecting me to interject at that point with some kind of *no problems mate, whatever*. There was a long, awkward silence.

'I wanted to be with her,' I said eventually. I was quite sure Matthew was under no illusions about how I felt about her.

'Yeah, sorry, mate. You know, it's ...'

'Yeah.' Every man for himself, evidently.

I'd stood at the window watching Matthew's Mercedes roll down the driveway and pass through the front gates, turning left to head back to the real world.

That'd been two weeks ago.

'Hey, are you heading home today?' Chelsey said now, spotting me staring out of the same window. 'I forgot ... here ...' She reached into her pocket and pulled out a pen and a scrap of paper. She scribbled something on it. I knew what it was.

She smiled as she pressed the note into my hand. 'Let me know if you ever want to catch up on a Friday evening,' she said. 'I finish work at six.'

I nodded. I wasn't sure if that was even legal. 'Thanks, Chelsey. Thanks for looking after me.'

'Hey, no problem.'

I couldn't believe she wanted to go out with me, after seeing me at my absolute worst on more than one occasion over the past two months. Chelsey was out of the league of the man I was in there. I was happy to see the back of her, actually, because she reminded me of him. Without her looking back at me each day with my reflection in her eyes, I had a chance of forgetting that I was and had ever been that pathetic, crying, screaming, sweating creature.

CHAPTER 35

I walked into my office the following day with as much of my old swagger as I could muster. Which was, in summary, not that much. I felt like everyone was staring at me. The only one who spoke to me was Sally. She handed me a coffee and updated me privately on the nature of all the rumours that were flying around about me. I told her I was grateful, which I was. It was the nicest thing she'd ever done for me. Rufus welcomed me back, but his tight-lipped grimace gave me the impression he'd resolved to withhold judgment on whether letting me come back to work was a good idea until I proved it to him.

I wondered how long I had available to achieve that. A day? A week?

'Right, well, best get cracking,' I said to him, giving him what I hoped was a confident grin. 'What've you got for me?'

'Come into my office,' he said. 'We need to talk.'

Matthew pretended he hadn't seen me as I followed Rufus past his cubicle, making out like he was totally engrossed in his document even though it was only twenty past seven and I knew Matthew wasn't due to do any substantial work for at least an hour and a half. I felt like a kid getting busted by the principal, wishing I'd talked my mum into letting me quit school rather than return to face the music. The one good thing was that the detail of most of the rumours Sally had collated was actually better, not worse, than the real situation.

I stared at Rufus across his desk.

He stared at me.

'Am I going to regret this?' he demanded eventually.

I felt tired already. 'I don't know, Rufus.'

He said nothing for a while. I wasn't sure what he expected from me, since I'd answered his question. 'Do you intend to make any attempt to convince me I've done the right thing by letting you back here?' he asked eventually.

'I don't sense anything I say will give you much comfort. I can only prove myself to you by getting back to work. Which I will do as soon as I'm excused from this meeting.'

My boss's brow furrowed as he glared at me. 'Alright. Fine. Sam Godfrey has pleaded guilty to both the Frazer and the Constantine murders. He'll be sentenced on all charges next Thursday, along with Robilliard. I want you to meet with the prosecutor and the investigating police on the murders, and the guys from the Online Child Exploitation Squad and help prepare for the sentencing. The charges are quite disparate. We need to make sure the homicide submissions don't contradict those for the child exploitation charges. And *you* need to make sure neither of us have missed anything.'

I was confused. The OCE Squad? *Child exploitation*? Had Rufus mixed up Godfrey's charges with the Schneider case? Godfrey was Schneider's lawyer, not his co-accused. In any case, Schneider had never sold any of his productions online. He was too stupid to work out how to use the internet. 'What does the OCE Squad have to do with Godfrey?'

Rufus frowned. 'Didn't Richard tell you? There are some extra charges against Godfrey.'

'Extra charges? About what?'

Had they charged him for sending the Schneider pics to me? Surely not without speaking to me first. Unless ...

Was it photos that he emailed?

'He was *selling* the photos we sent him?' I wasn't sure why it was such a shock. After all, we knew the guy was a murderer. But this seemed ... just too awful.

Rufus reached into his filing cabinet and pulled out a thick file. He passed it to me. I opened it to find two confronting photographs of young girls. Rufus hadn't bothered warning me, presumably because he was pissed at me. The photos looked like Schneider's style, but they weren't ones I'd seen before.

'The same day you were charged over the Schneider pictures being emailed to you, Crime Stoppers got a call from a woman who later agreed to be identified as Angela Constantine,' he said, while I flicked through the remainder of the file. 'She gave them two pieces of information. Firstly, she told them she'd had the opportunity to look at the personal laptop of someone she knew. She noticed he'd downloaded two unusual programs. One was a private browser called Tor, which is of course a browser used to access the dark web. The other was a metadata removal tool. As you might know, the presence of Tor on its own doesn't mean much. Anyone can download it and although it can be used to visit the dark web, it's also commonly used by law-abiding people to protect their regular browsing habits.'

'Okay.'

'But the metadata stripping software is a bit unusual. A standard operating system's built-in functionality for clearing EXIF data from images is more than sufficient for most people wanting to upload a few pics to Facebook without giving away where they live. Angela knew the man she was calling about was not a professional or amateur photographer and though he might need to view metadata from time to time in the course of his work, he certainly didn't need to strip it.'

'And the second piece of information?'

'Was the fact that the man she was calling about was the same man you were at that time alleging had emailed child exploitation material to your email address from your work computer.'

That must have been around the day I met Angie outside The Den and told her what I believed Sam had done to me. I'd seen something in her eyes that told me she'd remembered something. Now I knew what it was. She'd remembered seeing that metadata stripping program installed on Sam's laptop. She'd gone home and either that night or the next day, she'd called Crime Stoppers to tell them what she knew.

I wondered why she'd done that.

She had a barrage of problems at the time. She was dealing with her drug addiction and likely serious money problems arising out of that, the grief and anger associated with her sister's violent death, the threat of Sam coming after her too. Worry for her family, regret over everything that'd happened with Sam, anxiety about whether to pursue charges over what Sam had done to her. It seemed far-fetched to think she rang Crime Stoppers to try to help me. If anything, I was making her problems worse.

No, I reckoned she'd rung Crime Stoppers because she was sick of Sam Godfrey abusing her, and though she wasn't quite ready to sit in the witness box and be called a liar, she was ready to fight back. The moment she knew she had something on him, she fought back.

'So, the OCE Squad thought that was interesting enough to call Richard and ask about your complaint,' said Rufus, getting to his feet to stick a pod in the Nespresso machine he'd installed in his office in my absence and which apparently no one else was allowed to use, even if they brought their own pods. 'They asked to see what we'd found on your computer and recognised it all from prosecutions on which Godfrey had been engaged. On the strength of that, along with Angela's tipoff, and the fact that Richard and Jessy had confirmed Godfrey was most likely in your office at the time the emails were sent, and had lied about his departure time, they decided to set a trap for our Mr Godfrey. The cops manipulated the metadata to look authentic then used image steganography to encode a message into those photos you just saw. Then they sent the images to us and we disclosed them to Sam Godfrey in the Schneider proceedings. Subsequently we told him we wouldn't be proceeding in connection with those photos, but of course they were in Godfrey's hands by then.'

I doubted Angie understood at the time she first saw it what the presence of that software on Godfrey's laptop might mean for him. If she had, she'd have known from the start she was Sam's real target. I wondered what she said to him at the time. Was it a question? *How* come you need to remove metadata from photos? Or a throwaway comment? *You should lock your laptop while you're on the john, Sam. Anyone can see what shit you're up to.* Or did he simply walk into a room and come across her on his computer? Did he glance over her shoulder and see she'd found the program, seconds before she slammed it shut and apologised for snooping?

Whatever it was that was said that day, he knew that she knew about the program. And that was enough, I had absolutely no doubt, to motivate him to make the decision to kill her. Our conversation outside The Den was the moment she realised what Sam might be doing with the photographs he'd been supplied as evidence in prosecutions against his clients. Perhaps she'd wondered then, if only for a fleeting moment as I started to tell her about my email getting hacked, whether her sister's husband had tried to murder her.

'How'd they find the images again?' Trawling through the dark web looking for two images in particular sounded like a gruesome job. Allocating it to one or two individuals could leave them scarred for life.

'The dark web is not as large as people think,' said Rufus. 'It's actually small compared to the rest of the web. And they did have help from the FBI and other international partners, and some software that helped. They found them alright. He'd uploaded them within hours of receiving them from the cops. He'd stripped the metadata, as expected, but he wasn't expecting steganographic content in the images.'

'Even if he was it would've been hard for him to find,' I observed. I didn't know much about ciphers, over and above what every enthusiastic teenaged boy devours about cryptography, the Enigma machine and World War II. But I did know that digital image steganography – the encoding of a message in an image – was very difficult to detect even with the right programs. It involved manipulating single pixels, so that, for example, the colour of every hundredth pixel might be changed to correspond to a letter in the alphabet. The changes to the image would be invisible. 'I think it comes down to statistical analysis, doesn't it? And we all know lawyers are not good at maths.'

Rufus shrugged. 'Yeah, well anyway, they got him with it. They compared the data files for the images they'd located on the dark web to the original images supplied to Godfrey to easily reveal their little steganographic message. They could then trace back to Sam Godfrey the site where they found the images. It was a busy enterprise. He's been raking in the Bitcoin off the back of the evidence disclosed to him by the DPP every time he takes on a new child abuse case. We'll see what a sentencing judge makes of all that, but I think he or she will be impressed with the police work at least.'

'What did the message read?' I was sure the nerds at the OCE Squad would've been keen to insert a message which they considered to have some poignancy. Something like *Sam Godfrey is a pervert* would've been the obvious choice, but the DPP would have patiently explained to them that the message couldn't be something that might improperly influence a jury, lest the evidence be ruled inadmissible.

Rufus had made his coffee too hot, so he was cooling it by slurping it. Which was fine, since he was the boss. 'I don't know,' he said. 'It'll be in that file there somewhere. You know what those techie guys are like. It's probably something about *Star Wars* or *Star Trek*. I can't tell the difference between the two.'

I didn't know what to say to that, other than that I doubted the techie guys would've been willing to besmirch the name of either of those revered productions by having them associated with Sam Godfrey's grotty side-hustle. Whatever the message was, it'd be all over the papers in due course, so it would probably have been carefully conceived with help from the government's public relations guys.

'So, who's prosecuting?' I was ninety-nine per cent certain I knew already, what with the way my luck had been running for the past few months.

'Matthew Bridges.'

'Right. Of course. Good.'

'Talk to Matthew to find out when he's scheduled the meeting.'

'Of course.'

~

By ten o'clock that morning I was sitting at the far end of the meeting table while I waited for the others to turn up. Matthew, not surprisingly, didn't seem keen to indulge in idle chitchat so he'd gone out to the foyer to wait for the cops. I peeled yellow post-it stickers off a pad one by one and tore each into the smallest pieces I possibly could before sweeping them into my hand and then scattering them on the floor under the table.

Lil was dead. I was alive. I wished I was running through Kings Park, or out on the water right now, so perhaps I might feel it.

I looked up as Matthew, Richard and Jessy entered the room and took seats at various spots around the table. Jessy looked at me for a long moment, then looked away. She seemed anxious. They all murmured a greeting and I murmured one back.

The OCE guys arrived seconds later and took a seat. There were three of them. A woman and two men. I'd met one of the guys before. Chris Lim was his name. I was in awe of them all, really. I'd never want to have to do their job. All of them had probably spent many hours sitting at a computer pretending to be a teenaged child, slowly reeling in a paedophile, playing the long game to ensure he didn't slip off the hook. I remembered Chris had told me once he loved what he did, despite the ugliness of it all. He loved the thrill of the chase and he loved nothing more than finally landing a big fish so he could watch him suffocate on the shore.

'Listen, the first thing we want to say to you, Andrew, is that you've done a good job with this,' said Richard. 'I doubt anyone would've been convicted of any of these crimes, ever, were it not for your efforts.'

'Thank you, Richard,' I said, wondering since when Richard had ever given two shits about recognising the efforts of anyone, let alone a lawyer. It seemed weird that he wanted to be nice to me. 'I appreciate that you credit me with the demise of Godfrey's website, but I really didn't do anything on that other than make him mad enough to get careless with the uses he put these photos to. All credit for that one needs to go to Angela Constantine for calling Crime Stoppers.'

'Yes, but he wouldn't have been mad at you if you hadn't been pursuing him for the Constantine murder,' said Jessy. 'Look, we just wanted to say, we know you've sacrificed a lot, personally, to achieve this result. So it's important to us that we secure an appropriate penalty now.'

On hearing her voice, directed at me, I turned to look at her. Part of me was angry at her, but I knew I had no right to be. What could I say to her? Jess, look, I think it was really a bit bloody unfair that although we were in a deep and committed relationship of at least three weeks duration, you couldn't stick around through a couple of minor challenges. Granted, I was at various times suspected of a murder, obsessed with avenging the death of my last hook-up, unable to have proper sex, wanted by the police on child exploitation charges, addicted to prescription drugs and completely absent from the relationship emotionally, and generally also physically, for the duration of Operation Get Sam and my subsequent rehab. But geez, relationships are a two-way street you know, Jess. We each have to make a *bit* of an effort to make them work. 'I'm committed to securing an appropriate penalty,' I said to her. 'That's why I spent all morning reading your sentencing brief.'

She nodded. 'Have we missed anything?'

'No.'

Matthew watched the two of us observing each other for ten seconds or more before speaking. 'Yeah, well, Rufus wants us to go through it together, right? So, let's get started. Detective Simms? Detective Lim? Do you have the edited videos for us to review?'

The interview on the two murders alone had gone on for ten hours, so I sincerely hoped the videos had indeed been heavily edited. All the stuff about the offences against me would've gone, including the two and a half hours Jessy had devoted to grilling him about my bashing even though I'd told her not to bother, since he'd never confess in the absence of any evidence against him. 'Our one's been cut down to an hour,' said Richard, reading my mind.

'Ours is an hour and half,' said Chris.

Matthew nodded. 'Good. When we're all comfortable we've got the editing right on both we'll get them off to Godfrey's lawyer to check.'

So, I sat in an air-conditioned room with polished wooden furniture and panels on the walls, and a jug of water with seven glasses in the centre of the table. I watched the videos, and made some notes, and said nothing. I thought about water-skiing. I thought about the cool depths of the lake down south, the whisper of the ski sliding across the water, the sun striking the orange buoys, how the world tipped and rolled from side to side each time I set the ski onto the opposite edge and sliced across the wake.

That was six at thirty-five off, man. Fucking awesome! Can't believe you're skiing like a demon when you look like a hundred per cent shit.

The buoys, that day, two days before the Schneider trial and a week before rehab, were all I wanted, my whole and sole goal in life. I needed them; I threw myself into them with all the energy and determination of a man without options. I got one, and as soon as I did, I abandoned it in favour of the next, approaching each with increasing desperation. *Two. Three. Four. Five. Six. Gate. Slam dunk!* I pumped my fist into the air as the curtains of water I'd sent towards the sky with every turn settled back onto and into the lake like rain. I sunk below the surface.

I am alive. Lil is dead, but I am alive.

'Excuse me for a minute,' I said, standing. 'Can you pause? Sorry, yes, thanks Richard.'

I left the room, ignoring the stares of the others, and walked down the hallway to the end, where a glass window not designed to be opened offered an expansive view of the city. I looked beyond the high-rise buildings, to the escarpment.

'Hey, Drew, are you okay?'

I turned to see Jessy standing behind me. She was so small, so light. I felt enormous next to her. I could pick her up with one arm and toss her over my shoulder. I thought about the last time she'd allowed me to touch her, the last time I'd properly been able to make love to her.

It seemed like a lifetime ago.

'Are you sure your boyfriend will be happy for you to be out here talking with me?'

Her eyes, suddenly, were icy. 'I don't have to answer to you, Andrew, about who I date.'

I nodded, regretting saying something so childish, not to mention possessive. 'I know. I'm sorry.'

'I like Matthew.'

'Yes, he's a really nice guy. Do you want to go for a ski?'

She stared me like I was bonkers. 'What?'

'You know, water-skiing. Have you ever thought about trying it?'

She frowned. 'No, Drew, I haven't. But even if I wanted to, going water-skiing with you would be a date. I can't go on a date with you, because I have a boyfriend.'

'Oh, right, yeah. Sorry.'

This wasn't going well, but I supposed I had nothing to lose, so who cared. 'I know what you're thinking,' I said, turning back to look out the window. I knew she could walk off and leave me there, talking to myself, but I felt calmer when I looked up at the escarpment, shrouded by haze and with the promise of the rest of the world beyond it. 'You're thinking: *I won't let Andrew into my heart until he proves to me that he would fight as hard for me as he did for Lily Constantine.*'

She didn't reply.

'But I'm not going to stalk you, Jess,' I said. 'I'm not that kind of man. I'm not going to prove myself to you with flowers and chocolates and love letters you didn't ask for.'

'Good,' she said, her voice tiny. 'That's good news.'

I turned around to face her. 'I want you to dump Matthew and be with me. And I will prove it to you then. I will prove to you that I will be your best friend and the lover you deserve, and I will be the man you can always count on, no matter what happens. If you have a hard day at work, I will be there to listen. If you kill someone, I will give you an alibi. Jess, you're all I want.'

I wanted desperately to touch her, as she stood there trembling.

But she wasn't mine to touch. Matthew came out of the room and scurried up the hallway. He looked troubled to see Jess and I facing each other, not speaking.

Anything he said would've been lame, so wisely he chose to say nothing.

'Let's go back,' said Jessy. 'Get these submissions finished.'

I nodded. 'Sure.'

We sat through the rest of the videos and re-read forty pages of materials. Finally, Matthew wrapped up the meeting. As he tried to extract a police DVD from the audio-visual equipment – not an easy task for a fuckwit such as he was – Jessy took a yellow sticky note off the pad sitting on the desk in front of me and wrote something before passing the note to me. I slipped it into my shirt pocket. My pulse thudded through my veins.

'You're looking much better, Andrew,' said my new best friend Richard as he and Jessy left together, and Matthew ran after them to *see them off.*

'Yeah, thanks Rick,' I called after him, then sat down to read the note, my heart still beating hard like a schoolboy's.

Let me have a think about it. You, that is, not water-skiing. That one's a definite no.

EPILOGUE

SANTA
IS
REAL

They were the words – the *plaintext* as it was apparently called – that had been inserted into the bogus Schneider images by the tech gurus at the Online Child Exploitation Squad. Santa Claus, of course, evolved from the original historic Christian Saint Nicholas, the patron saint of children who was well known for his work in protecting them and their dignity.

He was also, I recalled from Sunday School, the patron saint of repentant thieves, though I doubted the OCE Squad knew that.

Coincidentally, Rocco Schneider was sentenced on the same day as Sam Godfrey and Leon Robilliard. Schneider was first on the list and I presented submissions on behalf of the prosecution. Audrey Simons was gracious enough to agree to represent Schneider on the sentencing, even though he'd previously sacked her in favour of Godfrey. She was briefed and funded by Legal Aid by reason of a serendipitous downturn in Schneider's personal fortunes since blowing all his money on Godfrey and winding up in prison when his bail was revoked following his trial.

Despite being armed with an extensive psychological report detailing his own childhood abuse and consequent problems, Schneider got seventeen years, with the possibility of parole after fourteen.

Godfrey and Robilliard were listed for after lunch. Godfrey had a token lawyer, though I expected he'd be making all his own calls without considering his lawyer's opinion at all. Robilliard was represented by Legal Aid even though I'd no doubt he had plenty of sources of income.

Godfrey wisely hadn't pushed for a psychological assessment, since it would not reveal he was driven by any factors arguably beyond his control, but rather that he was a man from a background of privilege who absolutely knew right from wrong. By his own admission he was prepared to off anyone who presented an inconvenience to him, and a psych report would probably assist only to identify a misplaced sense of entitlement and self-worth. His mother and father attended court. They were quite elderly and seemed confused by the proceedings. This despite the fact we hadn't even got started yet. They were assisted by a lady wearing a t-shirt emblazoned with the name of a pricey aged care facility in the western suburbs. She sat with them and tried to explain what was going on.

Amanda and Angie sat beside each other in the public gallery with their parents and their two brothers. The brothers were giving their funeral suits a second outing and both looked tired and stressed. Amanda's children weren't present. I saw Amanda reach for Angie's hand and squeeze it. Angie gave her a weak smile.

Millie was present for the sentencing of her son's killer. She was in her flogged-out old wheelchair. It was a heavy steel one, not one of the modern featherweight aluminium variety. Ashwin was with her, but he was struggling to get her wheelchair into the viewing gallery. I expected security would assist him, but they didn't. I helped him lift the chair, with Millie in it, up a couple of changes in level until we'd got her to a spot where she could see the proceedings. I was pretty sure Millie could've walked that last bit but she didn't see why she should and I supposed that was fair enough. I was glad I'd been working out while I was at rehab. I was sweating by the time I slipped my jacket back on and returned to sit behind Matthew at the bar table.

A throng of excited journalists filled the remaining space. This was, it seemed, the biggest news story of the year. It obviously wasn't just Richard who loved to see a defence lawyer hung out to dry.

Robilliard was the first to be led into the dock. Having not surprisingly been refused bail pending sentencing, he'd been transported to court that morning in a secure vehicle and come straight from the holding cells to the court room. He didn't look particularly worse for wear. Prison life was obviously something to which he was quite accustomed and had slotted straight back into with relative ease. After Audrey's plea in mitigation and submissions from Matthew in response, he was sentenced to twenty years for murdering Lil, with credit for time already served awaiting sentencing and discounts for a guilty plea and rolling on Godfrey. He flipped the bird in the direction of the judge, got another three months cumulative for that and was then led back to the cells to commence his time in maximum security.

Richard had told me he and Jessy felt there was realistically no chance of a successful prosecution on the assault against me, given I'd been in Robilliard's home. I didn't care that they weren't going to proceed with that. I wasn't keen to explain to a magistrate why I was there in the first place, and there was actually something extremely satisfying about the fact that a complaint that could never succeed was what had brought them both undone.

Godfrey was led out next. Unlike Robilliard, he seemed uncharacteristically flustered. I expected he'd be quite a popular man in prison due to his ability to advise all the prisoners on how to prepare their own defences and appeals. That assumed of course that he was able to get his act together and do so even if he wasn't being paid a thousand bucks an hour, or in fact anything, for his time. But he did not seem to be seeing the bright side. He wore the same suit he'd been in on the day he was arrested months ago, and it seemed way too big for him now, and needed a dry-clean. He looked thin and haggard. Possibly even, one could argue, beaten. The image of Lil's crime-scene pic flashed into my mind, and I reflected on the fact that everything Godfrey was going through and would go through in the future was thoroughly deserved.

But it was good his children weren't there to see him like that.

The facts in relation to all three matters – Lil's murder, Frazer's murder and the four hundred and forty-seven charges arising out of the distribution of child exploitation material via his website – were read to the court. Godfrey's lawyer presented a plea in mitigation by reading a prepared statement and Matthew presented the prosecution's submissions. An hour and a half later, and also with the benefit of a discount for early pleas of guilty, Godfrey too was sentenced to twenty years on Constantine with credit for time already served awaiting sentencing, with a further fifteen years added in respect of the Frazer murder, to be served largely concurrently. Happily, the sentence on the website was made cumulative. That, along with the non-parole period imposed, meant that despite Richard and Jessy promising Godfrey he wouldn't spend the rest of his life in jail if he cooperated with them – which was absolutely the case at the time they promised it – he would actually never experience freedom again. Angie's efforts had seen to it that her family would never need to front a parole board hearing and argue against the freedom of the man who had murdered Lil.

Following the sentencing, Ashwin and Millie left straight away. Ashwin didn't need my help to get out of there, since the changes in floor level were now downhill, so he just pushed Millie over the edge of each step and waited for her to stop bouncing. They were gone before I got the chance to say another word to either of them.

Matthew asked Lil's family to follow him to a private interview room to avoid the media. Although I was not family by any stretch of the imagination, and was technically meant to be back at work, I followed them and, due to a shortage of chairs in the poky room, leaned up against the doorframe as he spoke to them.

'We're happy with the sentence,' said Lil's mother, and her father murmured his agreement. 'It's in the region we discussed.'

Matthew nodded. 'I don't think it would be appellable.' He glanced up at me. 'What do you think, Andrew?'

Matthew had been very nice to me since Jessy had ditched him for me. He took it so well, I wondered if he'd been feeling a bit out of his depth with her in the first place. 'I agree with you. It's not the best-case scenario but it's far from the worst. And the judge's reasoning was sound. There was nothing in the decision that indicated she'd missed the thrust of any of the submissions we made.'

'Yes.' It was one of Lil's brothers who'd spoken. The older one, I thought – he too stood but on the opposite side of the room to me. I looked across at him. 'I reckon he got what he deserved,' he said.

I froze.

Next time you'll get what you deserve.

Oh man. I recognised his voice. From those five words he'd spoken to me while he wore a balaclava on his head, shortly after beating me almost to death.

There were three of them, and now I knew who they all were. Leon Robilliard, of course. And Lil's two brothers, all three convinced by Godfrey to do his dirty work. Robilliard would've been told in no uncertain terms that his further assistance was required to prevent Godfrey – and consequently himself – being outed by me as involved in this crime. But Lil's brothers, well, who knew what had been going on in their heads as they exacted such violence against me? Perhaps they'd been manoeuvred into believing that they had to do this to me in order to protect their family, in order to honour their sister. Perhaps they just agreed with Godfrey that I was sticking my nose in where it wasn't wanted, and I needed a bit of a touch up.

As we stared at each other, the brother who'd spoken seemed to realise his mistake. He glanced down at his mother and father. He wanted to protect them from the truth of what he'd done. The other brother, who was seated, looked up at us both and, without another word being exchanged, seemed also to realise they'd been sprung. I blinked, and I was back in the car park, curled up defensively, crying with pain, taking kick after kick to already broken bones from these two men in the room with me now.

'Andrew, we didn't get the chance to speak to you at the time all this happened,' said Lil's father.

With difficulty, I dragged my attention back into the room. I turned to face him. 'Sorry?'

'We wanted to tell you how grateful we are. You know all we wanted was to find out who did this to our Lily. You gave us that. Our family will never be the same, but now we are comforted by the fact the killer is found and he will be punished. Now our family can start to heal, all of us, together.'

'Oh. It's ... thank you.'

'You gave us an invaluable gift,' Lil's mother added. 'Even though we were strangers to you. You fought for our daughter. You gave her a voice, when she was silenced. You were her advocate.'

'Yeah, I just ...' I stopped, not feeling able to continue. I swallowed a couple of times and took a deep breath. 'I'm sorry I couldn't protect her that day. I wish I'd taken the phone call more seriously.'

'There's nothing more you could've done.' It was Lil's dad again, though his mouth seemed to be moving slower than his voice was coming out. 'Andrew, you'll always be welcome in our home. We've lost our daughter, but you will be like a son to us.'

'Right.' I felt like throwing up. I looked across the table in the centre of the room to the older brother. His black eyes stared at me, his expression a combination of regret and fear. 'What's your name?' I asked him.

'Jack.'

'Jack. Can we talk privately?'

'Yes. Of course.' He threw his parents a reassuring glance and followed me out of the room. We walked to the end of the hallway. He glanced back to make sure no one had followed us.

I looked at him and waited for him to speak.

'Listen, Andrew, I'm sorry. We're both sorry. We didn't realise ... we had no idea Sam was manipulating us.'

'What did he say to you?'

'He said the cops had let you go because you had an alibi, but that he knew from experience that time of death couldn't be accurately determined, really. I believed ... we both believed at the time that you were the one who'd killed our sister, but that the cops were letting you off because you worked with them.'

'You believed I murdered her, then wrote her a note with my mobile phone number on it?'

He looked distressed. 'Andrew, I'm sorry, we just ... we weren't thinking straight, and we trusted him, we trusted that he knew about this stuff. Legal stuff. I know you want to go to the police, and I don't blame you. Honestly, I don't. But we'll go to jail, both of us, for what we did to you.'

'Yes. I expect you will.'

'It will kill my parents. They've already been through so much.'

'Do they know what you did?'

'No. No one knows except Sam and Robilliard.'

I leaned against the wall. 'I think you're asking too much of me. I think I've already done enough for you people.'

'Think about it, maybe, Andrew. Maybe think about it overnight. I mean, I'd rather lie there for twenty minutes letting you do the same thing to me than have my parents find out about this. I want to protect them. It's all I've ever wanted to do, protect my family. Now I'm powerless to stop you from hurting them all over again.'

I frowned. 'Well, you're not powerless, really. I mean, you and your bro can come round and kill me a bit later on. You can't do that now, since we're in a court building and all, but if you can convince me to shut up at least until I get home tonight you can come around and finish me off in relative privacy.'

'I'm not a murderer.'

'I don't think I'm overstating it, Jack, to say you damn near killed me.'

'Yeah, I know,' he said, looking away from me then as he stole another glance down the hallway to make sure no one was starting to wonder what was keeping us. 'That's how I know I'm not a murderer.'

~

I want a new fucking car. That's what I wanted to say to Jack Constantine. *Yes, I got insurance money, but I had to spend it all on drugs and rehab thanks to you.*

But a new car didn't seem to be in the offing and ultimately, I wound up having to make a choice. I felt angry because I owed those people nothing, and they owed me a lot. My body felt angrier than my mind. In my mind I felt as though it was all too hard anyway and couldn't be undone even if Lil's brothers went to prison, and Jack seemed like a nice bloke, and who cared, really. But my body was still greatly aggrieved by the attack on me. It wanted to fight back. It wanted justice.

Jessy and I lay together in my bed and I didn't tell her about identifying my attackers. When she slept I looked at her peaceful face. I wanted to put all my energy into her, into our relationship, into taking care of her. Prosecuting Jack and his brother would strip me of my focus and energy for possibly even a year, if they pleaded not guilty. Which, let's face it, they would since there was hardly any evidence against them to speak of other than an unreliable voice identification and Jack's confession to me which would probably be inadmissible in a court, not the least of the reasons being because no warning had been given.

Maybe Lil's brothers had saved my life, in a roundabout way. Maybe if they weren't there to witness it, Leon Robilliard would've killed me.

Jessy had taken a chance on me because I'd promised her I would fight for her. I made my decision. It was time to start keeping my promises.

ACKNOWLEDGEMENTS

Thank you from the bottom of my heart to my parents, Geoff and Marian McLean, who worked the land to give me opportunities, and to my husband Simon, who backs me unconditionally as I pursue those opportunities.

My most heartfelt thanks to my fabulous and talented best mate, Sarah Hay. As well as being my inspiration, you took my writing to the next level, and your ruthless but loving criticism was so important to me throughout the evolution of this book.

Thank you also to my wonderful friends Renae Poot and Emma Wood for all your feedback and encouragement.

Thanks also to my early fans, especially Emily Waller who gave me the courage to believe I could engage a reader, and, going back a bit further, the inimitable Mrs McIntyre, who parted with a rare 10 out of 10 for a story I wrote in high school and sowed seeds in my mind.

Thank you to Georgia Richter at Fremantle Press, who needed no convincing to back me, and whose advice has been invaluable, and patience admirable.

And finally thank you to all the people who make up the vibrant community of Kalgoorlie–Boulder. The support I've had for this book from friends, clients, colleagues and acquaintances has blown me away. You guys are the best.

I would like to acknowledge the traditional owners and custodians of the Goldfields where I live and write, and pay my respects to elders past and present and the emerging leaders here.

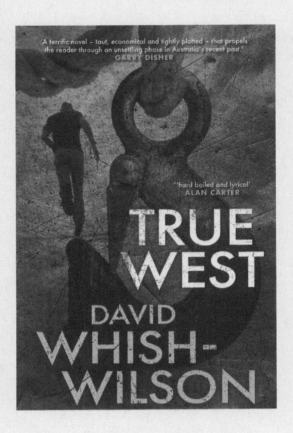

Western Australia, 1988. After betraying the Knights bikie gang, 17-year-old Lee Southern flees to the city with nothing left to lose. Working as a rogue tow truck driver in Perth, he is captured by right-wing extremists whose combination of seduction and blackmail keeps him on the wrong side of the law and under their control.

As the true nature of what drives his captors unfolds, Lee becomes an unwilling participant in a breathtakingly ambitious plot – and a cold-blooded crime that will show just how much he, and everyone else, still has to lose.

'But for all of Whish-Wilson's skill with impactful action and white-knuckle suspense, True West ultimately reveals itself as a complex morality tale about the tenacious spread of prejudice.' *Books + Publishing*

'[This] story of a hardened boy with a good heart facing violence and danger at every turn is among other things a clear-eyed look at the genesis and the effects of toxic masculinity at its most extreme.' *The Saturday Age*

AT ALL GOOD BOOKSTORES

Cryogenicist Dr Georgette Watson has mastered the art of bringing frozen hamsters back to life. Now what she really needs is a body to confirm her technique can save human lives.

Meanwhile, in New York City, winter is closing in and there's a killer on the loose, slaying strangers who seem to have nothing in common. Is it simple good fortune that Georgette, who freelances for the NYPD, suddenly finds herself in the company of the greatest detective of all time? And will Sherlock Holmes be able to save Dr Watson in a world that has changed drastically in 200 years, even if human nature has not?

'Very different to Warner's usual rural noir novels, this is an enjoyable, clever mystery that moves briskly along and offers some good suspense and nice touches of humour. Terrific fun.' *Canberra Weekly*

'[W]hat *Over My Dead Body* has in spades is a fun, entertaining story, with great supporting characters.' *AustCrime*

First published 2021 by
FREMANTLE PRESS

Fremantle Press Inc. trading as Fremantle Press
PO Box 158, North Fremantle, Western Australia, 6159
www.fremantlepress.com.au

Cover images: Tempura, gettyimages.com;
Aaron Burden, unsplash.com; istockphoto.com.
Cover design: Nada Backovic, nadabackovic.com.
Printed by McPherson's Printing, Victoria, Australia.

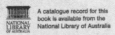

A catalogue record for this
book is available from the
National Library of Australia

ISBN 9781925816730 (paperback)
ISBN 9781925816747 (ebook)

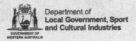

Department of
Local Government, Sport
and Cultural Industries

Fremantle Press is supported by the State Government through the
Department of Local Government, Sport and Cultural Industries.

Publication of this title was assisted by the Commonwealth Government
through the Australia Council, its arts funding and advisory body.

MIX
Paper from
responsible sources
FSC® C001695